Angeline

BOOKS BY ANNA QUINN

The Night Child
Angeline

ANNA QUINN

Angeline

BLACK STONE

PUBLISHING

Copyright © 2023 by Anna Quinn
Published in 2023 by Blackstone Publishing
Cover and book design by Alenka Vdovič Linaschke

The characters and events in this book are fictitious.
Any similarity to real persons, living or dead, is coincidental
and not intended by the author.

Printed in the United States of America

First edition: 2023
ISBN 979-8-200-75663-6
Fiction / Literary

Version 2

CIP data for this book is available
from the Library of Congress

Blackstone Publishing
31 Mistletoe Rd.
Ashland, OR 97520

www.BlackstonePublishing.com

"I also am other than what I imagine myself to be. To know this is forgiveness."

—Simone Weil

Chapter One

Meg lies prostrate on the stone floor. Her body, a cross. Incense curls around her white gown and spirals up like tiny resurrections. When she rises, they dress her in black and call her by a new name: Sister Angeline. It is the twelfth of December, 2014. She is twenty-three years old. She is now, after six years of discernment, officially a bride of Christ.

The bishop, dressed in reds and blacks, slides a gold band on her ring finger. A choir of nuns sing the psalm "De Profundis," a celebration of her death to worldly things. They sing something beyond the swell of human voice, something closer to white birds wrapping her in silk and promising to be there when she emerges.

And she stands there among them, head lifted toward light pouring through stained-glass windows. It is then, when she opens her eyes, she sees the baby floating in the perfumed clouds of smoke, a crown of lilies on its tiny head. Sister Angeline wipes her eyes, her face, and whispers *I love you*, and the baby flies away through the night.

Chapter Two

With the exception of singing and chanting and an hour of conversation each day, the twenty nuns live together in complete silence. Their daily lives divided by bells, moving them from one prayerful hour to the next, reminding them to pay attention to the moment. Even though there are no cell phones, computers, televisions, or radios, and the windows are frosted, a cloistered nun can become distracted.

The first bell rings at 12:30 a.m. for Matins, and Sister Angeline rises from her bed, kneels, and places her forehead on the floor. Attempts to relinquish ego. Washes her face. Dresses in full habit but leaves her feet bare. It is a breach of discipline to hurry, so she moves steadily, not with haste, and strives to stay in a perpetual state of prayer.

Once the nuns are gathered in the chapel, the prioress, Sister Josephine, exposes the Blessed Sacrament. She opens the door to the tabernacle, and there in the form of wine and wafers lies the body and blood of Christ.

Sister Angeline absorbed by this metaphor. The thought of

all becoming one body—no one separate from the other—but there are those who drink the wine and eat the bread who still feel alone, afraid, hungry, desperate, and ashamed.

She is one of those.

The nuns chant then, an ancient Latin call and response, creating a primal echo, a oneness of heart, extinguishing a silence that can sometimes suffocate.

Afterward, they return to their cells for three more hours of sleep. Sister Angeline undisturbed by this bifurcated sleep pattern—she hardly sleeps anyway. To fall asleep means ghost bodies crawling in and dead sparrows floating in coffins filled with blood.

Another bell at 5:30 a.m. The nuns gather to pray the Rosary. Father Condon arrives at 7:00 a.m. to say Mass. He has a heart condition and a kind temperament and must be helped to walk. Sister Angeline likes that he drinks the consecrated wine from the golden goblet with such gusto.

After Mass the nuns eat breakfast, usually eggs and buttered toast—sometimes there's blueberry or strawberry jam—and freshly squeezed juice and coffee. The only sounds: chewing and drinking and the muffled throb and scream of traffic through the double-paned windows.

Once the nuns clean up the kitchen, they pray for an hour in solitude. Sister Angeline prays in her cell, on her knees, head in her hands. She prays for the suffering, the sick. She prays to be with the ones she lost. She prays to be forgiven.

After prayer she assists with the laundry and cooking, polishing, sweeping, sewing, and gardening in the tiny, enclosed plot behind the convent. Sometimes, while she works, rappers perform on the other side of the brick wall. It seems to her that rapping requires an incredible grasp of human nature. Also, fearlessness and urgency.

Today a young man recites words rapidly, "These streets are shit, why can't I speak, I ain't telling you how to survive, ain't telling you, babe, when to cry, when to die, these streets are shit, why can't I speak?"

She can hear him breathing hard, and she feels an ache of pain for him, and it makes her call out, "I hear you," and there is a sudden silence, and then he says, "Thank you, whoever you are."

Lunch is the biggest meal. Never meat, but sometimes fish, usually lentils and rice, and if it's a feast day, they might have cookies.

They eat in silence except for one nun who is appointed as reader. The reader reads aloud the story of her choice. Whenever it's Sister Angeline's turn, she chooses a biography of a female saint—there are hundreds of these stories, and she wants to learn from all of them. These are women who didn't flee from suffering, who chose to live their entire lives at the edges—without possessions or power, undergoing hardship for the sake of others. Who stayed true to themselves even in the gravest of circumstances, even if it meant being burned at the stake.

After lunch more prayer and manual work. At 4:30 p.m. they sanctify the day with Vespers, by singing and chanting psalms. They must sing louder at Vespers because of the yell and bellow of rush-hour traffic.

The evening meal always consists of soup—the idea is to fast with only liquids until morning. Fasting is not an end unto itself, but a means of sharpening their minds and bodies for spiritual growth.

For an hour after the evening meal, the nuns may use their voices for conversation, though Sister Angeline doesn't participate. She prefers to use her free time to pray, not because she feels spiritually superior, but because she feels she owes a great debt.

In the beginning she'd waited for Sister Josephine or one of the other Sisters to say something about her lack of interaction, to insist she socialize, but no one ever said a word to her. Though, once, Sister Leon whispered *ice princess* as they passed in the hall, and Sister Angeline's throat tightened, and for a moment she was back in middle school where the bullies lived.

She'd been harassed in school for her strange eye colors, one blue and one brown. Kids passed rumors, said she was a witch, said she cast spells, blamed her for everything from bad test scores to a teacher's suicide, pushed her up against walls, and once, an older girl, a girl she'd only seen in the hallways, held a lit cigarette to her neck in the bathroom and said, *I never want to see you using this bathroom again or I'll burn you hard, Meg.* After that, she only used the bathroom by the nurse's office.

The doctor explained that she has heterochromia—a difference in coloration in two structures of the eye that are normally alike in color. He said it wasn't a negative thing.

Yet.

There was always someone within striking distance who made it so.

The bell for Compline rings at 7:30 p.m. More prayers, a hymn, and an optional examination of conscience. Though they are nudged to let the Ten Commandments guide them, Sister Angeline has her own set of questions.

Have I been distracted from prayer?

Have I knowingly hurt anyone?

The final bell rings at 9:00 for bedtime.

Prayeatchantcleancookreadprayeatchantcleanprayeatchantclean-
cookreadprayeatchantcleancookprayeatchantcleanreadpraypra-
yeatchantcleancookreadprayeatchantcleanprayeatchantclean-
cookreadprayprayeatchantcleancookreadprayeatchantclean-
prayeatchantcleancookreadprayprayeatchantcleancookreadpra-
yeatchantcleanprayeatchantcleancookreadprayeatchantclean-
cookprayeatchantcleanreadprayprayeatchantcleancookread-
prayeatchantcleanprayeatchantcleancookreadprayprayeatchan-
tcleancookreadprayeatchantcleanprayeatchantcleancookread

The monotony drives some of the nuns away. The monotony kills some of them.

For Sister Angeline, the surrendering, the predictable rhythm
carries its own body,

its own blood,

its own redemption.

Marriage between humans is a dare, a summons, a trial.
Marriage to God is a microscopic introspection, a quantum
leap, a release. A chrysalis.

Chapter Three

When Sister Angeline is twenty-four years old, only a year after taking her final vows, the Archdiocese of Chicago runs out of money to support the Daughters of Mercy. The foundation crumbling, stained glass shattered by bullets. The once-solid neighborhood collapsing into crime. And the number of nuns

> dwindling
> > dwindling
> > > dwindling.

The archdiocese closes the convent down. Heartbreak for the small band of women. Seventeen of the brides over seventy. They've lived and prayed here for decades, believed this was their home. Now they will be sent to nursing homes or families with extra bedrooms. The three younger nuns will be transferred to convents around the United States.

"I'm sending you to Light of the Sea convent," Sister Josephine says to Sister Angeline. It is morning, and they are sitting in her small dark office. The room has only two tiny, square stained-glass windows. The one above the prioress's head is open slightly, and the morning breeze whispers its way into the room and touches Sister Angeline's face. But now the cry of sirens, and they both close their eyes and whisper a Hail Mary. When they open their eyes, light slants in and lands on the papery hands of the old nun—the crinkled fingers clasped together on the worn oak table between them.

"Light of the Sea is on Beckett Island in the Pacific Northwest," Sister Josephine says. She is in her late seventies. A strand of gray hair hanging loose from her wimple. The heavy slump of her shoulders. The authority gone from her body. She will go to live with her sister in Michigan and volunteer at Our Lady of Refuge, the local Catholic elementary school, twice a week.

"They are looking for another nun to join them," Sister Josephine continues. "When their director, Sigrid, wrote to me, I immediately thought of you." She moves her hands, tucks them under her scapular, and the light flashes now on the silver crucifix hanging from her neck, illuminating the entire body of Jesus.

"But the Pacific Northwest is thousands of miles away." Sister Angeline stares steadily into the old woman's eyes, an overwhelming feeling of dread creeping throughout her entire body.

"There's more," Sister Josephine says.

"More?"

"Light of the Sea is *not* a cloistered convent. There are five Sisters, and they have contact with the outside world, and they're—they're quite radical. They've started their own community and no longer follow canonical law. They define their convent as a deconstructed one, an intentional spiritual community inclusive to all."

"They're excommunicated?"

"Yes. The pope has removed his blessing, but it doesn't mean they are stripped of God's blessing, remember that. They left of their own accord, and they, well, they just have their own vision about how things can be done." Sister Josephine shuts her eyes for a moment, inhales deeply, and then opens them.

"Their own vision?"

"Their abbess, Sigrid," Sister Josephine says calmly, "is a dear friend of mine, and you are like a daughter. I want you to be with her. I've prayed long and hard on this and I believe it's the right place for you. You'll love Sigrid." She clears her throat, rearranges her fingers into a shaky steeple. "She used to live here with us, but over time, she decided she couldn't live with the Vatican's stance on homosexuality and abortion, the subservient role of women, the cover-ups, so she left and started her own convent—it's been going for over forty years." Sister Josephine's face soft with pride. "She was, still is, the Gloria Steinem of nuns. She marched in civil rights protests, campaigned for the Equal Rights Amendment. She even says the Sunday Mass for the locals."

"Without a male priest?"

"Without a male priest."

Sister Angeline looks at Sister Josephine and takes this information in. Something sparks inside her. The kind of flicker she hasn't felt in a long time. She remembers how often her mother had shouted about the Church's subjugation of women—she'd hated the fact women didn't have the same rights as men, didn't have rights to their own bodies, were rendered illegitimate to deliver the words of God. She'd even flown to Rome in the '70s for a women's conference and marched in front of the Vatican, wearing a pink pantsuit, and carrying a sign that said, Open the Door! Open the Dialogue!

Meg and her mother came together on the Church's issues, one of the few subjects they agreed upon, and more than once, before Meg took her solemn vows, she asked herself why she would join a convent connected to an oppressive Church. She likes to think at some unconscious level it was because her mother often said, *Don't run, stay and fight.* But the truth is she joined because all she'd wanted was to atone for her wrongdoings. In the cloister, life is designed for atonement and prayer. Except for the tiny garden out back, she's never left the convent. The dentist comes to them. The doctor comes to them. The groceries come to them. Sometimes if you want, a relative even comes, but Sister Angeline requests no one and no one requests her, and she wants to keep it that way.

Sister Angeline knows her vow of obedience means she needs to listen to the prioress, but she also knows that since Vatican II this vow no longer means she need serve blindly. She need only listen intently—to hold open the possibility that others might know what's best for her and who she is meant to be. And she trusts Sister Josephine. Admires her wisdom and fairness. But this. This is too much. She needs to be in a place where she can focus all her energy on prayer, not designing posters for protests and campaigning for politicians. She needs to pray without interruption.

Outside a motorcycle roars its engine. A guy shouts, LOOK OUT, ASSHOLE!

"I'm not going," she says.

"Sister Angeline, do you remember the conversations we had when you were going through your six years of discernment? I expressed to you then that I didn't feel you were here for the right reasons. I believed that you, like most novitiates, were having doubts, but you were so passionate about prayer, I allowed you in. However, my sense now is that your doubts, your unhappiness, have only grown stronger, and hiding in a cloister is not the means to spiritual growth."

The walls collapsing on Sister Angeline, the cells in her body simmering distress, her chamber of solitude and privacy dissolving fast. "Am I supposed to be *happy?*" she says. "Or am I supposed to draw closely to the suffering of others? Was Catherine of Siena happy? Rose of Lima? Joan of Arc?" She immediately wants to suck these words back into her mouth, the arrogance and absurdity of comparing herself to saints deeply embarrassing.

"Listen," Sister Josephine says. "I know the sacredness of the cloistered vocation. I also know how enclosures and locked doors can fool you into believing isolation and prayer are the answers. But those women, those saints—they had a fervor, a fire burning within. They did not stay behind walls—they were out in the world."

For a few moments, Sister Josephine says nothing, just opens and closes the steeple of her hands. Then she says, "I believe you are ready for what's coming next, I can feel it. To follow a doctrine that isn't yours is a tremendous burden."

Angeline bows her head. Tears begin to fall.

"I want to tell you something," Sister Josephine says, more softly. "Something very personal." She rises from her chair and walks toward the large oil painting of Mary. She stumbles slightly, even though the floor is bare.

Sister Angeline waits, her heart working to control itself. In the seven years she's lived here, she's never heard Sister Josephine reveal anything personal. Not a word in the halls, not a whisper at meals, not a sound except for chanting and song and an occasional reprimand should someone fail the vow of silence.

"Decades ago, when I was a young nun in Ireland, I was assisting at a facility in Galway operated by nuns who sheltered orphans and cared for babies and unmarried mothers, a Magdalene institution—you've heard of those, yes? The home babies?"

"Yes."

"Once the babies were born, we were to care for them until they were adopted. At times, there must have been at least a hundred."

Sister Angeline's hands reach for her belly, and she enfolds it.

"But the conditions were horrible," Sister Josephine says, "the rooms damp and cold, all the babies whimpering, the stench of urine so strong you had to hold your hand over your nose, and there was hardly any staff, and I knew . . ." Sister Josephine's voice catches, and there is a small silence before she continues, her voice barely audible. "I knew many of the babies were sick, starving of hunger, but I never saw a doctor or nurse come near the place."

Sister Angeline's hands clasp her belly tighter. *No, don't think about her. No no no. Inhale, exhale.*

"And sometimes the tiny ones would disappear and I'd never see them again and when I asked, 'Where are the babies?' I was shushed and glared at and told to scrub or polish—" Sister Josephine crying now as she speaks, her shoulders trembling, and Sister Angeline thinks she should run to her, hold her, but she can't, she can't move from her chair, can't feel her legs.

"When I heard last March the authorities found all those bodies, almost eight hundred baby bodies in Tuam, the tiny bones of them dropped into an old septic tank in the backyard of the convent, I knew I should have done something, I should have spoken up. Instead I hid. I prayed. I told myself prayer was enough. Maybe if I'd—"

"Stop," Sister Angeline cries. "Please stop!"

The older nun turns then, alarmed, and moves to Sister Angeline, takes her into her arms, and whispers, "I'm sorry. I'm only trying to say that sometimes you must do more than pray. Sometimes closing yourself off also closes you off to God. I want you to trust me. I want you to go to Light of the Sea. If it doesn't work, we'll find you a different placement, I promise."

But Sister Angeline isn't listening, she's weeping inconsolably.

"It's all right, it's all right," Sister Josephine says, and the two women fall to their knees, still clinging to each other, weeping for the missing heartbeats, weeping into the broken places, bodies shaking, bodies remembering. Angeline murmuring, *The babies, oh the babies.*

Chapter Four

Sister Angeline travels by ferry to the Light of the Sea convent on Beckett Island, an island among hundreds between the mainland and Canada. Only four islands of the four hundred are accessible by ferry—Beckett is one of them.

She grips the rusted railing, the vibrations rattling through her body. Sweltering in her black habit. A few people stare at her. Others lower their heads in a deferential way. She hates to be looked at and turns away.

It is August, and the water flashes heat.

All this water.

All this sky.

All this blue.

In Chicago, outside her window: grime and sirens and beat-up buildings and wrecked cars and people. In the South Side, it wasn't hard to remember suffering.

And now Sister Josephine's words: *I want you to look forward, not back. You must find your own path. Your heart knows God's desire for you.*

God's desire.

Sister Angeline was seven when she'd first encountered God.

At school the nuns had spoken about what it was like to be called by God—how you would be visited in some unique way—that you would *know* it was God. They said that receiving a call was an uncommon thing, an exceptional thing.

She'd been straddling a thick branch in a white oak, secure and safe in the shape of the tree, when she noticed a dead moth in the curve of a branch. She'd touched the delicate white wings of it with her index finger, and her eyes flooded with tears. "Please, God, wake her up," she'd repeated.

All at once a consuming heat enveloped her, and her eyes began to sting violently. She squeezed them tight, and when she opened them, a heat surged from her entire body, and she saw the moth's antennae vibrate and its wings quiver faster and faster until the vibration became so intense that she could feel the breeze of the wings on her face. She sat motionless as the tiny creature lifted from the branch and fluttered in front of her, emitting a bright violet light, its large eyes a brilliant green. It circled the tree at least five times before disappearing into the distance.

When the moth came back to life, Sister Angeline *knew* it was God, but she didn't tell anyone. It wasn't anything she had words for. It wasn't a *he* or a *she* or anything she could picture in her mind. It was a holy secret she wanted to be alone with.

As she grew older, she would contemplate God as:

A radiating sensation without limits, without shape, like water.

Something knowable and unknowable, like love, light, and truth.

Something beyond time and nature.

When she was twelve, she'd been standing on the shore of Lake Michigan, praying for her little brother, Ricky, who was in the hospital on a ventilator. She'd repeated, "God, please save my brother," and once again the dazzling light had surrounded her, washing her body with an extreme warmth. Her eyes had stung as if someone were shooting tiny needles into her pupils. She'd felt herself floating higher and higher toward the sky, her entire body vibrating. She'd watched as her tingling hand reached up to touch a cloud, and it was then she knew Ricky would be okay.

She'd returned to the hospital just in time to see Dr. Meadows place the tips of the stethoscope in her ears, the chest piece on Ricky, and say, "Well now, that's strange."

"What's strange?" her mother said, standing at the doorway, unmoving.

The doctor tapped her stethoscope, listened again.

"His lungs are almost clear," she said, looking at Meg's mother. "I only hear a slight congestion. But that's impossible. Yesterday the ventilator was breathing for him, and his blood tests showed a severe mycoplasma infection." Dr. Meadows scrunched her pretty face, cocked her head to the side. "I don't know what to say. I've never seen anything like this."

Of course, Meg knew—her prayers had worked. Two days later Ricky came home.

When she was fifteen, she'd dreamed her father's plane crashed on the way home from a music gig in Ireland. His band, the Jackhammers, had traveled to Dublin to play at an all-boys boarding school and were expected to return Sunday night.

In church, the morning of her father's flight home, as she prayed for him to miss his flight, and as the choir sang "Ave

Maria," her eyes began to burn again. Electrified, she prayed
even harder. The familiar heat surrounded her head, and within
seconds she became conscious of her body absorbing the music,
the heartbeat and holiness of it, and her face and chest, arms and
legs began to slowly fold into the bodies of all the people in the
church, folding and folding, until they'd all become one body—
one bright, amorphous mass attached by a silver thread to her
father. Meg saw him there, In his neon-orange pants and black
leather jacket, the silver thread wrapping around and around
him. And then abruptly, as the last musical note faded into the
haze of incense, the sacred sensation released her, and she was
at once herself again—a girl blinking and dazed, kneeling on a
wooden pew in a church.

That night on the news, she learned the flight that her father
was supposed to be on had crashed over Iceland and there were
no survivors. Within moments, her father called. "It's okay, baby,
I'm safe. The school asked us to stay and do an extra gig—whew,
that was a stroke of luck!"

Meg was certain it was more than luck; it was God, it was
prayer. She began to read everything she could find on prayer
and ultimately decided her requests to God carried an energy
with its own potent wave frequency and could influence the
state of particles in other human beings or things. She'd written in her notebook:

Prayer is its own language.

Prayer can impact the external world.

The possibilities of prayer made her tremble.

And she'd written down questions:

Does prayer for a person who is a continent away have the same
effect as prayers for a person who is inches away?

Does the prayer skill level of the person praying influence the outcome?

Can a thousand prayers be more powerful than one?

Does it matter how you say the prayer? How focused do you have to be?

Can people who died feel your prayers?

What conditions are necessary for prayer to work?

On the ferry now, a crowd has suddenly gathered, children jumping up and down, pointing to the water, people raising phone cameras.

Sister Angeline inches toward the crowd, and there, in front of them: three whales erupt into the air, black-and-white bodies big as houses twist high, snort and sound their presence, then land heavy, slapping blue everywhere. Sun lighting up wet black skin. They are so close, she can see their open mouths and rows of teeth and pink tongues, the holes on top of their rounded heads spurting water.

For a moment, Sister Angeline is eye level with one of them. The whale's eye, a blue-black bead in a massive body, looking straight at her, its grace and power seeping into her.

Her breath held.

And then the whale is gone.

She is filled with the flooded sense one gets after something extraordinary happens. Something that makes you feel a deep attachment, a knowing that you are right where you are supposed to be, and in that moment, she feels slightly more at ease.

A little boy beside her is jumping with excitement, shouting, "Wow, wow, Liam, did you see that?" He is holding hands with an older teenage boy in a gray hoodie, who she assumes is Liam.

"That was c . . . c . . . cool," Liam says, and now the little boy turns to her, still bouncing, and puts his small hand on her skirt and tugs on it.

"Have you ever seen a whale that close?" he says to her, still holding on to her skirt.

Stunned by the experience, all the emotion around her, emotions she's not used to, Sister Angeline looks at the wide-eyed joy of him. His red sneakers with their purple laces. His yellow backpack. She opens her mouth, but nothing comes out, and she can only shake her head no.

"Well, now you have!" he says happily. He keeps looking at her. "Hey, you're a nun!"

She nods.

His enthusiasm is not to be squelched, but at least he has released her habit. "We have nuns where I live on Beckett Island. But they don't dress like you. They dress like us. Well, except for one who dresses like you. Her name is Edith. She's kind of mean and she never says hi to me. Are you mean?"

"Dude," the older boy says. "D . . . d . . . don't be rude."

"I'm sorry," the little boy says. "Can I tell you something about whales?"

Sister Angeline can't help smiling.

"Those were orca whales, and some people call them killer whales, but orcas don't actually kill people. Mostly, they just kill seals and salmon. Sometimes they vomit up the fish they've swallowed, and the vomit floats on the surface and attracts seagulls, and when the seagulls are eating, the whale comes from under the water"—and he sweeps his arm up like a whale surfacing—"and chomps its jaws on the gulls to drown them, and then the whale eats them."

This little boy reminds Sister Angeline of someone—her brother. He reminds her of Ricky, the innocence and animation of him. She immediately feels bereft and needs this boy to go away.

Liam pulls his hood down, exposing his thick black hair. He looks at her and says, "Hi, I'm Liam, and this is M . . . M . . . Michael."

"I'm Sister Angeline." She thinks she should reach out formally with her hand, but she keeps them clasped under her scapular. It feels like a challenge she isn't ready to meet.

"Nice to meet you," Liam says. "Michael and I live on the island. I babysit him. He's a bit of a pain and never stops talking, but he's okay."

Michael makes a face at him and says, "Well, you are a huge, gigantic pain!"

Liam laughs and ruffles Michael's blond curls, and the action strikes Sister Angeline as extremely tender. It also occurs to her that Liam is about the same age she was when she entered the convent. How young she'd been. How lost her soul.

Liam pulls out his phone, scrolls, puts it back in his jean pocket. "C'mon, little d . . . d . . . dude," he says. "We n . . . n . . . need to go if you want that C . . . c . . . coke before we land. Maybe we'll s . . . s . . . see you later," he says to her.

"Yeah, maybe we'll see you later!" Michael calls out and waves as Liam pulls him toward a vending machine.

"Bye," she says, waving a little.

The ferry horn blasts now, startling her, and a man's voice blares through a loudspeaker, "Now arriving, Beckett Island."

Heart pulsing fast, she looks out, and there it is. A brief interruption in an eternity of blue. The unspoiled beauty of it.

Trees with glossy leaves and peeling orange-red bark line the sandy bluffs. Gulls keening and gliding everywhere. The surge and release of waves against the shore. The sun warm and soft on her face. She almost turns away, a sliver of guilt rising, already realizing how easy it is to be sidetracked, but now Sister Josephine's words, *Stay open, stay present to each moment.*

A young girl stands on the stony beach, watching the ferry arrive. She is wearing a lemon-yellow dress, and even from here, Sister Angeline can see it is at least two sizes too big. The girl waves at her and she waves back. She hasn't waved at anyone for seven years, and twice today she's swished her hand at someone.

The captain blasts the horn again. Maneuvers the white beast into the narrow slip. The boat bangs into the pilings, making her grip the iron railing. Deckhands release hydraulic ramps and secure rope to steel cleats.

A light breeze lifts her veil, and she closes her eyes. The enormity of what she is doing threatens to steal her courage, the massive roar of it mocking her confidence, but here she is, what else is she to do? She uncurls her fingers from the railing and prays, "God be with me."

Sister Angeline picks up her suitcase, squares her shoulders, and marches down the ramp. She walks, head raised. Beneath her habit, sweat leaks through blazing skin and drips under her breasts and between her thighs. New life set in motion.

Chapter Five

A woman with short gray hair, wearing a button-down Hawaiian shirt with a floral graphic, rushes to her, pumps her hand, and says, "Yo! I'm Sigrid."

"Lovely to meet you, Sister Sigrid."

"Sigrid. Just Sigrid. No formal titles here. But you're welcome to use Sister if that makes you more comfortable."

Startled, Sister Angeline says, "I think—yes." She needs her full religious name—needs to keep the symbolism, the need to become someone else.

"What was your name before you took your vows?" Sigrid asks, waving at a woman in a red halter getting into a VW Beetle the color of a robin's egg.

"Meg." She is feeling too exposed now, incongruous. Speaking about her past to a woman she met not thirty seconds ago amid a flurry of people and revving car engines is disorienting and disappointing. Sister Josephine said she would love this woman.

"And who chose Angeline?"

"I did." But that's all she says. She doesn't want to say that Saint Angeline was also orphaned and accused of being a witch though, of course, she was not.

Sigrid looks at her curiously and then says, "Whoa, Sis, you have one blue eye and one brown."

Sister Angeline stands there, unsure of what to say. She doesn't trust her voice right now, a thick knot forming in her throat.

Sigrid says, "Our dog, Anu, whom you'll meet shortly, also has a blue eye and a brown eye. We call them ghost eyes because she can see heaven with the blue eye and earth with the brown eye at the same time. We say she's blessed."

Mostly, they've been a curse.

"Well, let's go, you've got plenty of folks to meet!" Sigrid walks ahead of her, her body springy with charisma. They arrive at the car, a rusted orange Volvo, and Sister Angeline freezes.

"Yeah, it's not much to look at. Salt does a number on vehicles around here." She opens the trunk. "Throw your bag in, and we'll be off!"

It's been eight years since she's been in a car. Eight years since the accident.

For the journey to Beckett Island, she'd avoided taking a taxi to the airport by taking a bus instead, and because the bus was much larger than a car and very crowded, she was able to stay calm enough. In preparation for the trip, she'd sat on her bed in the cloister each night, closed her eyes, and imagined herself a passenger in a car. She'd prayed the Rosary while the imaginary driver took her places. Touching each crystal bead, the repetition of the words guided her into an untroubled place, and she was able to move through more and more beads. Sometimes she could pray all the way through the Joyful Mysteries before the frightening images arrived to haunt her. Once, she made it to the Sorrowful Mysteries. She'd used this technique on the bus, and she'd been able to disappear into her meditation. When the bus arrived at the airport, she'd walked off, seemingly undaunted, as if she rode it every day.

But now here she is, and she doesn't believe closing her eyes and praying the Rosary will help for even a minute.

"Getting in, Sis?" Sigrid yells from inside the car.

Sister Angeline places her suitcase in the trunk and slams the lid shut. She walks to the passenger door, reaches for the door handle, her fingers trembling.

The way her mother's blue eyes looked through the shattered windshield. The smear of blood across her little brother's cheeks. Her father's lifeless arm—the exposed white bone and angle of it.

"Sister Angeline?"

She forces herself to yank the door open. Slides into the front seat. Shuts the door. Buckles her seat belt. Reaches for her rosary and brings it onto her lap. Intertwines it between her fingers.

Give me courage.

She makes herself look out the front window while she touches each bead. Reminds herself she is here on this island for a reason and not by chance. But she wants to fling herself out the door. There are no speed limit signs anywhere, and Sigrid is driving too fast. A bug splats on the windshield, and Sigrid turns on the wipers and smears the creature across the glass.

Sister Angeline is nauseous. She shuts her eyes. She wonders if she should say something—say she needs to get out—whether this would be the right thing to do or the cowardly thing.

That's when Sigrid says, only one hand on the wheel, "Say, did Josie tell you I was your age when I first arrived here? Drove this very Volvo from Chicago. Of course, it was bright and shiny at that time. Josie thought I was so courageous, but I was terrified, leaving the cloister. I'd been there ten years after all. Ten years in a two-thousand-square-foot enclosure!" She shakes her head in disbelief. "And to think I never left it. Ever. Not for my sister's wedding or my father's funeral or the birth of my niece. And then to also leave the pope, the rules, the secrets. Felt kind of like a criminal, you know? I had nightmares of archbishops tying my hands behind my back, telling me to remain silent, that anything I say could be used against me in a court of law. I had such stomachaches, swallowed Tums like candy, worried maybe I'd misread my heart and now my entire life was ruined. But Josie put a cooler of ham sandwiches in my back seat and said, 'Sigrid, you're doing the right thing and I am so proud of you.' The best thing was her face. She looked at me like I was the sunrise or something."

Sister Angeline opens her eyes.

Light slants through twisted branches of extraordinary, fantastical trees. Two people, a man and a woman, are picking up shells from the rocky beach, the blue of water spreading wide beside them. She lowers the window a few inches, and a salty breeze touches her cheeks, moves her veil.

Sigrid points out things while she drives the potholed road: "There is the library, the church, the grocery store where we sell our herbs and apples, jams and vegetables."

A deer leaps across the road now and Sigrid abruptly swerves, veers into the other lane, barely missing the animal, and Sister Angeline gasps aloud and her whole body seizes, her mouth an

inaudible scream—*how is this happening how is this happening*—
and then a tremendous crash of metal and glass and pain and
airbags exploding white and Sister Angeline frozen, eyes closed
tight. A deathly quiet.

Her eyes open slow.

No shattered windshield.

No red lights flashing.

No sirens screaming.

Sigrid has pulled the car over to the side of the road. She
stares at Sister Angeline, mouth agape. "For all that's good and
holy," she says. "What happened?"

Sister Angeline's face flushes. Eyes brim with tears. Her
mouth opens, but the words won't form into shapes, into sounds.

"You're shaking." Sigrid reaches a hand to touch Sister Angeline's arm but draws it back when she flinches.

"I— I—"

"Listen, honey, you're in for a lot of changes," Sigrid says,
her weathered face tinted with warmth. "It's no little thing to
be thrust out of serene seclusion into the hullabaloo of civi-
lization where cloister rules don't apply, to be whisked to an
island where who knows what's going to happen and, on top of
that, be strapped into a rusty orange car zipping around sharp
corners. And ya know, I should've known better." She smiles
gently. "Sorry 'bout that, kiddo."

Sister Angeline turns away. She is not ready to smile. She
is not ready to be called *kiddo*. Not ready for this place with its
whimsical trees and ocean-smell trickery. Everything unpredict-
able and erratic, one moment heaven-sent, the next hellish. She
clenches her rosary with both hands.

"Whatever you've been through," Sigrid says, "everything

that's happened to you, has brought you right here to this place, and I, for one, am glad you've arrived. Shall we keep going? I promise to lighten my lead foot."

Sister Angeline stares straight ahead—her face drained of color, her eyes following the road to the next tight curve, the bright yellow arrows warning drivers to slow down or else. "Keep going," she says, determination vibrating between each syllable. "Keep going."

Chapter Six

The Light of the Sea convent consists of nine small yurts sitting atop a grassy hill, a rickety fence defining the border. Each yurt covered in a different shade of green or blue fabric. The gentle curve and grace of them. Each wooden entry door painted a different color—red, yellow, turquoise, pale green, forest green, blue, indigo, violet, and purple. Nothing in Sister Angeline's imagination could have created anything this enchanting, and the charm of it momentarily quells any residual shaking.

In the center of the nine yurts, a life-size stone statue of Mary. Garlands of tiny white flowers wind around her crown. Pockmarks on her face and body make her look like she knows pain, like she knows more than one language.

Beyond the yurts, a large garden, chicken coops, chickens and goats everywhere, and acres and acres of apple orchards. Past the orchards, the Strait of Juan De Fuca leads to the Pacific Ocean. In the distance, the Olympic Mountains reach quiet to the sky.

A tall brown woman with her head wrapped in a bright

orange scarf stands at the entrance of the first yurt, holding the collar of a Siberian husky. The dog tugging and barking.

"That's Kamika," Sigrid says, "and there's Anu—the dog I told you about."

Sister Angeline steps out of the car, and Anu bounds to her, bumps her nose hard into the young nun's legs. Sister Angeline keeps her arms folded under her scapular, but she crouches to meet the white-and-black dog.

Its eyes. One blue. One brown. Sister Angeline flooded with a longing to touch the dog—to bury her face in the black fur of its neck—but she's not ready. She needs to pace herself, so instead she only whispers, "Hello, sweet soul." Anu looks straight into her, eyes alive with tenderness and curiosity and tries to lick her face. Sister Angeline can't help then but to reach out a hand and stroke Anu's head. When the dog wags its tail wildly, Sister Angeline's other hand comes out of hiding, and she rubs behind Anu's ears. The heat of the fur is the warmest place she's touched in years.

She used to have a cat named Nacho and a dog named Chip, but they disappeared after the accident. Her aunt said when the authorities went to her parent's house, there were no animals present. Neighbors hadn't seen them. Sister Angeline imagines Nacho and Chip wandering, thin and confused around Chicago. Tears well in her eyes. She blinks them away and quickly removes her hands and rises. The look in Anu's eyes: pure affection.

The woman in the orange headscarf, her thick black hair hanging loose to her bare shoulders, extends her hand and says, "Hi, I'm Kamika." She is wearing a lavender tank top and a long green skirt, and her face opens like a summer flower. Before Sister Angeline can return her greeting, two more women emerge from separate yurts. They gather around Sister Angeline and introduce themselves.

One woman reaches in, takes her hand, surprising her with an enthusiastic grip. "Hi!" she says. "I'm Gina." She is beautiful, with her short curly black hair and thick lashes framing dark eyes. Silver rings on every finger. Her lips painted a deep shade of red, her nose pierced, her cargo pants torn at the knees. She is barefoot and her toenails are painted turquoise. Everything about her suggests fresh air and small, spinning planets.

"Aren't you roasting in that habit?" Gina says, not unkindly, but suddenly Sister Angeline panics. Everyone paying her too much attention. She wants a bell to ring, reminding them of prayer. She wonders what time it is. It must be late afternoon. It must be time for Vespers.

Do they even have bells here?

Sigrid puts her arm around the waist of the woman who hasn't yet introduced herself and says, "This is Alice. She's taken a lifetime vow of silence."

Alice is at least seventy. She is black, with silver dreadlocks touching her shoulders. She wears a pink blouse and a gray skirt. Smiling at Sister Angeline, she hooks her white cane on her wrist and holds out both hands. Her wrinkled fingers long and graceful.

Without thinking, Sister Angeline lays her hands in Alice's, and there is immediately between them a warmth, a harmony, a familiarity—as if they've known each other forever. Alice knows her, she can tell. She can also tell that Alice can see her—knows she is scared. Knows she wants to disappear.

Gina says, "So that's everyone, except Edith. She's probably in the garden—not much for a commotion. You'll meet her later. For now I'll give you the grand tour!" The rings on her fingers dazzle in the sunlight.

Alice squeezes Sister Angeline's hands, and her eyes say, *Go. You will be all right.*

Sister Angeline turns to Gina, says, "Okay." She will not allow the panic breathing room.

They enter the chapel first. Above the front door, a wooden plaque: *Dwell in God's tent: an open door, which no one is able to shut.*

From the ceiling, light drops from a hole open to sky. The fabric held taut as a drum by a wood frame. There are four small windows made from aquamarine glass, shining like jewels, like the sea, equally spaced apart around the circumference of the yurt. The faint scent of incense. A wooden altar with a white candle in the center. Three rows of wooden pews. No statues or a cross with naked dying Jesus.

On the wall four huge, colorful banners:

Air
Earth
Water
Fire

The Air banner urges her to inhale. Earth presses her feet into ground. Water wets her lips, makes her swallow. The flames on Fire look like they would burn her if she dared touch them.

The potency of this place insisting she drop to her knees and pray.

As if reading her mind, Gina says softly, "Let's pray." She

faces the small window looking toward the ocean, folds her hands, and closes her eyes.

But when Sister Angeline closes her eyes, all she can see is her baby flailing her tiny arms like a sparrow who's lost its way and sits perched alone on a wire.

And now Gina whispers in her ear, "We'd better keep going?"

Sister Angeline used to see the baby all the time—the tiny body of her, sometimes a skeleton baby, sometimes an alive baby with eyes like her own, one blue, one brown, eyes looking out at her, the tiny red mouth opening and calling *mama mama mama*, but gradually the skeleton baby and the alive baby had melted away. She is startled to see she has returned.

Gina behind her, saying softly, "It's a lot, I know." She takes Sister Angeline's arm then and gently escorts her to a yurt with a yellow door and climbing green ivy painted all around the edges. Gina opens the door wide and exclaims, "And here is the kitchen!"

The intoxicating smell of this place. Bundles of dried flowers and herbs hang on long purple ribbons from the ceiling. Gina naming them as they walk by: dill, tarragon—how Sister Angeline wants to touch the yellow buds!—mint, chamomile, thyme, red roses, lavender, rosemary, and sage.

White ceramic pots of herbs line a counter under the window, the sun illuminating the veins branching through the green leaves.

"Sweet basil. Oh, you have to taste it!" Gina says, plucking off a tiny leaf and holding it out for Sister Angeline.

Sister Angeline touches the leaf to her lips, the mild spiciness of it tingling her tongue—it tastes like grass and cinnamon and the anise extract her mother used to drip into her hot chocolate when she was sick.

On a round wooden table in the center of the room: huge yellow bowls of strawberries, apples, tomatoes, cucumbers, and lemons. A vase of purple flowers. An open newspaper and a stack of mail. Around the table, five painted blue chairs.

Gina pulls the oven door open. "Rosemary potatoes and garlic," she says. "All from our garden! You'll love it! And wait till you see what we have for dessert!" She walks to the counter under the window and, like a magician, lifts a yellow flowered towel off a golden apple pie.

Sister Angeline bends down and breathes in the sweet, warm fragrance, the edge of her veil brushing the sugar sprinkled across the lustrous crust.

"Are you hungry?" Gina asks, looking at her with a bright, childlike face. "We have melon in the fridge! And figs!"

Sister Angeline's mouth waters—but what is she thinking? She is barely off the ferry, and here she is, already dreaming of licking sugar off her lips, falling fast for this fairy-tale place, this place where everything seems intended for someone who doesn't want to be a nun. She draws away from the pie. "No. Thank you. I'm not hungry."

This is a lie. She hasn't eaten since her flight nine hours ago, and even then she'd only eaten a few peanuts, turned down the free gingersnaps in their sparkly cellophane package. She will stay committed to her vow of three small meals a day. She will be disciplined. This proverb in her mind: *Do not become the woman who eats and wipes the evidence from her mouth and says she has done nothing wrong.*

"You sure?" Gina asks.

"Yes, I'm sure, thank you." She feels slightly stronger now that she's dodged a temptation—minor seduction that it was—still, she'd done it, and this makes her believe, even in this place, devotion to her vows might be possible.

The next yurt holds the library. Inside, floor-to-ceiling bookshelves line the perimeter. To the side a propane stove surrounded with deep cushioned armchairs. The bamboo floor covered with a worn Turkish rug. Books, newspapers, and magazines piled all over the place. Sister Angeline moves toward the shelves, fingers the book bindings: Austen, Baldwin, Brontë, Dickinson, Merton, Morrison, Plath, Rilke, Steinem, Walker, Woolf. So many names she hasn't read, and a few she remembers from high school. In the cloister she was only allowed to read the *National Catholic Register*, the *Catholic Herald*, and *US News & World Report*—here it seems they can read anything.

She loves to read. The way words can be arranged into meaning, into art, into something unfamiliar, can open or heat or freeze her body, send it into chaos, can become living things that fall and fly across the page, burrow into her skin, into the marrow of her breastbone, sometimes splitting her open, leaving her humbled, renewed, reborn.

She used to write too. She used to show her stories to her father. Only to him. And every time, he'd say they were extraordinary, she was remarkable, she must graduate and go to college. Then he died, and she didn't graduate and didn't go to college, and she stopped writing.

"Okay, c'mon, I want you to see your space!"

The self-assurance of this young woman is startling.

They arrive at Sister Angeline's yurt, and Gina spreads her arms dramatically as she opens the blue door. "Welcome to your new home!" Anu races across the grass when she sees them, runs into the yurt, spins around in circles. Sister Angeline can't help that's happened to you, has brought you right here to this place, and I, for one, am glad you've arrived. Shall we keep going? I promise to lighten my lead foot."

Sister Angeline stares straight ahead—her face drained of color, her eyes following the road to the next tight curve, the bright yellow arrows warning drivers to slow down or else. "Keep going," she says, determination vibrating between each syllable. "Keep going."

Chapter Six

The Light of the Sea convent consists of nine small yurts sitting atop a grassy hill, a rickety fence defining the border. Each yurt covered in a different shade of green or blue fabric. The gentle curve and grace of them. Each wooden entry door painted a different color—red, yellow, turquoise, pale green, forest green, blue, indigo, violet, and purple. Nothing in Sister Angeline's imagination could have created anything this enchanting, and the charm of it momentarily quells any residual shaking.

In the center of the nine yurts, a life-size stone statue of Mary. Garlands of tiny white flowers wind around her crown. Pockmarks on her face and body make her look like she knows pain, like she knows more than one language.

Beyond the yurts, a large garden, chicken coops, chickens and goats everywhere, and acres and acres of apple orchards. Past the orchards, the Strait of Juan De Fuca leads to the Pacific Ocean. In the distance, the Olympic Mountains reach quiet to the sky.

A tall brown woman with her head wrapped in a bright

but smile at this happy dog and this happy young woman with her curly hair and fluttery eyelashes.

She looks around the bright room. Takes in the ivory skin of the yurt. The smell of soap, salt, sanctuary. Filmy curtains fluttering from three small windows, the plump coverlet on the bed, the painted desk and chair. Everything white, except a lamp shade rimmed with blue and green sea glass and a small black propane stove sitting quietly in the center of the room and a simple wooden cross on the wall above the bed. The golden wood floor smooth and free of rugs—sunlight gleaming across its surface. This place is simply beautiful. Uncomplicated. Unadorned.

Is it too beautiful? Will she be a hypocrite, praying for the suffering while she kneels in this milk-and-honey place?

She opens one of the curtains, and a slight breeze caresses her face. The air astonishing—the thick, fishy, elemental heat of it. And there is the ocean, a vast cerulean body, and it is then the temptation to run to the water fills her body, and she yearns to strip off her habit and dive into the water's glittering brilliance—

"Oh, and hey, here's the bathroom," Gina calls from across the room.

Sister Angeline turns, and behind a pine wardrobe, a private toilet. A private shower and bathtub. White towels. Sprigs of lavender in a vase. Over the sink, a mirror. And because she hasn't seen a mirror in seven years, the mirror startles her more than the private toilet and shower. Sister Angeline turns from it, a panic seizing her—she is not ready to see the "I" she's attempted to expunge for so long.

"I know, I know," Gina says. "I felt that way about the mirror too, when I first arrived, but then Sigrid said maybe it's not all about self-denial? Maybe it's about self-knowledge?"

No, no, no, no. The whole point is to waive self, leave self behind, become self-less. When she entered the convent, for the sake of eliminating past identity, she'd surrendered all evidence: iPhone, computer, makeup, jewelry (even the pearl earrings from her father), money, street clothes. At first it was hard to give up these things, but then she'd finally understood the vow of poverty. She'd thought it meant lack of things and destitution and worrying about tomorrow's meals, then she'd understood it was the waiving of individual ownership. Everything in the convent was for the common use of all, and she need not own one single thing, and it was more about how you live together, how you pray together, how you go about your daily life.

She'd also relinquished her hair. The oldest nun in the cloister had snipped strand after strand, piled it on a silver platter, Sister Angeline's own hand setting the hair on fire, the room filling with the sulfur ghosts of her past, satisfaction welling inside her as she watched an aspect of her femininity spiral into oblivion.

Anu rubs against her leg now as if to comfort her, and she bends down and wraps her arms around the dog. She is weakening. She is becoming too tired to worry about fighting desires.

"If it makes you feel better," Gina says, "there's no internet. We're off the grid. We share one cell phone, and there's a landline in the kitchen. All our electricity comes from solar panels on the barn roof and those poles you see near the chapel yurt. And maybe you noticed that small tower right next to each yurt—the thing with the windmill on top and solar panels on each side? That's your own little power plant. Edith designed and built each one herself. In her first convent, she got an engineering degree—she's crazy smart. Anyway, don't worry about the world's noise smothering you here."

Sister Angeline stands and brushes the dog hair off her habit. Her wimple damp against her forehead. She longs to remove it and replace it with a cool, wet towel over her face.

"Also," Gina says, "you don't have to wear that torture chamber of a dress. Remember, um, Vatican II? You can wear jeans and a T-shirt here."

Waves of uneasiness rise within Sister Angeline. There is no way she is going to wear jeans and a T-shirt. She loves wearing her habit, needs the reminder of it, the autonomy, the safety. It reminds people to keep their distance.

"And you can let your hair grow back!" Gina says with a wide grin.

Sister Angeline's brows furrow. Shaving her head is a renouncement of conceit—a way to let go of herself.

"You're thinking it's vain?" Gina says. "An instrument of seduction? You might not advance spiritually?" She pulls a curl of her black hair straight, cocks her head, and says with a friendly smirk, "Girl, it's just hair."

They both smile then, though Sister Angeline's is wobbly.

An orange cat with a tinkling bell around its neck appears and curls around Sister Angeline's ankles. Its tail a lofty brush of fluff.

"That's Joan. As in Joan of Arc. She's nineteen, been with us since she was a baby. In the beginning we thought that name might be a bit too much pressure for her, but she's lived up to it!"

Sister Angeline strokes the cat's head. Her finger touches a scar where an ear should have been. "Oh," she says and looks at Gina.

"She had a bit of scuffle with a coyote when she was younger. Edith watched the whole thing out the kitchen window. The coyote had a squirrel in its mouth, and Joan tried to save it. She lost her ear but saved the squirrel, scared the coyote off." Gina shakes her head. "Once, some guy started hassling Sigrid when she got out of her car out front, and Joan shot from the bushes, hissed, and jumped on him, clawed the guy like crazy." Gina laughs. "Dude ran away, shouting obscenities."

Sister Angeline continues to stroke Joan's head, causing the cat to press harder into her leg and purr in a deep, guttural way. "Why was the guy hassling her?"

"He'd heard she'd invited a bunch of people to the convent library to stitch together some Pride flags for the parade. He wasn't too happy about that—not a fan of LGBTQ celebrations, I guess. Anyway, here's your dome opener," Gina says, reaching for a steel pole near the door. She holds the pole up high, inserts the hook into the window's clasp, winds it. A little flap in the ceiling opens, and sunlight pours onto the bed, drenching the white duvet.

They stand together, gazing at the beam of light.

"It's a blessing to be here," Gina says, barely audible. She turns and moves toward the blue door. "I'll see you soon—at Vespers. You'll hear four bells."

"Yes. Okay. Thank you for all this. Could you—could you tell me the rest of the schedule?"

"Yeah, sure. Just didn't want to wear you out. We follow the traditional schedule, except that we skip the middle of the night prayers, and there's an hour of personal time right after each meal. Oh, and the hour before Vespers? Like right now *ha!*, which is why I have to get going, we practice Tai Chi on the lawn if it's nice out, otherwise we meet in the library. Are you familiar with it—Tai Chi?"

"It's a martial art, isn't it?"

"Yup. The oldest, and a super internal one. When you're ready, maybe come try it with us someday? It's sublime. Kind of a flowing body, mind, spirit thing."

Sister Angeline's head dizzy with the rush and whir of *things*. The shifting of *things* in her mind, *things* rearranging, sorting themselves, but mostly bumping hard into themselves and falling into various lumps on the ground.

"It's a lot, I know. I should go so you can rest." She pauses and looks Sister Angeline straight in the eyes. "I think you're brave," she says and bounces fast out the door with Anu and Joan by her side.

For a moment there's an unfamiliar opening in Sister Angeline's heart. She isn't sure if it's a promising window or a perilous crack, but there's a hint of illumination to it.

Chapter Seven

Once Gina leaves, Sister Angeline looks around the gauzy space, her body an assemblage of contradictions.

She moves around the room, runs her hand along the cold cast iron of the propane stove, the pale cotton tuft of a candlewick, the rounded weathered edges of the blue and green sea glass lining the lamp's rim. "What's your story?" she whispers to a frosted green piece with a slightly pitted surface. "What were you before the waves washed you ashore? A bottle? A plate? A window?"

She walks then into the tiny bathroom. Its clean, sparkling space, with its private toilet, sink, and shower, shames her a little. In the cloister seventeen women shared two dingy toilets and two dingy showers in one bathroom with dim lighting. There were no sprigs of lavender in a white vase or fluffy duvets and hotel towels. Things made sense there.

Excess, Sister Josephine always said, *is a synonym for greed, an antonym for restraint. How can you be equipped to know the poor, the forlorn, if you don't live in their shoes?*

Sister Angeline looks into the mirror, thinking this is just another test to pass, thinking she needs to prove the mirror is no longer necessary, thinking if she doesn't look, the mirror will obsess her thoughts and make it hard for her to sleep and pray.

Her legs tremble.

She removes her veil and wimple, scapular, tunic, and undergarments.

She looks into the mirror. Makes eye contact with herself. Her body startles and shudders. She is surprised and also pleased to see that her outer self reflects her inner self. Her skin is pale and white, but not like a summer cloud, more like a chalky corpse. The shaved head, the hollowness of her cheeks. Her mother would have loved this face, this half-starved body. Her tall, thin, fashion-photographer mother loved angular faces and bodies better than round faces and bodies.

When Sister Angeline was little, they'd have fashion shows, she and her mother, but eventually, her mother gave up rolling out the red carpet because her daughter showed scant aptitude for the panache and vision of style and wouldn't even try to be thin. Meg did try—she tried so hard, spooning spaghetti sauce over raw spinach instead of pasta, running in place ten minutes for every extra hundred calories she'd eaten, writing every single calorie down in a tiny pocket notebook—but then the cravings would come after she crawled into bed, and she'd be downstairs in the dark kitchen at two in the morning, spooning peanut butter and ice cream fast into her mouth.

Once, her mother found an empty candy wrapper in her bedroom and had flown into the living room, high heels clicking on the laminate, the olive bouncing madly in her martini, her long red hair swept back and sprayed into waves, shrieking, *How could you?*

Sister Angeline runs her fingers along the map of her skull, then traces the shape of her lips. Her fingers start out soft but then get mean, press hard into the lips, the lips of betrayal, the lips that are to blame for everything. She opens her mouth slow, and there is the ugly tongue—no, that is not a tongue, that is a knife, a sharp knife, *don't forget that, you stupid girl*. The knife decides what it will cut, when it will cut, who it will cut. She watches as the tongue creeps out as if it is going to lick the lips and convince them to say something wrong, something false and dangerous.

Her hand rips the mirror off the hook and shoves it behind the toilet. Her heart pounding fast, she moves toward her suitcase and lifts it onto the bed and unzips it and reaches inside. She feels around for the metal. And now she kneels. She places her forehead on the floor. And now she flings the chain links hard over her bare left shoulder. Once. Twice. Now twice over her right shoulder. And then back to the left, the right, the left, the right. Again and again and again. Metal whipping skin and spine until she's certain there's blood, until she can feel the heat of the red breaking from under the skin, her mind gone white, her mouth murmuring, *Hail Mary, full of grace, love is with thee . . .*

And when she's repeated the prayer over and over, the fingers open slow and the whip falls to the floor and the body is shaking violently, and here, *oh look! here is my baby!* Her baby naked and bright on the bed, and Sister Angeline, her eyes wet with adoration, reaches in tentative, reaches in to smell its honeysuckle hair, the baby's eyes wide, the baby recognizing her, quiet as a blossom, but now the tiny body is turning into dust, and when Sister Angeline tries to stop the baby from disappearing, tries to say, *Please, I want to touch you, I want to hold you, I want to know you, I want to name you,* the baby dust falls through her fingers and dissolves into thin air, and all she can murmur is *come back come back come back.*

Chapter Eight

Sister Angeline wakes up, disoriented, astonished to see she's on the floor, astonished to see that she's naked. Naked in a bright, very white room with light blazing through the three little windows. Women's voices sing psalms somewhere in the distance. She feels like a madwoman in a death dream.

But there is the whip, and now she remembers. The taste of the sluttish tongue still in her mouth. She stands, snatches her bathrobe from her suitcase, and wraps herself tight in it. Hides the whip under the bed, frightened someone will take it from her. Sister Josephine hadn't known she'd used the whip, had fiercely condemned self-flagellation as a form of penance, but she hadn't known the enormity of Sister Angeline's transgressions. She wouldn't have understood how the pain brought her closer to her beloveds.

She walks into the bathroom. Brushes her teeth and her tongue hard. Notices the mirror behind the toilet and realizes removing it was a mistake. The mirror had given her a critical reminder last night, revealed ego not yet annihilated. She places it back on the wall. The mirror is her ally.

There is a knock at the door then, and a soft female voice asks to enter. Sister Angeline pulls her robe tighter. Her portion of the world much larger now, a place where anyone can knock on the door at any time. She takes a deep breath and forces herself to sound confident and ready for what lies ahead. "Come in," she says.

It's Kamika, holding a big yellow bowl of raspberries. "Good morning! Hope I'm not intruding."

Sister Angeline lies, says, "No, of course not."

"You must have been exhausted—you slept right through dinner and morning prayers and Mass."

"What! Oh no!" In seven years Sister Angeline has never missed prayers, never missed Mass. Receiving the Eucharist is a very necessary thing for her. She relates to Jesus, even though she's only seen his face on crosses and in books. This is someone who knew something about death and brokenness and suffering. And she needs the blessed wafer, the way it strengthens her, makes her a sturdier conduit for prayer, makes the rage in her shrink a little more each time she swallows one.

"It's okay, it's okay!" Kamika flashes Sister Angeline a warm smile, her dark eyes wide and amiable. She is wearing what she wore yesterday—a lavender tank top and green skirt to her ankles and an orange batik scarf tying up her long black hair. A tiny diamond in her nose glints light. "You've had a huge trip! A flight from Chicago to Seattle, a ferry here—that's no small thing. And to come from a cloister to this place?" She shakes her head and smiles. "Gina called your trip *epic*." Kamika holds out the yellow bowl to her. "Raspberries? They're wild—they grow like crazy on our property."

Sister Angeline smiles briefly, vaguely. She reminds herself that this is her life now and in this life people might bring her yellow bowls of raspberries whether she deserves it or not. Still, she doesn't need to accept them, even though the wild sweetness of the red berries tempts her. It is a new day, and she is determined to keep her vows. "No, thank you."

"Okay. Well, breakfast is in an hour. You'll hear three bells, and breakfast will begin fifteen minutes later. I'm making brown rice with figs and fresh thyme and rosemary from the garden. It's my mother's recipe. She served it every Saturday morning when we lived in Iraq, and it's delicious. I think you'll love it!"

Kamika's eyes wander around the room, and to Sister Angeline's horror, there is the handle of the whip, sticking out from under the bed, exposed. She sees Kamika fall into a sudden silence.

Sister Angeline's face blazing.

"I'd—I'd better go," Kamika says. "Don't want the rice to burn. See you soon, okay?" As she turns to leave, Sister Angeline can see a bluebird in flight inked onto her left shoulder, and something about that tells her Kamika will keep her secret.

Sister Angeline moves to the window, slides the glass open wide. Water like the silver blue of music, tipped with white froth, the glissando between waves, the slow hymn of orange rising into sky, a sailboat sliding toward the horizon. The scene delivers a sudden ache, an agitation. Three bells ring now, and she is taken by how soft they sound, comforted by the exquisite dignity, almost tenderness of their purpose.

She takes a quick shower and dresses. White panties, white bra. The hooks of the bra catch on a wound from the whip, and she flinches. She prays, "Please do not let anything force me from prayer and into distraction today. Clothe me in the spirit of making amends."

Now the black tunic and scapular: "Clothe me in the spirit of subduing bodily desires and keep me from being distracted."

She links her rosary to the small hook on the belt: "Unite me with those I love. Please make the links strong enough to never again break."

Next, the black shoes: "Today may I offer all my movements to God."

Finally, her hands fasten the black veil to the Velcro of the white wimple: "Whatever awaits outside this door, give me courage to face it with strength and love and calm."

Chapter Nine

Sister Angeline walks to the kitchen yurt, repeating, "Whatever awaits, give me courage to face it with strength and calm," unsure if she'll be able to quiet her pulse, but as soon as she enters, the scents of sweet fruit and cinnamon, garlic and onions, envelope her, bring her a sudden composure. Four women, Sigrid, Kamika, Alice, and Gina, rise from the wooden table, smile, and say good morning. The fifth woman—the tall, big-boned one dressed in full habit, who could be forty or fifty or sixty—stands with her arms folded, her face a grimace. A few faded red strands of hair poke from her rigid wimple.

"Sister Angeline, this is Edith," Sigrid says.

Sister Angeline extends her hand, resonating immediately with Edith because she has also chosen to wear the habit. "Lovely to meet you," she says.

Edith, however, keeps her arms folded and her lips tight. Sister Angeline draws her hand back, embarrassed and slightly taken aback. The glare in this woman's eyes unnerves and disappoints her.

"Seems you've finally decided to join us," Edith says. "How nice."

"Oh, for crying out loud, Edith, seriously?" Sigrid says, shaking her head. "C'mon, y'all, let's sit down. Honestly," she says, glaring at Edith.

Sister Angeline mortified. Gina pats the chair next to hers, and Sister Angeline sits, prays, *Give me strength.*

"Edith," Sigrid says evenly, "will you say the prayer?"

Edith stiffens but closes her eyes and folds her large hands. The others bow their heads. Sister Angeline shuts her eyes and makes the sign of the cross.

"For the nourishment and abundance provided here," Edith says, "we thank you. May we be energized and able to work hard for others, to do more for them than ourselves. May our hearts seek out ways to help and leave our own needs behind. Amen."

The softer tone of her prayer, even with its skew of accusation, relieves Sister Angeline slightly. To know that Edith can express concern for others unlocks her throat enough so that she is able to say amen.

The women open their eyes. For several minutes there's silence. Sister Angeline glances around at the faces and then studies the feast in front of her, not knowing what to do. Is she supposed to say something? Do something? Her empty stomach shudders with hunger.

"This is the recipe I told you about," Kamika says to her, breaking the quiet. "The one with the fresh figs and rosemary. Oh, and feta!" She passes Sister Angeline a big wooden spoon and a blue bowl of pungent brown rice. Once Sister Angeline spoons a tiny bit onto her plate, Gina offers her a basket of bread. "Gluten-free—super good for you," she says.

"Based on little or no evidence," Edith says, heaping a large portion of rice onto her plate.

"Well, it makes me feel better," Gina says. "So there's that."

"Sister Angeline," Sigrid says, redirecting the conversation, "we aren't going to bombard you with questions about yourself or tell you about us. We'll just let all of it come out in its own time. We know your way of relating these past seven years has been completely different to ours—so we'll pace ourselves. Does that make sense?"

Sister Angeline nods. Relieved. Speech isn't coming naturally for her—living in silence for so long, communicating only with sign language. She lifts a forkful of rice to her mouth. The fragrant smell. She tastes it. It's like nothing she's ever tasted before—the honey-like sweetness of the fig layered with the salty feta, the bitter rosemary and creamy rice awakens her taste buds, and she immediately takes another bite, another, and another.

"Guess you like it!" Kamika says, grinning.

"It's—it's wonderful." Sister Angeline realizing then how fast she's eating. She notices Edith's raised eyebrow, the sympathetic look on Alice's face, and quickly sets her fork down, wipes her mouth with her napkin.

Hunger is a cunning thing.

"So I want to talk about something," Sigrid says, looking around the table. "Apparently, folks don't want to have another Women's March in January because the last one was *ineffective.*" She shakes her head. "Largest protest in all of history, and that's what they're saying."

"Yeah, well," Gina says with a shrug, "I'm sure people said that about the Boston Tea party too, and the American

Revolution, am I right?" She licks a drip of honey off her finger, smears a thick slab of butter on a large chunk of bread.

"It's beyond me why anyone would say that," Sigrid says. "Protests are the foundation of our country—morale builders, a way to open conversations—"

Edith waves her hand dismissively. "C'mon. It was a bunch of weekend revolutionaries making themselves feel better—let's see if they have what it takes to keep going beyond knitting their pink pussy hats and inventing catchy slogans for their signs."

"Is that what you think we are?" Gina asks, her dark eyes daring Sister Edith. "Weekend revolutionaries?"

"Listen," Edith says now to Gina, everything about her unbending. "In the '90s, when you were still a toddler sucking on cherry lollipops, thousands of us marched in DC demanding LGBT rights—the Q wasn't even a thing then. But the decade went marching right on by, and nothing happened for fourteen years. Fourteen years! Even when something did finally happen? The new policy only protected rights in the workplace, not the bathrooms, which, you know, would have been, like, totally crazy!" Edith has trouble keeping her voice steady. "Let's face it, we've lost our ability to influence anything, and to think differently is completely delusional."

"Well, you weren't there," Gina says, shaking cinnamon angrily onto her rice, black curls trembling. "We were unstoppable. We were a force."

"Let's see if that unstoppable power finds its way to the voting booths," Edith says, brushing crumbs off her mouth with the back of her hand. "Sheesh, this stuff tastes like cardboard." She puts what's left of her gluten-free bread on the edge of her plate.

Sister Angeline nervously swallows orange juice from a jam jar, the scene passing before her like a stage play. Her thoughts move fast through feelings: first, astonishment at the level of freedom these women display, the lack of reserve and inhibition to say whatever they want; and now captivation; and now dismay at how little she understands the workings of the current world; and now nostalgia, this conversation evoking dinners with her own family.

If there was one thing to be envied about the Gorman family—the closely knit unit of mother, father, daughter, son—it was the deep level of affectionate banter and intellectual conversation around the dinner table, the place she'd learned about wonder and beauty and the strengths and failures of humans. Picasso, Matisse, O'Keefe, Plato, Curie, Dante, Brahms, the Beatles. They were a happy family. Except when her mother poured her third or fourth glass of wine and her father sucked down his third Jameson and it was as if a switch had flipped in their house and Meg had to hide Ricky in her closet, holding his hand until the awfulness was all over.

"You know, when I studied American History before I left home," Kamika says quietly, slowly peeling an orange, "I read about the women in 1840 who gathered in New York— the Seneca Falls Convention. I couldn't stop reading about them—their courage and—I mean—" She stops short, looks around the table at each of them, her face animated with passion. "I mean, those kinds of protests are unheard of where I came from." She takes a deep breath, and her eyes well. "To march with all of you, with thousands and thousands of others who cared so much about human rights—" Her wide, wet eyes stay with Edith's now. "It was—it was everything.

During the hours we marched, for the first time in months, I felt like I belonged."

Alice writes something fast in her small notebook. Her hand lifting the page to Kamika, who reads it aloud in a whisper, "You do belong."

The sound of ocean coming through the windows.

"Thank you, Alice," Kamika says and kisses the old woman on the cheek.

"And you," Edith says to Sister Angeline with an edge. "How do you feel about protests?"

Sister Angeline's temper triggered. She wants to snap at this woman, shoot her a barb, shout, *What's at the heart of this hostility! You don't even know me!* but then,

May all my movements be toward love.

"With all due respect," Sister Angeline says carefully, "I—"

Before she can say anything more: outside, a scream pierces the air.

Chapter Ten

Sigrid, Edith, and Gina run down the driveway toward the scream. Alice walks slowly with Sister Angeline, and Kamika holds her elbows to keep her steady. The scream coming from a girl pointing to the prayer box, a wooden structure nailed to an oak tree—the box a place where people leave notes of need, things they want the nuns to pray for: a dying mother, food, a longing. The girl quiets when she sees the nuns.

"Amelia! What is it?" Gina says. "What's wrong, honey?"

Sister Angeline recognizes Amelia as the girl she observed on the beach when she first arrived—the girl in the oversized yellow dress.

Amelia's chin trembling. "It's dead. The squirrel is dead." By her side, Anu jumps on the tree and barks madly.

"What squirrel? Down, Anu, down, girl," Sigrid commands. The dog obediently retreats, and Sigrid peers inside the box. Flinches. She takes out a note, unfolds it, and reads aloud, "'Go away. No one wants you here.'"

The others take turns looking, stepping back from the box, their faces whitening, mouths forming *O*'s.

Sister Angeline doesn't want to look, but she does. In the box, a squirrel lies on its stomach, motionless. Blood burbles from a tiny hole in its head. Its eyes flat, fixed on nothing. The vulnerability and innocence of it sinks into her belly like a punch. And there is a faint, raw smell—a smell that scrapes her throat, chokes her breathing. She wants to touch the tiny creature, stroke its silver-gray fur, wake it up. She reaches her hand toward the squirrel, and that's when it happens. For the first time in a long time, her eyes tingle in the way they had when she'd prayed as a child for the dying moth, for her brother to heal, for her father to come home.

"Don't touch it!" Edith shouts. "You're tampering with evidence!"

Startled, Sister Angeline jerks her hand away, and the tingling in her eyes abruptly disappears. Slightly disoriented, she drops the lid on the prayer box, backs up, and brings her hands together in a clench under her scapular.

Amelia stands next to her. She touches Sister Angeline's arm and whispers, "Is it dead?" The girl's face gaunt, blue half circles hang beneath her round gray eyes. A small white scar on her right cheek. In the light of the sun, the scar looks like a flickering sliver of moon.

"Yes, I'm afraid it is."

Amelia's small face crumples.

Sister Angeline bends down then and whispers in her ear, "I believe when someone dies, they become a star. I think this squirrel will become a very bright, beautiful star!"

Amelia gives her a tremor of a smile. She looks so incredibly young.

"Who would do such a thing?" Kamika cries.

"There are possibilities," Edith says. "Probably Collin's boy, Liam. Or one of his friends. You've seen their BB guns, and that's a BB gun hole if I ever saw one."

"Don't jump to conclusions, Edith," Sigrid says. "There are plenty of folks with BB guns around here. And why would those boys put a dead squirrel in the prayer box? We've never had a problem with them before."

"Take the blinders off, Sigrid. Kids will do anything when they're bored. And when they're angry like Liam—"

"Sweetheart," Kamika says, touching Amelia's shoulder, "did you see anyone around the prayer box?"

Amelia chews nervously on her stringy blond hair. "No. I—I just wanted to put this in the box," she says, holding up a scrap of white paper. "And I—I—"

"This is what happens when you don't have police," Edith says. "A place goes wild. Not that they'd be able to do much, since we've completely trampled any footprints that might have been helpful." She releases a deep, annoyed breath.

Sister Angeline turns to Gina. "No police?"

"Nope. They have to come from Madrona Island, and it has to be a super serious thing for them to come and it takes them forever to get here, so most folks take care of themselves and each other. There's an EMT, Collin Brown, who lives down at the marina and helps out if someone has a heart attack or something. All in all, though, we rarely have scary situations."

"This is scary," Amelia says in a tiny voice.

"Amelia, do you want to give us your note?" Kamika says.

"No, I don't." The girl runs down the road then, clutching the paper, the white of it fluttering in her hand like a lost bird.

Chapter Eleven

The sun beating down, Sigrid rolls up the sleeves of her flannel shirt and pulls the bill of her baseball cap to the front for more shade. "I'm sorry for this distress on your first morning," she says to Sister Angeline as they walk back. "Please don't think any more about it. Edith and I will take care of things. Your job is to get used to your new home, deal?"

"Yes, okay, but—" Sister Angeline wants to tell someone the mysterious energy has returned, wants to ask about—

"But—the girl, Amelia?" Sigrid takes a deep breath. "There's something really sad about her, isn't there? I just don't know that much about her, except she's new here. Her father recently bought the oyster farm on the other side of the island, and so far they've pretty much kept to themselves. There's a twelve-year-old brother named Jack, who seems a bit of a rascal." She takes another deeper breath. "I do wish we could have seen Amelia's note."

"I'll pray for her," Sister Angeline says quietly. *Does she have a mother? Does anyone else notice her sadness? Her father? Her teachers? How could they not?*

They arrive at the blue door of Sister Angeline's yurt. Nearby, Edith is already getting to work mowing the lawn. For the second time that day, a spasm of annoyance flashes through Sister Angeline at the sight of this dominating woman. She watches Edith push the mower up the grassy hill, can see the tightness in her broad shoulders, the rigidity of her neck, visible warning signals to stay away. But then Sister Angeline detects something else—an aloneness, a grief in the body of this bristling woman, an apology even—and in that moment her judgment about Edith softens slightly. She vows to remember this scene— the way contradictions weave between appearances.

"That's Edith praying," Sigrid says. "And you have an hour of personal prayer time now too. Pray anywhere you wish and in any way that makes sense for you. The chapel is always open, or you can stay in your room, walk on the beach, wherever you feel called."

Sister Angeline looks out beyond the grassy hill to the ocean spreading wide in front of her, the blue catching the morning sun and shooting sparks of light into the sky. She remembers then how her mother always said, *Someday, Meg, we will go to the ocean and walk on the sand in our bare feet with the spacious sky over us instead of these grimy clouds and we'll breathe air so clean it will hurt.*

"Thank you, but I'll stay here, in my room." She is not ready to feel the new world of ocean without her mother.

"Yes, of course," Sigrid says. "I get it." She reaches down to adjust one of the solar panels on the miniature power plant by the door. "It's no small thing the way silence changes you, how it can make you crave more and more of it. I found tremendous clarity and peace in the cloister."

Sister Angeline is surprised to see her wipe her eyes as she stands up.

"But I left, came here." She turns and looks at the small group of yurts clustered on the grassy hill. "I wanted to begin a new community—one of equality, no one's agency ignored. Now mind, we don't receive funding from the Seattle Archdiocese—they've disowned us—but we manage just fine with our gardening and the generous donations of neighbors. Anyway," she says, looking at Sister Angeline. "Listen for the next bell. It announces it's time for chores, though we're making an exception for you today. Kamika is taking you to visit St. Paul's Catholic Church. As I'm sure Josephine told you, we don't attend it—we hold our own services for the Sisters in our chapel and take turns offering the homily and the sacraments."

Sister Angeline transfixed by this woman in front of her, the words she's spoken. How does someone become unafraid like this? Fierce without a performance of thorns?

Sigrid points up the hill to the apple orchard. "See that big white barn behind the trees—the one that needs a hundred gallons of paint? That's where we hold our public Sunday services. We sing. We break bread. We pray." She stops now and looks again to the ocean. "If that feels like too much for you," Sigrid says, "which is completely understandable—you can attend Mass at St. Paul's. No judgment." But something shifts in her face now, her smile thins. "You can check out the new priest, Father Matt. Fresh from the seminary." It looks like she might say something more, but she stops herself, then begins again. "His parishioners seem to like him—partly, I suppose, because he toes the Vatican line."

Weeks ago, in an unexpected desire to push beyond her fears,

Sister Angeline decided that if she were to come all this way to be part of Sigrid's community, if this is what Sister Josephine wanted for her, she would step fully into it. Until she knew what she wanted for herself. Until she knew what God wanted for her. Even if she only took one or two steps forward at a time. Even if she moved in slow motion. Even if she stood still and watched.

Though now the mention of attending a traditional Mass creates a craving within her. A craving for a place she's known all her life, a place so sure of itself, so predictable and efficient with its rules and rituals, a stained-glass place that smells

like boundaries,

like safety,

like father,

a place that, despite its faults and imperfections and cruelties, has somehow shaped and comforted her and become a place she could rest her head upon.

"I'll think about it," she says, and with that she slips inside her yurt and gently closes the door, restored to her privacy for the moment.

Sister Angeline lies on her bed and feels like her head might explode. It's not even noon, and at every turn she's encountered disturbance and turmoil. And despite the return of the mysterious energy, all she can see, all she can hear, is the frightened little girl asking, *Is it dead, is it dead?*

She shuts it out, shuts her eyes, attempts to breathe in peace, but disquiet has pushed open the door of her subconscious, a door she'd long since locked, and her nerves are so frazzled, she is unable to pray away the memories.

Her aunt Nell sitting by her in a beige room that smells like ammonia, her aunt saying things, horrible things: *Your mother is dead, your father too, your brother too, and you'll go home with me, you'll stay with me now, Meg, do you understand?* and pain firing through her body, and now the room is spinning with its bright ceiling lights and chemical smells and Meg's skin is burning and the sound of her pulse is loud in her ears.

And now
her aunt's
voice
moving away
                        moving away
and Meg touching her stomach and murmuring,
What about the baby the baby the baby the baby.

Chapter Twelve

Kamika and Sister Angeline walk the narrow road to St. Paul's Church—a ten-minute stroll from the convent. Anu runs ahead, nose pointed into the salty wind. Madrona trees with their cinnamony-red bark line one side of the road, their roots traveling under the asphalt and cracking it in places. On the other side of the road, the water, turbulent and frothing, waves slamming against stone, rattling them with every crash. Kamika points out a kingfisher, a great blue heron, and a Dall's porpoise.

Ahead in a field, a small bird with gray feathers lands on a cow's brown hide. The nonchalant way the cow looks at them as they walk by. Sister Angeline allows herself to absorb this loveliness, allows the sun to soak into her skin, tries not to worry that she is walking alone with another nun. In the cloister moving in twos was asking for trouble. It wasn't that they couldn't be there for each other—they were encouraged to build each other up—but pairing up suggested a particular friendship, a distraction from vocation. Such a relationship might cause discord or division within the community, or worse, a distancing from God.

"I have something to tell you," Kamika says quietly. She stops, removes her sunglasses, and blinks into the brightness. The tiny diamond in her nose sparkling. Since breakfast she has coiled her long black hair into a bun and braided a wide orange ribbon through it. "I didn't want to wait to tell you—well, I'm just going to come right out and say it. I'm—I'm not a nun. I'm not a Sister. I'm not Catholic. I'm Muslim."

Startled, Sister Angeline says, "Oh," but doesn't know what to say after that. She'd known this place would be unconventional, but this degree of nonconformity stuns her.

"The other Sisters know, many of the people on the island know," Kamika says, "and I wanted you to be aware too, because you might notice I don't say all the prayers."

I don't say all the prayers either.

Kamika removes her sandals and begins walking again, barefoot now, making Sister Angeline's black shoes feel heavy as concrete.

"I grew up in Baghdad," Kamika says. "When Saddam Hussein lost power, my family went into hiding because we'd be prosecuted, maybe killed. My father was part of Hussein's government—he had no choice; we needed the money. He ran the transportation department, and when the US captured Hussein, anyone who worked for him wasn't allowed to work for the new government."

She keeps looking straight ahead. "Hundreds of us went into hiding. So many disappeared or were executed—my little brother Amari, my father." She stops now, turns to Sister Angeline. Her eyes charged with pain. "It was a—a cleansing—of one Muslim sect by another."

The sun unbearably hot here. Here, where anyone can say

anything at any time. Kamika's words slowly reach into Sister Angeline's heart, her lungs, and she can only watch the words

executed

my little brother

executed

my father

executed

fall slow motion from the lips of this beautiful woman standing in front of her, words dropping from her tender mouth to the gravel near their feet, and Sister Angeline wants to gather the suffering up and transport it to the water, where the tide can absorb it into its own blue space.

But all she can do is murmur, "I'm sorry."

Anu licks Kamika's toes then, licks and licks, and then sits by her, pressing into her legs, and Kamika blinks away tears and rubs the top of the dog's head but keeps looking at Sister Angeline, holding her focus steady as if something might break should she turn away.

Finally, Kamika says, "When I was twenty-three, I got a job as a translator for the US Army. I moved to New York to help negotiate contracts, and because I worked for the US government for three years, I was given asylum to stay in America indefinitely."

In a very gentle voice, Sister Angeline says, "How did you— Why are you here?"

"When I was younger, I could hear the bells from Our Lady of Refuge Catholic Church from our house. Three times a day—6:00 a.m., noon, and 6:00 p.m. The bells gave me comfort.

One day I walked to the church and found a newspaper on the steps, the *Catholic Leader*, and I stuck it in my bag. Later I read an article in it about Light of the Sea convent. I was drawn to these women—how they'd been excommunicated, how they rebelled against patriarchy, how they questioned the contradictions in the Church without losing their faith, how they're creating a new way to be in community."

Her brown eyes shift suddenly, like dawn to morning, light spreading across her face. "I saved the article for years, and one day I wrote Sigrid, found out this convent was still alive and thriving, and well, here I am. I'm not planning on becoming a nun—I love my own religion too much—but I feel safe here."

"Where is your mother?" Sister Angeline had been afraid to ask this question, afraid that something worse than execution had happened. Then it came to her that maybe the mother was still alive somewhere.

"I—I haven't seen her in seven years," Kamika says. "She's hiding, I think, probably somewhere in Turkey, maybe even France, I don't know. We've agreed not to communicate until she's certain we're safe, but she'll come for me. I know it."

"How will she know where to find you?"

"There's a place, a newsstand in New York. I left a note with my address with a woman there who helps immigrants. It's like an underground information network. If my mother makes it somehow to New York, she'll go there and find my note."

"She wouldn't be safe in the United States?"

"I don't know." Kamika's eyes change now; they are not soft or warm—the brown of them almost black. "I dream of the day we're no longer worth searching for." Tears stream down her cheeks.

"I'm—really sorry for what you've been through. You shouldn't have to hide. And you shouldn't have lost your family."

She thinks maybe she should tell Kamika about those she lost too. But then she thinks *lost* is a strange word. I *lost* my shoe. I *lost* my book. I *lost* my way. I *lost* my family. As if your family is a shoe or a book or a direction. As if you haven't lost yourself.

Chapter Thirteen

Sister Angeline and Kamika arrive at the church. It looks like the kind of church a child might draw. It is a small, white square structure with a red door and a simple wooden cross on the steeple. It is also dilapidated. The paint is peeling, and one of the stained-glass windows is cracked. Sister Angeline can see how it used to be pretty, though. Behind the church is a small wooden house with a sign that says, Pastor's House.

"Even with people coming from all four islands, church attendance here is low," Kamika says. "But Sigrid's service? Hers is so popular, we've had to move the Sunday service from the chapel into the barn. It's astonishing really, that people don't seem to worry she's a woman, even though the Vatican declared the communion she offers invalid. People know this, and yet still they come, still have her baptize their children, still have her marry them."

It is astonishing, Sister Angeline thinks. To give up a religion so much a part of your core identity. The courage that must take.

She walks over to a life-size statue of St. Francis, the statue leaning against a madrona tree, the face gazing lamely into the sky. She tilts her head and looks into his eyes. St. Francis, the patron saint of ecology and animals. A stone dove perches on his shoulder, and an adoring lamb and wolf lie at his feet. She touches the saint's face as if it is a newborn, wipes the green moss off his cheeks, exposes the childlike eyes. Tranquility fills her.

"The wind must have blown him over. Shall we straighten him?" Kamika says.

As the two women struggle to lift St. Francis, Sister Angeline suddenly finds herself face-to-face with the statue again, his lips almost touching hers, his eyes no longer childlike, but startled as if he is surprised to see her there. She drops her hands, and he rocks back and forth for a moment, still gazing at her in a confused way.

Kamika pushes his bare feet hard into the original hole, covers them with dirt and rocks, pats a little extra dirt around the wolf and lamb. "There," she says. "He's steady now. We'd better get going."

Sister Angeline wants to stay with St. Francis, notices his expression has changed; he looks forlorn, troubled. She doesn't say this, only leaves him there and follows Kamika across the stone path and into the church.

The usual scents of incense and candle wax, the pews dark and grimy, and the cracked plaster walls need painting. Sister Angeline is surprised to see a grand piano in the corner. She walks over to the piano, lifts the dusty keyboard cover, and presses one of the ivory keys with her index finger. The sweet note floating up up up.

"Do you play?" Kamika asks.

"A little."

"You can play anytime you want," Kamika says. "Whenever there isn't Mass."

This news wakes up longing. Faint flames tingling Sister Angeline's fingers.

"Play something?" Kamika says.

But now behind them, a man clears his throat.

The two women turn around.

A priest. He is young, late thirties. This must be Father Matt. He is handsome. His wavy hair as black as his shirt—the shirt buttoned up to his neck, the black cloth sewn to accommodate a small white square at the base of his throat.

He grins and extends his hand to Sister Angeline. He is only a few inches taller than her. "Hello," he says, his voice filled with warmth. "I'm Father Matt."

She receives his hand. "Sister Angeline."

He squeezes her hand a little too hard, and she thinks maybe he is nervous, like her. It is not easy to be a new person in a new place, to be somewhere between the known and the unknown.

"A pleasure," he says. His eyes glint in a way that makes her feel as if he is looking right through her—she's not sure if this is a good thing or a bad thing.

"Afternoon, Father Matt," Kamika says.

"*Sister* Kamika," he says. And then, "Sorry. I keep forgetting y'all have dropped those formalities. Forgive me." Even though he's smiling, there is a tinge of derision.

She understands now why Sigrid's tone changed when talking about him. He's not a supporter of this liberal convent. But then why would he be? He's following the rules of the Church, like he's supposed to. Like he's vowed to do. Now she's vowed to do. She's on the side that's breaking them. What has she gotten herself into?

Father Matt turns back to Sister Angeline. "So you've joined the radicals, huh?"

Her cheeks heat up. She looks away. Quietly shuts the piano keyboard lid.

His voice softening now. "I'd love to have you attend my Mass," he says. "Give me a fair shot?"

What is she to say? He is so earnest, so serious. And maybe because he can see right through her and she is wearing a habit, he knows she has not fully committed to this change in her life.

"We need to go," Kamika says. "It's almost time for the midday meal."

"Think about it?" he says to Sister Angeline, who nods imperceptibly as she leaves the church.

"He's persistent, I'll give him that, doesn't take no for an answer," Kamika says once they're outside. "His congregation is very small—it's been diminishing ever since Sigrid opened our services to the public. The priest before him, Father Damian, had been here forever, and I'm not sure he even noticed the pews were emptying."

"Must be hard on him, Father Matt," Sister Angeline says. She thinks, too, that less than a year ago he'd probably been in a seminary with at least fifty other young men, and now, except for daily Masses, he is completely alone.

In the cloister, though solitude was the essential foundation, all the conditions were in place to clear the mind and body, to achieve the inordinate effort of freeing the whole self—there must be no interruption, nothing to distract from the expression of prayer. Still, part of those conditions included gathering several times a day with others, to pray, to sing, to eat. And the time spent, it seemed to Sister Angeline, was just the right amount of time—not too much and not too little. Just enough time to hear Sister Claire sing as if she were in a famous opera but didn't know it, just enough time for Sister Mary Regina to smile across the supper table as she offered to pour a cup of tea, the freckles across the bridge of her nose, little light beacons on her round face, just enough time to feel the pulse of Sister Therese as they touched elbows in the hallway. Just enough time to know she wasn't alone in the world.

Outside she goes to St. Francis again. He gazes at her steadily as if he is alive with a heart and lungs, muscles and bones. His eyes are no longer gray but very white and strange and beautiful, opening and closing, making her feel suddenly shy and awkward. It is then she feels her own eyes begin to change, begin to sting—first the blue one, then the brown one.

A hot violet light envelops her now, makes her light-headed, and she moves her hands to touch the open hands of St. Francis. The heat of absolute tenderness spreads from her body to his. She is completely attentive, watching his eyes turn into a bright fire of orange, then paling into a pool of blue. Little by little the statue's face changes. Softens.

The lips open in a hesitant way, and as she moves her face closer, she can hear small sounds, utterances slightly bent and misshapen, an Italian trace, and now words unrolling slowly from the mouth:

Do not fear your rage.

But now Kamika is calling, "Sister Angeline! C'mon, we have

to go!" and St. Francis suddenly goes stone cold, his entire face and body inexpressive. Sister Angeline doesn't say a word, only rubs and rubs her eyes until she can see again, and, distressed, runs down the road to the convent.

Chapter Fourteen

It's late afternoon, and the six women gather for Vespers in the chapel. They dip their fingers into the font—a white scallop shell attached to the doorframe—and make wet crosses on their bodies. Sister Angeline stands among them, listening to the summer rain pattering on the canvas roof, watching the drops trickling down the windows. How badly she wants to stand in the falling water, let it wash her face, let it wash away the awkwardness with Father Matt and the confusion of St. Francis.

Alice lights two tall white candles on the altar and blows out the match with a mighty *whoosh*, as the Sisters divide into two groups of three on each side of the altar. They chant a call and response, and even though it's in English, the prayer isn't one Sister Angeline recognizes.

"Just listen," Gina whispers in her ear. "You'll learn the words soon enough."

Sister Angeline's eyes close, her body still tense from the day, and she tries to listen, but the words *so you've joined the radicals* and *do not fear your rage* tangle through her mind and she's not sure which voices to listen to and it's impossible to concentrate.

She is not unsettled by the statue speaking to her—she's elated to have the mysterious energy returning in any form. She's unsettled because she doesn't understand why St. Francis would say this to her now.

Her pulse increases and she tries again to focus on the prayers and she thinks she hears the women sing *dive into unknown waters* or is it *dance into unknown stars*, but again and again her mind wanders, and again and again she brings herself back to the present until finally the Sisters are chanting in Latin, which she is familiar with and likes very much, the beauty and intensity of it, so that even when Vespers is over, she continues to chant Latin verses until dinner and in this way she passes several hours not thinking about Father Matt or St. Francis.

For dinner they have beet soup, garlic snow peas, and figs stuffed with goat cheese. With the exception of the rain drumming on the canvas and Sigrid saying grace and spoons clinking and chewing and swallowing and the tinkling of Kamika's bracelets, it is quiet. Is everyone's mind as crammed as hers? No matter, Sister Angeline is thankful for the silence—this is what she wants more than anything: the absence of questioning and disturbance and turmoil—space for contemplation, meditation, God. But she is too ravenous to fulfill any other desire than to consume food, too ravenous to remember her vow of poverty. She gulps every last drop of her soup, eats five snow peas and at least three stuffed figs before the statue's words again twist her mind, winding her brain so tightly that she is forced to murmur sounds aloud, the others saying, "What is it? Sister Angeline, what's wrong?"

It is Sigrid who finally shakes her and insists she leave the table and get some rest, and Alice who gently takes her hand and escorts her to bed, undressing her, and tucking her in like a child, even caressing and kissing her cheek. And when she feels Alice stroke the wounds on her back, hears her singing a lullaby, she mistakes her for her mother and falls into a deep sleep.

It isn't long before Sister Angeline awakens and the words are closing in again and she tries to soothe herself by repeating, "Ave Maria, gratia plena, Dominus tecum," but nothing works, and *why didn't St. Francis know it was my rage that destroyed everything I loved*, and she rises from the bed now, shame an overwhelming presence, and reaches for her whip. But abruptly she drops it, grabs the flashlight from her dresser, and heads out into the night toward the statue.

The rain has stopped, but the wind is wild, branches snap against each other, and the waves pound against the shore. A half-moon in the sky slants light across the road and illuminates the ocean beside her. Sister Angeline isn't frightened to be alone in the night. She is focused on her mission.

The road is longer and bends more than she remembers, and she worries she's gone past the church. But now, finally, here it is, red votives glowing from the stained-glass windows.

Behind the church Father Matt's house sits dark, and she thinks he must be asleep, and she is relieved. She shines her flashlight on the gate latch, flips it open, and walks quietly toward St. Francis, the wind becoming even stronger now, dead branches dropping everywhere, worsened by the shadows they cast, and she can't help but feel they are aimed at her, messages shouting that her presence won't be tolerated.

The statue glows in the moonlight, its unblinking eyes

inches from her face. She places her hands on his stone chest. "Please," she says. "Tell me—why did you say 'Do not fear your rage'?"

She waits. She waits for some sort of connection, some current to flow, some revelation.

Nothing.

No tingling of her eyes, no heat moving through her body.

Nothing.

The wind lobs branches like grenades now.

She moves her hands until they hold his face. "Talk to me," she pleads. "Talk to me."

Silence.

She presses his eyes lightly, touches his ears, his neck, his arms, traces the top of his head.

He remains mute, inanimate, defunct.

Particles of confusion and anger vibrate in her chest, the friction escalating, creating a heat that spirals fast into her legs, arms, neck, face.

"Rage is a destructive thing! A destructive thing!" she shouts, and now tears are flying, and her fists are beating beating beating against his chest

and he tips

and lands

with a dull crack

on the concrete path.

A part of his face has broken off.

Her hand over her mouth, she stands there in the dark, shaken and waiting as if she believes he might become suddenly unbroken and stand of his own accord. She doesn't know how long she stands there, hope evaporating, until finally, she decides to lift him—it is almost impossible, but somehow she manages to lean him against the church.

"Hey, what's going on out there?"

Father Matt.

Flickers of a flashlight beam.

She freezes.

It doesn't sound like he's moving toward her, though it's hard to tell, the wind drowning every sound but itself. When she's sure he's gone back inside, when she thinks she hears his front door slam shut, she picks up the stone fragment of the statue's face and runs fast back to her yurt.

There, she wraps the fragment in her mother's silk scarf and sets it on the dresser, whispering to St. Francis, "Forgive me, forgive me." Then she removes her coat and her nightgown, grasps the whip, lowers herself to the floor, and draws blood.

Chapter Fifteen

In the chapel, the thin wafer dissolving on her tongue, Sister Angeline imagines light surrounding her. She draws the light into every part of her body and then, on her outward breath, sends light to the squirrel and to whoever shot the squirrel and to Edith, who seems to be carrying a heavy weight, bullying her way toward her own God, and to Amelia and the white note in the palm of her hand, and to Kamika and to Alice and to St. Francis, but then the image of the statue, and she thinks, *Goddamn you, Angeline,* and she feels for the fragment in her pocket and wraps her fingers around it until an edge cuts into the palm of her hand.

After the service, the six women prepare breakfast. A morning breeze and the coo of doves float through the windows. Gina fries eggs in a large cast-iron pan, and Kamika cuts chives and parsley to sprinkle on top of the lemony yokes. Sigrid, in a faded denim shirt and purple suspenders, piles blackberries into a huge white bowl and sings "Fire and Rain" along with James Taylor on the radio. Edith grinds coffee beans, and Alice brews tea that releases the intimate scents of cinnamon and orange.

Sister Angeline lays down a flowered tablecloth and sets out blue plates and mugs. She attempts to breathe in all the comfortable sensations, but she's become unsettled again from the previous night, and the welts on her back are a stinging reminder of the damage she's caused St. Francis.

Once they are all seated, Gina reads a poem by Ada Limón, a poem called "Maybe I'll Be Another Kind of Mother," and Sister Angeline is comforted by the way the poet suggests a childless existence is not an inferior one.

Sister Angeline blows on her tea. Considers whether or not she should tell them what happened last night, afraid anything she says will confirm she's unbalanced, unhinged—that she was sent here because who else would have her?

This is the same nervous feeling she'd had with Mother Hildegard, the psychiatrist who had interviewed her for entrance into the Daughters of Mercy convent, the psychiatrist who kept asking her what she remembered about *the accident*, who kept saying, *What else, what else, what else*, even though Sister Angeline repeated, *I don't remember, I don't remember, I don't remember*. In the end, the psychiatrist approved her entrance, saying grief wasn't a crime.

Sister Angeline makes eye contact with Alice, and something about the flickering light in her eyes makes Sister Angeline think she should take a chance and confide in these women. Uncertainty and awkwardness shift inside her. In the cloister if she had a problem, she solved it privately, but then, in that isolated place where she followed and blended in, she didn't have this kind of a problem. *Still*, she thinks, *I'm here now, and I'll never know unless I try*.

"Something's happened," she says, looking around the table, her face flushing. "I've done something awful."

The Sisters stop eating and give her their full attention. Sister Angeline swallows, her courage threatening to coil tighter around her lungs if she continues to talk.

Edith breaks her silence. "Well? What? What did you do?"

Sister Angeline reaches into her pocket for the scarf holding the broken fragment of St. Francis. She lays it on the table and unwraps the cloth slowly, like a child bringing a dying bird into the house to show her parents, hoping they'll know how to revive it.

"Last night, I went back to St. Paul's because I wanted to ask St. Francis something, but I became so angry that I pushed him and I—broke him, his face. I just— I need some glue or something, and I need to go there and fix him before— I just can't—" She can hear herself beginning to sound slightly hysterical and stops herself from saying more.

"You broke St. Francis because you were angry? Well, maybe there's hope for you yet," Edith says, spooning blackberries into her mouth.

Edith's words throw Sister Angeline back into silence, and she breaks her toast into little pieces, struggling to hide her anger, feeling like a fly caught in a web. *Hope for me yet?* It's hard enough having expectations for yourself, but when others jump in, desiring to rearrange you into versions of themselves, how can you not dream of solitude, not dream of living as a hermit?

"Sister Angeline," Kamika says, "do you want to talk about what made you so angry?"

"No. No, I don't." Her voice cracks as she speaks. What is happening? Why does anger keep coming up?

Alice reaches over and squeezes her hand.

"I've got something that'll fix the statue," Gina says. "We'll go after breakfast. Meet me at my yurt."

Chapter
Sixteen

Sister Angeline's eyes pass over the objects in Gina's space: the embroidered cushions on the floor, the easels with their abstract paintings—there must be at least ten of them of all shapes and sizes around the room—the cans of paints and bottles of brushes filling floor-to-ceiling shelves. Under one of the small windows, a long wooden table splattered with blues, greens, purples, golds, and reds. Everywhere the smell of paint, vision, and creativity. It is enchanting here, and she doesn't ever want to leave. "You're an artist," she whispers.

Gina leans against the door. She's wearing a black cotton T-shirt, faded jeans with torn knees, and black flip-flops. Her black hair spirals wildly around her face. She smiles, shrugs. "It's really just how I stay sane. I mean, don't you find that with your writing sometimes? That it's a place to put all the confusion and chaos, the jagged edges, the grief, the anger?"

Anger again.

It's then that Angeline notices there's a loud black line, a jagged line, running through the middle of every single painting, splitting

the vivid abstract landscapes into two sections. She moves closer to
the nearest one, and her eyes follow the long narrow delineation.
She follows it through waves of a yellow the color of ripe lemon,
then through a purple helix of various hues—colors that seem to
be dancing, they feel that joyful—but as her eyes move along, a
feeling of sorrow pulsates through her heart, her chest, her eyes.
She stands there, blinking at the painting. This is her life. She is
the ugly black line. Beauty had been all around her, everywhere
there'd been joy, but her actions had ruined everything.

Tears stream down her face.

Gina touches her shoulder, offers a box of tissues. "Talk
about it?" she says.

Sister Angeline wipes her cheeks, silent for a few moments,
still staring at the painting. She doesn't know what to say. Where
would she start? She's never spoken to anyone about any of it.
She doesn't even know, really, what *it* is. She's tried to

write about it

but she always becomes afraid

of slipping off an edge.

"Sister Angeline?"

She turns now, looks into the warmth of Gina's brown eyes,
and says, "May I ask you a question?"

Gina sets the tissue box on the art table. "Please."

"What do the black lines mean to you?"

Gina pushes her hands into the pockets of her jeans, and a
flicker of anguish darkens her face. "Honestly, and you might
think this is strange—I'm not sure." She shakes her head slowly.
"There was a time I was afraid to paint because the black kept
inserting itself into my work; sometimes it wandered in sneak-
ily, sometimes the line plunged and cut, and without fail, it

felt—well, it felt kind of violent, like I was splitting apart at some subterranean level."

Gina's eyes take on a weighted sadness in that moment, a despair that makes Sister Angeline want to reach out to her, touch her, but discretion accompanies her impulse to touch; she doesn't know her well enough yet to cross that boundary. Instead, she says, "You're not afraid anymore?"

Gina reaches across the art table and brings out a folded piece of paper from inside a small clay bowl. She unfolds the paper, and here is a tiny black stone, slender as a dime. "A few months ago, I spoke to Alice about my fear of the black line, and she gave me this stone, wrapped in this note." Gina gently sets the stone on the table and reads the message aloud:

Dearest Gina,

Try to stay open. Sometimes our need to believe that something is true is stronger than the truth. Follow the line. Imagine the line as a road.

"I'd never thought of it that way," Gina says, folding the stone back into the note and placing both into the bowl. "I've always felt like the violence was pursuing me. I've always felt like—like I needed to flee."

"From?"

Gina takes a deep breath. "Let's talk about that another time," she says. "Right now we need to fix your statue, okay?"

Sister Angeline nods, her own pain dissolving, her heart opening wider to this woman standing in front of her—a woman who seems to know something about torment and sorrow.

Gina grabs a small can, a tiny brush, and a few rags from

her art table and stuffs them all into a canvas bag she pulls from her nightstand.

The drawer of the nightstand stays open, exposing a small silver gun.

"Oh," Sister Angeline says.

Gina sees her see it. "My father's," she says. "I keep it to remind me of things"—she pauses for a second, biting her lip—"but also because there are no police on the island."

Sister Angeline falls silent. This place is the opposite of Chicago, with its thousands and thousands of police. In Sister Angeline's neighborhood alone, there were at least ten officers patrolling, maybe more. "You—you know how to use it?" she says.

"Oh, yeah." Gina picks up the gun, polishes it with the little red cloth it was sitting upon. "This is a revolver, a .38 Special. My father was a cop, and he made sure I knew how to use it." She imitates her father now, her voice deep and mocking and startlingly cold. "'You need to get over your fears, missy. Staying afraid keeps you a little girl. Facing your fears makes you a woman.'"

Sister Angeline stiffens. She hates guns. Hates that bullets can enter a life and bleed it out. Her mother carried a small silver gun in her purse. When Meg was seven, she'd found the gun when looking for dimes and quarters. Her mother had thrown her hard against the wall then. *If you ever tell your father.* And from that moment on, whenever her parents raged at each other, whenever her mother raged at her, she feared her mother would take that little silver gun from her purse and end her father's life or her own.

Gina holds the gun out to her. "Do you want to see what it feels like? It's heavy, better to hold it with two hands."

"No!" Sister Angeline cries, the gun too close too close too close, and she backs away, holding both palms up.

"Okay, okay, I'm sorry. Didn't mean to scare you." Gina places the gun in the nightstand, shuts the drawer. "Listen, I get it. Lots of people hate guns. There's a lot to hate about them." She shakes her head. "Still, the police can't protect us if they're not here, so here I am! A nun with a gun!" She throws her arms up in a cheerleading way, flutters her extraordinarily long lashes, and it's impossible for Sister Angeline not to smile a little.

"Hey," Gina says, dropping her arms and looking at her watch. "We'd better get going if we're going to make it back for midmorning prayer. Also, if we're lucky, we'll finish before Father Matt's daily Mass lets out."

Chapter Seventeen

Sister Angeline and Gina arrive at St. Paul's. The riotous wind from the night before has ended, and sunlight filters through the canopy of cedars surrounding the church. Leaves are glistening wet, the air fragrant with moist earth and ocean salt.

"Oh, I just love the smell after it rains!" Gina says. "Did you know there's actually a name for it? It's *petrichor*! Isn't that wonderful?"

Sister Angeline too anxious to feel delight or savor sweet smells in this moment. She lifts her skirt and steps gingerly over a large tree limb. "What if Father Matt sees us?" she says.

Gina touches her arm, Sister Angeline instinctively flinching. Gina removes her hand, looks straight into Sister Angeline's eyes, and says with incredible self-assurance, "We've got this. Breathe. Besides, Mass is in session, which means we have at least thirty minutes."

Hail Mary, full of grace. Be with us now. Please be with us now.

"St. Francis is awfully close to that open window though.

We'll have to be super quiet," Gina whispers, opening the gate slowly. "But at least he's off to the side and behind that tree—no one will see us from the road."

Someone has moved St. Francis and thought it necessary to chain him to the cedar tree, wrapping the chain around his body and the thick tree not once but twice, securing all of it with a padlock. When Sister Angeline sees the chain and the broken face of St. Francis smeared with dirt, her heart sinks.

In the church someone is playing "Now Thank We All Our God" on the organ, and Sister Angeline's eyes widen. This is the song her father sang to her so many times when she was small. She remembers how she'd thought the *our* in the song's title was *are* and how shocked and disappointed she'd been when her father told her the difference, even though at the time she wasn't able to articulate why.

Later, she'd realized the revelation had upended her own belief that God's light and power was within everyone and not about one entity possessing the other. This realization hadn't changed her beliefs, but it had made her genuinely doubt God's internal workings and made her wonder if she'd imagined the violet light and the vibrations as a way to express her fears and sadness and make her childhood more tolerable, more magical.

She reaches into her pocket, retrieving the stone fragment, and Gina opens her canvas bag and brings out two small white cloths and a jar of clear liquid. "Water," she whispers. "We need to clean his face first." She gives Sister Angeline one of the cloths. "I'll wash and you dry."

Gina pours a little water onto the white cloth and rubs the crown of his head. She pours more water onto the cloth and rubs the open eyes, ears, nose, the curve of his lips, and finally, with the last of the water, she washes the entire edge of the wound, the missing cheek, and Sister Angeline dries and dries until his face is bright as new linen.

Next, Gina brings out a small can, sets it on the pine-needled ground. With a blunt knife, she pries off the lid, and there inside: liquid gold.

Sister Angeline gasps.

"Gorgeous, huh? I mixed powdered gold paint into an extra strong adhesive," Gina whispers. "Bonding stone to stone is tricky, especially if the stone is exposed to heavy rain, but I've used this before with concrete and it worked superbly, and this is such a small piece, so—"

"It's beautiful, but—the statue is—white."

"Kintsugi," Gina says softly, stirring the mixture with a wooden stick from her bag. "The Japanese art of creating precious scars—the idea that damaged objects are not something to hide, but to be illuminated—because well, there's beauty in the broken things."

She turns her face up to look at Sister Angeline now, her eyes hopeful, but still, there it is again, the flecks of something painful lingering, flickering scarlet in the brown iris.

Sister Angeline unwraps the fragment and holds it out to her.

Gina takes it and kisses it. She lifts it up to Sister Angeline's lips. "Kiss it too," she whispers.

Surprised but deeply touched by the gesture, Sister Angeline closes her eyes and kisses the stone as if it's a child's wound. The stone still warm from being wrapped in her mother's silk.

Now Gina carefully spreads a thin layer of the golden

substance onto the back of the stone. A faint smoky smell drifts from it—it's surprisingly honeyed and mellow, like a pleasing memory or an apology. She positions the cheek into place, holds it there for a moment. "For this next part, I'm going to need you to keep pressing gently, firmly, and keep up the pressure. It dries super fast, like within minutes, but still. We have maybe fifteen until Mass ends, so hold it at least another five."

Sister Angeline holds her breath so she can be as steady as possible and presses the fragment firmly into the face, releasing her breath slowly.

Gina dips her tiny brush into the gold and, with an extraordinarily unwavering touch, paints a hair-thin line along the crack. They are so close together, their shoulders brushing, and Sister Angeline can feel the warmth of Gina's body, can feel her concentration, can feel the energy vibrating through Gina's arm into her hand into her brush into the gold, can feel the pulsation guiding the brush, working to restore awaken resurrect save.

When she's done, Gina steps back and studies her work. "Perfect," she says. "Wait till you see it from here! But don't move yet—just a few more minutes."

It is then they hear Father Matt talking loudly about the vandalism at the church last night. They freeze, listening intently. "Some hoodlums," he shouts. "No, a thug! A thug knocked over the statue of St. Francis, broke his face, and left him there!"

Sister Angeline's hand, the one pressing the stone, almost quivers. Her body seizes, guilt pulsing frantic until now she feels the impulse to run into the church and confess, ask forgiveness. Explain herself. Explain about St. Francis speaking to her. Explain why his words frightened her. Explain why she pushed him over. How she didn't mean to break him.

As if reading her mind, Gina shakes her head. "Don't you dare," she whispers. "You don't owe anyone in there anything."

Sister Angeline unsure what to do, Father Matt expounding about moral emptiness, lost values, lost souls, how no one can see what's happening to the Church, to God! but she thinks Gina is right, because who would want to go in there and confess to complete strangers?

Inside, the voices are singing the "Prayer of St. Francis," singing, "Make me an instrument of your peace, where there is hatred, let me sow your love, where there is injury, pardon," and now she can hardly bear herself—

"Don't go there," Gina says. "Just don't."

Watching her beautiful friend stand there examining her work, gold smeared on her fingers, her nose, Sister Angeline experiences an unexpected surge of love and pulls her attention away from the voices and focuses on the statue.

"Okay, I think you can remove your hand," Gina says.

The fragment stays in place. The church silent now. The two young nuns move to stand in front of St. Francis. A hushed astonishment moves through Sister Angeline.

The glittering line
running down his cheek
falling
from his eye
catching the   sunlight
circling his cheek
flamed with   loss
deepening history
beauty almost throbbing

and now it's as if the crescent scar burns on her own face, and her fingers reach to touch it, to see if it's really there, and when she feels the heat of it, some cracked place within her chest fuses together and she hears St. Francis saying, *I am here*, and she knows now—she knows to permit faith, that in time—

But now Father Matt proclaiming, "The Mass is ended, go in peace."

The church bell clangs three times.

"Shit," Gina says. "They're all gonna want to see the damaged statue, since he made such a friggin' big deal of it." She grabs her canvas bag and pulls Sister Angeline around the side of the church behind a huge rhododendron bush. They huddle together, holding hands, adrenaline flooding Sister Angeline's body.

Minutes later, they hear voices near the statue.

"Oh my," a woman says. "How beautiful."

"God's work," another says.

"The face of an angel," says a woman with a gravelly voice.

"Why is he chained to the tree?" a child asks.

And now, "How is this possible?" Father Matt says. But his words are not filled with awe but thick with indignation.

"C'mon," Gina whispers. "Follow me. There's a trail over there that will take us back to the convent."

Chapter Eighteen

It's the first Tuesday of the month, which means political letter writing day. The six women sit around the large wooden table in the library. Today, they are writing letters to seventy corporations, insisting they lessen their environmental impact and use their billions to fund climate change research—to do the right thing, not just for themselves, for others, and Mother Earth.

Sister Angeline copies her letter from Sigrid's template, thinking how she doesn't know anything about the greenhouse effect, damaging gases, and carbon emissions, but she wants to learn, wants to help save the planet.

As a child she'd spent all her time outside with the trees and the grass, the birds and the sky—even though in Chicago the smells and sounds had been nothing like this—there was Lake Michigan and her favorite tree she'd climbed often, the beautiful oak where she sat up high in enormous branches, the sacred tree where she watched the lifeless moth fly again, and in the winter she'd skated in spirals across the lake and in the summer picnicked on the shores with her family, the four of them swimming and diving deep into its blue, her mother happy, her little brother throwing stones into the water, trying to hit a log, the two of them making dandelion crowns for each other—

"Sister Angeline, are you with us?" Sigrid says.

"Yes, yes," Sister Angeline says, and she surfaces from the tender reverie, though she thinks she hears her little brother calling for her, then realizes it's only a gull screeching outside the window.

"And tomorrow," Sigrid says, shaking out her hand during a short tea break, "we write Pope Francis. Whether he supports us or not is not the issue. We need to keep pushing for women's rights, trans rights—"

"Pounding our heads against rock, you mean," Edith says, waving her hand dismissively. "I've said it before and I'll keep saying it—if you think he'll undo Church doctrine, my name is Peaches and I've got a bridge to sell you."

Kamika laughs out loud, the sound like a thousand fluttering golden leaves, and the ease and freedom of it startles Sister Angeline.

How can she still laugh? How can she lose her entire family and still laugh?

"You never know how someone can change things," Kamika says, catching her breath. "He's so different than the others—"

"He's the first pope to even acknowledge that maybe, just maybe, abortion isn't a convenience," Sigrid says, stuffing letters into envelopes, but now something in her stumbles, setting off a deeper silence in the room, and she suddenly excuses herself, says she needs to be alone.

There are things people don't talk to each other about. There are things they save only for God.

Chapter
Nineteen

Sister Angeline kneels in the herb garden, yanking weeds. The cat purrs next to her, stretched out long and lazy in the afternoon sun. "You like it here, Joan?" she asks the cat, stroking its back.

How much has changed in only six days. She's gone from a place with walls and rules—a place she'd loved, a place she'd felt completely on the right path—to a place without walls and rules, and a path she's unsure of, a path with five women who speak of protests and poetry, who drink cappuccinos and wine, a path with a dead squirrel in a prayer box, a forlorn girl named Amelia, and a statue who speaks.

She plucks leaves of basil, brings them to her nose, and breathes in the pungent scent. She thinks how she is a nun with a cat and a yurt and an ocean. She thinks that if she wants to, she can remove her veil and let the sun warm her scalp. She can do this. But if she did, she might forget things. Moments to pray might fly away like frightened sparrows.

She's hardly prayed deeply since she's arrived—not because there hasn't been the time or space, not because she hasn't spent hours on her knees, hands folded, but because she hasn't been able to quiet her mind. She is overstimulated, and her ability to concentrate falters easily under these enormous changes. New thoughts and images from the last few days tug at her heart, begging for her attention. Prayer is a conversation with God, and she can't seem to shake the agitation within her enough to listen, to accept, to allow a deeper inner consciousness to awaken, to be heard. In an attempt to rest the voices, she repeats St. Teresa of Ávila's words, "Let nothing disturb you, nothing affright you. All things are passing . . . ," but then *do not fear your rage* sneaks in and the hair on her arms rise up like a million needy egos. Life has quickly become complicated outside of the cloister walls.

Her thoughts are interrupted now because Alice arrives and kneels next to her. Alice is dressed in jeans and a white linen blouse and a big straw hat. When Sister Angeline smiles at her, Alice smiles back and gives her a note.

Sister Angeline removes her gardening gloves and reads it, silently, nervously.

> *The other Sisters know this, and I wanted you to know too. I had a son who was killed, shot when he was twelve. His name was Talik. It was always just the two of us, and when Talik died, whenever I tried to speak, I couldn't. Sister Angeline, I think you may have lost someone too. I'm here. If you want to talk, I will listen.*

Sister Angeline's eyes well, and she looks at Alice. "I'm—I'm so sorry your son was killed," she says, a tremor in her voice, not sure if she should ask more—she knows how hard it is to tell these things, how dark and silent horror can become.

Alice, eyes watering behind her glasses, gives her a photo now.

Here is a child, wearing a red T-shirt, his hands in his jean pockets, grinning out at her. The way his wide smile, his gentle brown eyes, resemble Alice's. To see this child. An alive child silenced by violence.

"He's beautiful," Sister Angeline says. The photo pulling images from her memory, threatening her vision.

I think you may have lost someone too. I'm here.

Just the thought of telling Alice, hearing the words out loud, feels like too much to bear. But then a memory of her mother whispering to her father in the dining room, *Something's going on with Meg. She's become so secretive. Has she told you anything?*

Maybe if she'd told her mother earlier, they'd all still be alive.

And now Alice's arm around her, the warmth and protection of it. Something inside pushes Sister Angeline to tell, and suddenly she is saying, "My family, my mother and father—my brother, died in a car accident—and I was—pregnant—and the baby—she was three months old—the accident. I—I—lost her." But that's all she can say, and she's left so much out. Alice takes her hands in hers like a prayer, the folded note and the picture between their palms, and looks her in the eyes. The look holds such knowing, such comfort and intimacy, and now Sister Angeline presses her face into Alice's shoulder, and grief breaks to the surface like a long-held breath, violent sobs shuddering out, and the older nun rocks the younger as she would have rocked her very own child.

That night Sister Angeline stands outside her yurt, breathing in the weighty smell of salt water and pine. She looks at the stars for the first time since her arrival. Never has she seen a sky like this. Everywhere, stars like tiny milk teeth floating, a landscape of angels.

She touches her belly with one hand, and with the other she points to one trembling star after another and whispers:

There is a baby.

There is a baby.

There is a baby.

There is a baby.

There is a baby.

Baby, my baby, where are you?

Chapter Twenty

It's almost three weeks before Sister Angeline finally touches the ocean—or to be precise, according to Edith, the *strait*, but still, the proximity to the ocean is only miles away, enough to make the thought of going without her mother unbearable, to walk here without her mother, who despite all her flaws, she deeply admired, she loved. Her mother, whose entire dream was to touch the ocean. *If I could just touch it once, that would be enough*, she always said. *If I could just touch it once.*

But there was something about the moment with Alice, something about weeping in a way she'd never wept before, something about these women, that has Sister Angeline wondering if maybe she has no idea what atonement means, no idea how to make up for what she's done, no idea why she lived and they died, no idea why God would show up here—here as she reached for a dead squirrel, here as she listened to a stone statue tell her not to fear her rage.

Something propels her forward, and so she walks toward water, walks through tall beach grasses, giant purple flowers and

Queen Anne's lace on each side of her, shoes crunching on sand, an extraordinary aliveness overtaking her, the brilliant blue in front of her with its small whitecaps fluttering like birds. She keeps walking, moving closer and closer to the water, thinking, *I will touch it for her*, and then, *I will touch it for you, Mama*, and she is comforted by this thought, the hope that thinking about touching the ocean for her mother might somehow vibrate up to her mother in the stars.

Finally, here she is. She stands at the water's edge and squints into the brightness. Breathes in the salty blueness, allows the waves to kiss her shoes, not realizing the white line of salt it will leave, how hard it will be to remove that line. She stands there, taking it in, and all the words come to her— unpolluted, uncontaminated, unspoiled—the air so distinctly green and rugged and perfect, the sounds of birds and waves and nothing else. She bends now, touches her fingers to the water, lightly stroking the surface, the silver cold silkiness of it, and it is at once stunning and gentle and tragic. *Mama, can you feel this? Can you?*

But the water suddenly turns violent, biting and snapping at her fingers, the tender gone brutal, and here is her mother's face floating there, red hair spiraling like serpents around her skull, the painted red mouth saying, *No, Meg, foolish girl, I cannot feel it. I cannot feel anything, anything at all*. Sister Angeline jerks her fingers out of the water.

She turns to run up the trail—all she wants to do is hide in her room, feel her whip's harsh lashes on her back—but now Anu is barking hard, and she looks and there is the dog far down the beach, the dog standing beside a child—a child sitting alone on a log, hunched over and rocking.

Chapter
Twenty-One

Sister Angeline makes her way toward the dog and the girl, her body carefully negotiating the slippery rocks wet with seaweed, her mind still floating underwater, her mother's face suspended there, her voice relentlessly saying, *I cannot feel anything, anything at all.*

As Sister Angeline draws nearer, trying to blink the blur of it all away, she sees the girl is the one who screamed by the prayer box, the one in the yellow dress, Amelia. The girl, still in the same yellow dress, clutching something to her chest and crying hard, and there is Anu, trying to lick her tears, but the licking only makes the girl shout angrily, "Stop it! Stop it, you stupid dog!"

"Anu! Come!" And the dog immediately comes to Sister Angeline's side and whimpers.

"Your dog licked me," Amelia says between sobs. "What a stupid, stupid dog. I hate your dog."

Sister Angeline crouches next to the girl. "I'm so sorry. Her name is Anu, and I think she's just worried about you."

Amelia's blond hair hangs in limp strings over her eyes. Sister Angeline can see now she is clutching a Barbie doll.

"Amelia, do you remember me? Sister Angeline? Can you tell me what's wrong?"

Amelia keeps her eyes on her clutched arms. "My—my father won't let me play with my Barbie anymore. He says I have to get rid of it because I'm too old for dolls." She glances around nervously as she speaks, and Sister Angeline looks too, but they are alone on the beach.

"Oh, Amelia, that's awful. I'm really sorry."

Amelia stares at Sister Angeline. "I'm not even that old. I'm only eight. It's okay to have dolls when you're eight, right?"

It's hard not to notice the bruises. Bruises in the shape of fingerprints on her arm, the dark circles under her eyes. This child has been through something, something more than a doll being taken away.

"Yes, of course it is. I kept my dolls until—"

"Until what?"

She lies. "Until I went into the convent." Of course, she cannot tell this child that after she miscarried, after she lost the baby, the baby she knew in her heart was a girl, the baby she dreamed would play with her own childhood dolls one day, of course she can't tell this wisp of a girl that she'd stuffed all her dolls into a Hefty bag and carried them to the Goodwill, thrown them into a deep metal bin.

Amelia stares at Sister Angeline for a moment as if deciding whether to continue, then she says, "I don't want to give her up, and I—but I can't—I can't bring her back home, if I bring her back, he'll—"

Sister Angeline's heart aches for this little girl in her

paper-thin dress with its frayed hem. "Amelia, what if we hide Barbie in one of those big hollow logs over there, and you can come visit her whenever you want? I could help you."

Amelia's pale blue eyes widen. "You would help me?"

"Of course I would."

Amelia wipes her cheeks and studies the logs.

"Which one do you think would be best?" Sister Angeline asks.

Amelia points to a gigantic hollowed-out log way down the beach. The opening is big enough for both of them to crawl into.

"And it's above the high tide line," Amelia says. "So she'd be safe."

"Ah, smart girl."

Amelia studies Sister Angeline for a moment. "And you won't tell anyone she's there?"

"I promise."

"And nuns always tell the truth, don't they?"

Sister Angeline can only nod, guilt spreading across her skin as she thinks about all the things she's kept hidden.

As they walk toward the log, Amelia fills her pockets with sticks and oyster shells. "We'll need camouflage," she says.

Sister Angeline smiles at the child and begins to fill her own pockets with splinters of driftwood and shivers of seaweed, praying that whoever Amelia keeps looking over her shoulder for doesn't show up.

When they get to the log, Amelia climbs in first, holding her doll close to her chest, and Sister Angeline follows, awkwardly on her knees, pulling her skirt up, splinters pricking her shins, trying not to drop her driftwood.

There's very little light, but the musky scent of wood radiates warmth and safety. As they kneel side by side, Sister Angeline asks Amelia, "Is this okay?" and Amelia nods while Anu watches intently outside, before lying like a guard at the entrance, facing out, ears alert.

Amelia inspects the space for the perfect place to hide her doll. She crawls a few feet deeper into the log, touching various nooks, until finally, she reaches down and places her whole hand into a narrow crevasse. "I think this is a good spot, it's soft and dry," she says. Sister Angeline crawls behind her, touches the woody nest, and nods in agreement.

Amelia lays her Barbie down. The doll is dressed in a torn green evening gown, the shimmering fabric clinging to the plastic body, the blond synthetic hair in shreds, the face smudged, one plastic arm gone.

"You'll be safe here, Barbie, and I'll check on you every day," Amelia says, stroking the length of the doll's body, smoothing its hair. "And tomorrow I'll bring you some really warm blankets."

Together they cover the doll with the sticks, shells, driftwood, and seaweed. When they're done, they look at the tiny hump of debris, and Amelia's eyes fill.

"Amelia, would you like me to say a prayer for her?"

"If you want," she says, a tremor in her voice.

Sister Angeline closes her eyes, bows her head, makes the sign of the cross, and folds her hands into prayer. *Dear God, please keep Barbie safe and protect her from harm and give her comfort and warmth, until Amelia can be with her once again. Amen.*

When she opens her eyes, Amelia is sitting back on her heels, staring at her. After several moments she says between sniffles, "Why do you dress like that and the other nuns don't? Aren't you like really, really hot?"

Sister Angeline smiles. "Yes, I am like really, really hot." It startles her that she can sound so hip.

"Then why?" Amelia asks.

"Well," Sister Angeline says—she's never had to explain this to anyone before, "it teaches me humility and compassion."

"I don't get it," Amelia says.

"It helps me concentrate on what matters most to me and to better understand the suffering of others."

Amelia picks at a scab on her arm. "I used to think God was real. Actually, I used to like God a lot, but now I hate his guts." She stops picking the scab and rearranges a few of the stones and sticks. "My grandmother read me Bible stories when I stayed at her house—I used to stay there sometimes—and I thought God was an extremely good storyteller."

She looks at Sister Angeline. "I mean, I really, really liked that God talked about crocodiles and trees that clapped their hands. Oh, and there's that scary beast in the Book of Job who has bones like bars of iron and was able to suck the whole River Jordan into its mouth! I love that! Don't you love that?"

Sister Angeline laughs softly. "I do. But—now you hate God?"

Amelia gnaws on a dirty thumb cuticle, then looks up. "God lets too many bad things happen."

"Maybe God's not a person," Sister Angeline says, though as soon as the words are out, she thinks maybe she is wrong to say this to a child, yet she was a child when she discovered God wasn't a person, so—

"Not a person?" Amelia says.

"Well, I think that God is like love—an energy we can send out to others or call to for help. Kind of like a chemical reaction, like a spark, like ocean waves traveling from my heart to your heart."

Now something cold and brittle crosses Amelia's face. "That's the stupidest thing I've ever heard!" she says, and she looks so vulnerable that Sister Angeline reaches out to touch her hand.

Amelia pulls her arm back angrily. "Don't touch me! Who said you could touch me?" She pushes past Sister Angeline, crawls to the opening of the log, shoves Anu out of her way, and disappears.

Sister Angeline stunned. She's made things worse, increased this child's distress. Why didn't she keep her mouth shut about God? She feels suddenly that what she believes about suffering is profoundly naive—the unending fasting, the draping of herself in heavy black fabric, the self-mortification—when here in front of her, here is a frightened bird of a girl, hiding her Barbie in a log under sticks and shells and stones, saying, *Don't touch me.*

Is it suffering if you choose to suffer?

She moves from her kneeling position and sits curled with her back against the log. Anu comes to her and rests her chin on Sister Angeline's knee.

Sister Angeline looks deep into the eyes that mirror her own, one blue and one brown. Anu makes a series of low, distressed sounds. It is then Sister Angeline's own eyes throb and blur, and for the third time since her arrival, here is the surge of energy— the radiating heat of love. Waves flash from her abdomen into her arms, into her chest, into her mouth.

Find Amelia, her mouth whispers. *Help her.*

Chapter
Twenty-Two

Edith is hanging sheets on the clothesline. It is windy, as it is most afternoons, and her black skirt and veil fly like birds against a strong wind, unable to move forward.

Sister Angeline, Anu by her side, runs to her, breathless. "Edith, I need to find Amelia. Can you—can you tell me where she lives?"

"Whoa, whoa, whoa," Edith says, struggling with the whipping fabric. "What happened?"

Sister Angeline grabs a clothespin and a flailing corner of a sheet, secures it to the clothesline, and turns to Edith. "I met Amelia today on the beach. She was really upset because her father said she had to get rid of her Barbie, and there were bruises on her arms, and her dress was torn and—"

"Her teachers have already filed reports with Child Protective Services," Edith says, pulling another soggy sheet from a basket and handing a corner to Sister Angeline. "There's a caseworker. But Amelia's family is new here, so it's going to take time."

"But—"

"Listen, you can call CPS too," Edith says. "The number is by the phone in the kitchen." She studies Sister Angeline for a moment. "And I assume you haven't used a phone in what, seven years? There are directions for that too, next to the list. It's not that hard." She reaches for another damp sheet.

Sister Angeline's heart hammering. "But I don't know anything for sure, it's—"

"You don't have to be certain—you just need to have suspicion, reasonable suspicion." Edith speaks more carefully, something wavering in her voice. "Your concerns will be added to the reports. Maybe it'll help speed things along."

Angeline's veil blows into her face. She gathers the fabric of it like a ponytail, holds it behind her head, thinks about the danger Amelia could be in *right now*, the mysterious energy still fluttering like adrenaline through her body. "I think I should go to her—"

"No," Edith says, moving closer to Angeline. "No. Don't even think of taking things into your own hands. Don't talk to her father on your own, don't stalk their house, don't follow Amelia home from school. If things aren't done right, it could make things worse for her."

Edith so close now Sister Angeline can see her eyes are bloodshot, and she wonders if Edith is tired, she works so hard, but now the unmistakable smell of alcohol, the sickly yeasty smell she too often smelled from her father. Her whole body tenses.

She hated when her father drank. He'd start in the morning, drinking beer after beer until it turned into whiskey after band practice at night. She watched the way it darkened him, the stench of it, how it changed him, made him break promises, slurred him until he could barely speak at all.

She turns away from Edith, her lungs pressing together tight, her mouth a hard line of memories.

"Listen," Edith says. "Amelia sells flowers at the farmer's market tomorrow. Why don't you go with Kamika and check on her? And if you're so worried, go call CPS."

A timer goes off inside Sister Angeline's chest, pushing out images—her hand dialing the police when her drunk father left the house to pick up Ricky from school, then her hand hanging up before anyone answered, how she'd pulled on her father's coat, begged him not to go, how her hand had tried again to dial the police but then, again, hung up fast, because who reports a father?

"Well? Are you going to call or what?" Edith says, steadying herself on the clothesline post.

"Yes, I'll call." Sister Angeline hurries away, head throbbing, her brain spinning between her father and Edith and Amelia. She walks down the hill straight to the kitchen yurt, thinking, yes, she will call. This is how things are done here, here in this place with its white yurts, women painting and protesting, a dog sitting by your feet, a place where the tides rise and fall naturally. And in this moment some small splinter of self-condemnation, some shard of resistance, falls away, and in its place a tiny sliver of alive.

Chapter Twenty-Three

It is nearly midafternoon prayer time, and the kitchen is empty and quiet and still smells warm from the bread of lunch. She finds the CPS number on the list tacked to the wall. Reads the how-to directions for the phone. Picks up the silver cold of it from the stand. All at once feeling inadequate and distressed. She takes several deep breaths to compose herself. Presses the numbers, resistance pulling at her, the urge to run and find Amelia insistent, but her mind saying, *Follow the rules,* and she presses green for go.

A woman with a smooth, official voice answers. "This is Carol. May I get your name, please?"

"It's . . ."

"Your name is held in confidence," Carol says. "We won't share your identity with anyone."

"It's—it's Sister Angeline from Light of the Sea convent."

"You're a nun?"

"Yes. At the Light of the Sea convent on Beckett Island."

"And why are you calling?"

"There's a child I'm worried about."

"And the child's name?"

"Amelia."

"Last name?"

"I don't know." It feels wrong not to know Amelia's last name. Mostly, it feels wrong that she's not looking for Amelia right now. Just thinking about this makes her heart—

"And how old is the child?"

"Eight."

"Where does she live?"

"She lives at the oyster farm on the other side of the island."

"Oh. Okay, yes. A man and two kids." The woman is silent for a moment and then, "Sister Angeline, we are already following this situation."

Situation?

"Does—does that mean you've already sent someone to help?" Sister Angeline asks. "I heard there was a caseworker, but I—"

"No, not yet. We're still completing the report. Sister Angeline, what is your relationship to Amelia?"

"I've only talked to her two times. Both times she was alone, and both times she was really upset."

"Do you know her family?"

"No. I've only met Amelia. I—I haven't lived here long either, only a few weeks."

"And what is the neglect or abuse you suspect?"

"There are several small bruises on her right upper arm and a few on her legs, and her dress is dirty and torn." Sister Angeline shivering now, even though it's at least eighty degrees in this room.

"Well," Carol says wearily, "kids play rough sometimes. Also, maybe their washing machine is broken, or it's her favorite dress and she wants to wear it every day."

Something hot rises within Sister Angeline, moves into the back of her throat.

Carol wants reasons not assumptions, facts not feelings.

She wants to say the bruises wrap around Amelia's arm like mean fingers, that they are definitely not from dodgeball.

"Oh damn, I'm sorry," Carol says, "I shouldn't have said that. It's been a long day already. That was unprofessional. You have no idea how many calls we get, and people wonder why we don't get anything done. Anyway, please tell me about the bruises."

"Like I said, they're on her right upper arm, and I think, well, they look like fingerprints, like maybe someone grabbed her."

"Did you see anyone grab her?"

"No."

"Sister Angeline, is there anything else you want to tell me?"

"Amelia—she looks over her shoulder a lot. She seems scared, she seems perpetually scared."

"Anything else?"

She wishes she had something else, but she can't think of any more facts, can't think of a way to explain her intuition, the lost look in Amelia's eyes. "I guess not," she says.

"Well, thank you for calling us, Sister Angeline. Really, thank you."

"Will you let me know if she's okay?"

"Sister Angeline, I can hear that you care about this child, and as I said, we're following the situation, but I have to be honest with you. So far there's no evidence of imminent danger, and we can't just walk in and remove her from the home. The family has rights too." She hesitates for a moment and says, "There are other things you can do. Like you can ask Amelia open-ended questions like, 'Can you tell me more about the bruises? Can you tell me why you're angry?' Things like that. If she tells you anything that suggests she is in danger, call us back. Does that make sense?"

What if waiting for things to make sense is too late?

"Yes. Thank you."

After the phone call, Sister Angeline walks back to her yurt, fingering her rosary and feeling scared for Amelia, hoping she's done enough. It is then, as she walks past yurt after yurt, that she hears delicate sounds floating through the air. She follows the sounds, and the sounds turn into words, and the words are coming from Kamika's open window.

Sister Angeline stands for a moment and listens. Kamika is praying aloud in Arabic, the lightly weighted sounds float out the window and drift all around her, over her, landing soft on her lashes, her lips, folding her hands into each prayer, closing her eyes, each note, each space between the notes lifting her fears, and now she recognizes the words *Mama* and *Allah*, and she holds her breath, stands absolutely still, and blows the beautiful vibrations like tiny, quivering wings toward Amelia.

Chapter
Twenty-Four

Kamika and Sister Angeline walk to the farmer's market, the sun blinking through the madrona trees on the beach side of the road. It is early, and there are several hours before the last of the August heat stifles everything and keeps them inside until evening. They've gone a mile or so when up ahead they see a man and two boys walking toward them.

"Hey, there's Collin," Kamika says. "And Liam and Michael. Have you met them yet?"

"I haven't met Collin, but I met the boys on the ferry when I first arrived," Sister Angeline says. "Collin's Liam's dad, the island EMT, right?"

"Yes, and you'll like him. Honestly, he's remarkable. He fixes everything from broken arms to fences." She pauses, the light in her eyes dimming. "He's also a widower, a single dad."

Voices behind them shout, "On your left!"

Kamika grabs Sister Angeline by the arm and jerks her off the road as a group of cyclists in matching lime-green shirts race by as if every second counts, their speed causing the air to shake behind them.

Before Sister Angeline can catch her breath, Collin and the boys have reached them.

"Hi, Collin!" Kamika says. "Hi, Liam! Hi, Michael!"

"Hey, Kamika," Collin says. He is a tall man in his early forties. Thick red hair waves across a forehead etched with deep lines. He is wearing jeans and a white T-shirt, exposing muscular, freckled arms.

"This is Sister Angeline," Kamika says. "She joined us several weeks ago from Chicago."

Collin extends his hand. "Nice to meet you." His face pleasant and unhurried. "Quieter here, I'd imagine."

Sister Angeline reaches back. The warmth and strength of his hand. "Nice to meet you too, and yes, it's very strange and beautiful to hear waves and doves instead of sirens."

"I'll bet," Collin says, smiling wide. He nods now to the boy closest to him. "This is my son, Liam, and his friend Michael."

"Yes, we've met. On the ferry. Hi, boys," she says, managing a smile, her mind distracted and troubled by the guns the boys are carrying. She sees, though, they are probably only BB guns like the one her little brother had. Still, she thinks of what Edith said—that the squirrel was most likely killed by a BB gun.

Liam has a gray hoodie pulled tight around his face. "H . . . h . . . hi," he says, and their eyes meet briefly before he looks back to the ground.

"Hey, I remember you!" Michael says. He is wearing his red sneakers, a Seahawks T-shirt, and matching baseball cap. "We watched the whale together!"

"That was really something," Sister Angeline says. She is

reminded then of Ricky shooting a rabbit when he was five and the way he'd cried and said, *I've made the rabbit dead, I've made the rabbit dead!* and how there was nothing she could do to comfort him, no way to explain that death was irreversible.

"We're going to the landfill," Michael says. "There's tons of bottles and shells there we can shoot and Liam's an expert and he's teaching me." He twirls the gun like a baton.

"Stop playing with that," Collin says, his smile tightening into annoyance. "And if I have to say it again, we're not going."

Michael's little face crumples, he cradles the gun close to his chest, and everyone is quiet. A breeze flows across the water, carrying heat and salt. Tiny birds skitter along the lip of the low tide. A blue heron standing one-footed on a log is startled by a woman speeding by on a noisy motorbike and goes airborne with a loud shriek.

"We heard about what happened at the convent a few weeks ago—the squirrel in the prayer box," Collin says now, looking at Kamika. "Edith paid us a visit. Said the Madrona Island police won't help, so she's checking on things herself."

"Sh . . . sh . . . she's always in my f . . . f . . . face," Liam says suddenly, his free hand forming into a fist.

This sullen boy is not the amiable one Sister Angeline met on the ferry.

"Liam," Collin says, batting his son on the back of his head, "show some respect." And then to Kamika and Sister Angeline, "It's been a rough time."

"It's okay," Kamika says. "I know Edith can be—"

"She's the meanest ever," Michael says, his heart-shaped face a scowl. "She came to my house too, and I told her I would never kill a squirrel. Never, ever. Besides, you can't kill squirrels with a BB gun, right, Collin?"

"Not likely, but not impossible either."

"You'd need a rifle," Michael says, "like the ones you and Liam have on the boat—the ones with real bullets, right?"

"Can you j . . . just sh . . . shut up?" Liam says.

"Okay, enough, enough," Collin says. "No one's shooting anything besides shells and glass. And for the record," he says, looking directly at Kamika and Sister Angeline, "the rifles were my grandfather's, came with the boat, and as I told Edith, they're always under lock and key, only take them out when we go to the shooting range."

"I would never believe either of you could kill anything," Kamika says to the boys. "You're both too wonderful, too kind."

"I never could," Michael says, still holding the gun close with both hands. "Ever."

"I could," Liam says, staring at his boots, kicking a rock.

Sister Angeline, startled, wonders what led him to say this, why he needs to shock them in this way.

"Anyway," Collin says, giving Liam a long, hard look. "Let's get going, you guys. Enjoy the day, Sisters." And with that he turns and walks away, the boys following.

"Can you tell me about Liam?" Sister Angeline asks after they've walked for a while and Kamika has stopped to pick some tiny purple flowers.

"I don't know what to say, really. I've never seen him like that. I know Collin's worried. We're all worried—this feels like more than teenage angst."

"Has he always stuttered?"

"Yes, but—something's changed lately, just in the last couple of months, and it's worse than it's ever been. Collin thinks it's the bullying at school, but Liam won't talk about it."

Pain waves through Sister Angeline's heart for Liam. She hasn't ever spoken of her bullying to anyone either. Couldn't bring herself to talk about it, not as a teen, not as a young woman. She hadn't wanted to cause alarm, more disturbance, backlash from the bullies. But now, in this moment, she realizes she kept the tormenting, the intimidations, a secret because she'd been filled with humiliation and shame. And with that realization she suddenly wants to tell Liam nothing is his fault. She wants to march down to that school and demand they make it a safe place. She wants to punch a hole through a wall.

Chapter Twenty-Five

The farmer's market on Beckett Island sits at the entrance to a long wooden pier. Oak barrels filled with purple lobelia and red geraniums, asters and primroses line the wharf, and skiffs of every color—yellow, red, and green—are tied up to pilings encrusted with oysters and mussels. The wharf crowded with people selling things or milling about on a summer Saturday. Teenagers lean against the railing, heads down, texting. A young man plays a fiddle, and children throw coins into the case at his feet. Three women sell rhubarb pies from a small fold-up table with a red checkered cloth. The ferry horn blares its departure across the vast blue, and people wave blithely from its decks. Everywhere a metallic, briny smell.

Sister Angeline's never been to a farmer's market, never been part of a small village like this, and if she wasn't so distressed about Liam, wasn't in such a hurry to find Amelia, she would have liked to move slowly through the colors and sounds and smells.

She sees Amelia. The child huddled on an upturned white bucket, surrounded with other buckets of yellow, orange, pink, and purple flowers. She's not wearing the yellow dress—she's wearing jeans and a pink striped T-shirt. And—her arm is in a cast.

No no no no no no.

Kamika touches Sister Angeline's arm. "Go. Oh, and here," she says, pulling money from her backpack. "Buy a bouquet—it will make it less obvious you're checking up on her."

Sister Angeline stares at the money in a way that is part guilt, part fear, and if she takes it, part failed nun. It's been forever since she's touched money. The whole point of the vow of poverty is to free you from your desire for material things so you are free to serve others.

"Hey, it's okay," Kamika says, pressing the money into Sister Angeline's hand. "It's not a vow to be impoverished, it's a commitment to live simply, to share things."

Sister Angeline folds the money into its original creases, shoves it in her pocket, and hurries to the child.

"Amelia, hi."

Amelia looks up, pushes the hair out of her eyes, and stares at Sister Angeline for a moment. "Hi," she says in a tiny voice.

"Oh my gosh, what's happened to your arm? Is it broken?"

"I—I guess so." She pulls a brown leaf from one of the red flowers, drops it on the ground.

Ask her open-ended questions.

"Can you tell me how you broke it?"

Amelia pulls off another dead leaf and another and another. "It—it was dark, and I wanted water because I was thirsty, so I had to go downstairs to the kitchen, and I tripped on Jack's shoes because he always leaves them in the way, and I fell all the way down the stairs." She doesn't look up as she speaks, just keeps removing dead leaves, and every word sounds eerily rehearsed. Sister Angeline can see she is chewing the inside of her cheek.

"Oh, honey, I'm sorry."

Amelia darts her eyes down the wharf and whispers, "See that man over there working at the oyster cart? That's my father, and he doesn't like me to talk too much to customers, so can you please go away?"

Sister Angeline glances over and sees a tall bony man pouring a large bag of ice over grayish rippled shells. His movements quick and jerky.

She can't leave Amelia yet. The anxiety in the child's pale blue eyes. The shape of the tiny white cast. "How about I buy a bouquet?"

Amelia is quiet for a moment, considering. "Okay. Which ones?"

"Well, how about the yellow ones with the orange centers— those look hopeful and good-hearted. What are they called?"

Amelia looks at her like she's strange, but in a good way. "Those are coreopsis. I grow them myself, and the bees and butterflies really like them. They're twenty-five cents each."

"I'll take a dozen!"

Amelia stands and, with her good hand, takes a sheet of newspaper and lays it on the bench next to her. She carefully chooses one flower after another and lays each one on the paper. Awkwardly, she wraps them all up and hands the bouquet to Sister Angeline. "It's a little messy, sorry."

"They're beautiful," Sister Angeline says, breathing them in. "And extra special because you grew them."

Amelia smiles a little. "You're really nice."

"So are you." Sister Angeline lays the flowers gently in her basket. "Amelia, I was thinking—if there's anything you ever want to tell me, anything you want to talk about, you could write it on a note and leave it in the log by your Barbie."

There comes over Amelia's face such an expression of despair that Sister Angeline thinks she might tell her what really happened to her arm, but her face suddenly changes, and she says solemnly, "That will be three dollars, please."

Sister Angeline sets her basket on the ground and retrieves the money from her pocket. Counts out three one-dollar bills. "Here you go," she says. "Amelia, did you hear me?"

Amelia takes the money and barely nods. She turns and reaches for a Nike shoebox under the bench. Opens it and places the dollar bills inside, sets the shoebox back under the bench, sits on her bucket. "Okay, thank you," she says and begins rearranging the flowers in the bucket.

"I hope to see you soon," Sister Angeline says. "I hope you write me a note."

When Amelia says nothing more, only keeps working on her flower display, Sister Angeline walks away, unsure of what to do next. The look in Amelia's eyes agitating her, urging her to do something besides wait for things to be okay. If only she'd done more yesterday. She contemplates introducing herself to Amelia's father, but Edith's warning to not take things into her own hands is still loud in her mind. There shouldn't be anything harmful in an introduction, though. She wouldn't confront him or anything—but here he is now, coming fast toward her. He is barely ten feet away when she sees the raw disgust on his face, his furious finger pointing at her.

He comes up close and says in a low voice, "You. Stay away from my daughter. Do you hear me? And tell that other nun of

yours to stay the hell away from my house. How dare she knock
on my door and accuse my son of shooting that squirrel—who
the hell does she think she is?"

Heat colors Sister Angeline's cheeks. His tone is so harsh,
his body rigid with fury. Looking over her shoulder, she sees
Amelia standing there, an expression of fear frozen on her face.
Do not fear your rage.

Sister Angeline straightens her back and faces Amelia's
father. "She has a broken arm," she says, her voice strained but
unwavering, her cheeks flushed with anger. "She shouldn't be—"

Kamika's voice behind her. "C'mon, let's go," and she
slips her arm into the crook of Sister Angeline's and walks in
the opposite direction. "Don't turn around. This isn't going
anywhere good."

"Amelia, she—" Her breath catching.

"She'll be okay. Call CPS right when you get home."

Kamika's probably right; there's nothing more she can do
here. She'll go home, call Carol. Tell her the facts. The broken
arm. The furious father. She'll pray hard, and then in the afternoon she'll check the log for a note from Amelia.

As they walk, in front of them, near a booth where a woman
with two long white braids and dangling earrings is selling raw
honey, offering samples in tiny paper cups, there is Father Matt.
A crowd has gathered around him. And though Sister Angeline can't hear what he's saying, he seems jovial as if he's telling
a funny story. He's not wearing his clerical collar, his black
shirt unbuttoned at the neck, the sleeves rolled up, the tails of
it tucked into jeans. He seems different—casual and happy as
if he's on vacation.

A woman wearing a turquoise halter top, a short yellow

skirt, and high-heeled white sandals is standing right next to him. She is holding a basket of Amelia's flowers and smiling and tossing her blond hair around as if she isn't near a priest at all.

"That's Lisa, Michael's mother," Kamika says. "Single mom, teaches fifth grade over on Madrona."

Sister Angeline can see Michael looks like his mother. The straw-blond hair and the way they both communicate enthusiastically with their hands. She watches as Father Matt touches the purple of the flowers in Lisa's basket and then dramatically pulls out a string of colorful handkerchiefs. Lisa laughs, and the small group applauds.

It is then Father Matt sees Sister Angeline and his face brightens.

She smiles back.

Clearly enjoying himself, Father Matt keeps going with the magic tricks. He pulls a seashell from behind the ear of an elderly woman licking an ice cream cone, and the group erupts again into applause.

"We should get back," Kamika says, swatting a fly from the pies in her basket.

"You go on ahead. I need a few more minutes."

Kamika raises an eyebrow. "You sure?"

"I'm sure."

As Kamika walks away, Sister Angeline moves closer to the front of the group to hear better. She hasn't seen Father Matt since their first meeting weeks ago. She's felt guilty not attending his Mass—she doesn't want to give him the wrong idea, that she's wavering, which of course she is; everything so fragile, so new—the least she can do is try to show him a little amiability. And maybe a magic show will calm her. She needs to calm down before she calls CPS. She looks back at Amelia and sees the child is still sitting on her upturned bucket, still selling flowers.

"Do another trick!" a little boy shouts.

At least ten people in shorts and sunglasses and sundresses have gathered on the grassy area in front of Father Matt. They are sitting, some with their legs sprawled, some with their legs crossed, the sun streaming heat upon their heads. Sister Angeline sits too. She stretches her legs out in front of her and pulls her black skirt evenly over her legs and down to her shoes. She folds her hands.

A young woman in a pink tank top, torn jean shorts, and pink flip-flops, smelling of coconut lotion and cigarettes comes and sits next to Sister Angeline. Red hair falls in waves over her bare shoulders. They are about the same age, and when they catch each other's eye, the woman nods, smiles tentatively, then turns away without a word. Sister Angeline is used to this reaction—likely a response to her habit—but something in this interaction stings more than usual and a pang of longing surges through her, a longing to abandon her heavy black cocoon and expose her head, arms, legs, and feet to the sun, feel the heat melt into her skin, her muscles, her bones, feel the summer grass under her thighs, slather coconut lotion on her bare shoulders, a longing for the freedom of flip-flops, a longing to be normal.

"Okay," Father Matt says to the little boy. "This trick is a hard one, and I'll need a partner. How good are you at math? Can you multiply?"

"I'm super, super good at multiplying."

"Can you spell?"

"I was third in the second-grade bee last month!"

"Do you know your states and countries?"

"Almost! My placemat at home is a map. I spilled juice on North America, and it wrinkled up, but my mom dried it and then laminated it, and now I can use it again."

Father Matt chuckles. "Come on up!"

The little boy, barefoot, all sweet eagerness, runs up to Father Matt.

"So, Mr. Spelling Bee Champ, what's your name?"

"Oliver!"

"Okay, Oliver, in your head pick a number between two and nine but don't say it aloud. Nod when you have it."

Oliver closes his eyes for a second. Opens them and nods.

"Okay, now multiply that number by nine—again, don't say the answer."

The audience is quiet. In the background, sailboat cables twang, and seagulls squawk, and people chat and barter on the wharf, but in this group, there is focus, concentration. Oliver chews on his lip, then nods that he is ready.

The crowd cheers and the child beams, his cheeks blooming red.

"Now, and don't tell us, but you have a double-digit number, am I right?"

"Yes!"

"Add those two numbers together."

"Smart kid," the red-haired woman next to Sister Angeline says, though something in her voice isn't right, it's dim and monotone, and when Sister Angeline looks at her, she keeps staring straight ahead. She has a colorfully threaded backpack of greens, blues, yellows, and purples on her lap, her hands folded on top, and Sister Angeline can see her nails are bitten to the quick.

"Okay!" Oliver says.

"Subtract five from that number."

Oliver hesitates for only a second. "Got it."

"Now don't forget your number. We're almost done. This last part might be a little hard, but I think you can do it."

"I can. I know I can," Oliver says. The boy's confidence and enthusiasm a delight. If Ricky were here next to her, he'd be in an excited state too, unable to sit, whispering the answers loudly into her ear, holding his breath in anticipation for what comes next. Grief swells within her and she would do anything to have him back and she fears she might begin weeping, but then something about the little boy with the sun-bleached blond hair and shining, alive face, something about this summer light, this grass and water and blue sky, something about all of this surrounds her sorrow, contains and encloses it, absorbs and softens it somehow.

"I know you can too," Father Matt says.

Sister Angeline smiles, tears dissolving within her. He is a Father acting like a proud father.

"Think about the alphabet," Father Matt says. "If A equals one, and B equals two, and C equals three, and so on, without saying anything, what letter belongs to your number?"

Oliver turns his back to the audience, murmuring, and everyone can see he is counting on his fingers. Father Matt hums the *Jeopardy* song, making the audience laugh. Sister Angeline can see he responds well to positive attention, can imagine him giving a sermon. His delivery is one of confidence and perfect timing.

After a minute, Oliver turns back and says, "I have a letter!"

"You're amazing!" Father Matt says. "Now the last thing I want you to do is think of a country that begins with that letter. And remember, don't tell us!"

Suddenly, the young woman next to Sister Angeline starts crying quietly. Before Sister Angeline can think of what to say or do, the woman stands and walks away, her arms wrapped around herself, her flip-flops making little slapping sounds.

"Got it!" Oliver shouts.

The young woman is on the beach now, pushing a silver rowboat over the rocks, into the water. Sister Angeline watches her step in, watches her row away, pulling slow, deep strokes. *Please, God, be with her.*

"Hmm," Father Matt says, and Sister Angeline turns back to him, sees him smiling playfully. He rubs his chin. "Is your country—Denmark?"

Oliver's mouth falls open, his eyes wide with amazement. "Yes! Yes!"

The audience bursts into laughter and applause, and Sister Angeline can't help but smile and clap too.

Father Matt takes Oliver's hand, and together they take a bow.

Once the crowd disperses, Angeline surprises herself by walking up to Father Matt.

"Good to see you," he says.

"Great trick," she says. "I haven't seen priests do magic tricks before."

"Well, unless you count transubstantiation." He grins, his eyes shining. "Magic is kind of my specialty—I like the look on people's faces when the unexpected happens."

"It's like we know we're being deceived," she says, "but we still watch and wait for the reveal."

His easiness gone in an instant. He seems crestfallen. Maybe she hurt his feelings by using the word *deceived*.

"That trick was just a little trick of math," he says in a wounded voice—a voice that is almost a child's. "When nine is multiplied by any number between two and nine, the digits will always add up to nine, so if you subtract five, the answer will always be four. And ninety-nine point nine percent of the time, people choose Denmark as their country."

"Honestly," she says, wanting to fix things, "it was great! Completely surprising."

"Speaking of surprising"—his voice is back to an adult voice—"you haven't yet attended my Mass."

She sucks in her breath, can feel the blush creeping into her cheeks. Her hand instinctively finds her rosary.

He doesn't wait for her to say anything. "You don't seem like someone who would break the rules," he says. "You don't seem like someone who wouldn't follow the authority of the Church. And those women"—his tone sending a chill through her—"they're selling an illusion."

That's when she almost laughs. The irony of saying *they're selling an illusion*. His condescension about the women she is growing to love, the women who have waited patiently for things to change, for decades. Everything they've fought for, summed up in his words: *my Mass. My* Mass.

"I'll be attending Mass at the convent," she says, blood pounding in her temples, her legs strong beneath her black skirt. "Mass there belongs to everyone, and it's where I want to be."

Chapter Twenty-Six

The next morning after prayer and breakfast, Sister Angeline finds a brown paper bag outside the entrance to her yurt.

No one in sight. The only sounds are birdsong, ocean waves, and her own breathing. It is nine o'clock and already hot.

She opens the bag and peers in. Here is a shiny bundle of blue fabric. She carries the bag into her yurt and sets it on the bed, reaches in and pulls out the cloth. A swimsuit. She can hardly stop looking at it. Diaphanous silver threads woven through indigo, and when she holds the suit up to the light, it radiates a soft tremulous luster and becomes the azure color of ocean.

She lays the suit on her pillow gently, removes her hand slowly as if too much movement will cause it to disappear, and she just wants to look at it a little longer even though she knows it's a temptation, even though she knows she must give it back, *but to whom?*

She looks again in the bag for more and finds a tiny white envelope.

The note in purple cursive:

Please meet me at my hideout for a swim today. 3:00 p.m. Map on the back.

                              Your friend,
                              Gina

P.S. Don't look so startled. It isn't immoral or wicked. It will be fun and divine and beautiful.

Sister Angeline smiles. A hideout? She looks at the map, and it's not far from here. A red *X* marks the exact spot.

She folds the note, places it back in the envelope, and sets it on the bed. She removes her shoes, her socks, her habit and veil. Her body is unbelievably sweaty, and the cool air feels so good. She removes her panties and bra. She lays them next to the habit and holds up the swimsuit again. The sense of cool blue water flowing over her skin.

The suit glides easily over her body, and she barely feels the lesions on her back. She's become thin these last seven years, though she's probably put on a little weight since she's arrived here. The Sisters are not sparing in their eating like the nuns in the cloister, and they never talk about the power of deprivation. They eat from their own gardens and with such gusto and appreciation that it's difficult not to take an extra bite or two.

Sister Angeline slides her hands over the stretchy fabric; the way it clings to her stomach and breasts sends a tremor

of pleasure through her. She lingers on her breasts, closes her
eyes, her hands sliding again and her mind tumbling

                                        backward

        backward
        backward
        until
        she is fifteen
        and in bed with Jonathan
        the boy she is beginning to love
        and he is saying
        you are so beautiful, so beautiful.

That boy is dangerous, her mother said repeatedly, though
she'd never even met him in person. Yes, he'd been suspended
from school three times. The first time he'd added salt to ethyl
alcohol without permission or safety glasses and caused a fire in
the science lab. He was suspended the second time for throwing
a chair at his math teacher, and the third (and final) time when
he was a senior for shoving a kid in the hallway and threatening him with a pocketknife.

Her mother didn't want to hear that the fire was an accident
or that the flames were small or that no one was hurt or that Jonathan loved science. She didn't want to hear that he threw the chair
because the teacher ridiculed his friend Billy for crying as he strug-
gled to read, or that the kid in the hallway had called his father a
fucking loser for the hundredth time. Her mother didn't want to
talk about how Jonathan lived alone with his father in a garage.

Just keep away from him, her mother warned.

She hadn't kept away from him. For a year they'd managed
to keep their relationship a secret. Meeting after school in the

garage on Mondays, when his father took the bus across town to the food bank, or Wednesdays, when his father played cards at the American Legion.

She'd told Jonathan she was pregnant when she was three months along and she was sure the baby was real. They were sitting with their backs against the headboard of his bed, and they were relaxed and happy and dipping french fries in ketchup, and it seemed like a good time to tell him.

But when she did his eyes became still and dark, and he couldn't form a sentence, and red crept into his neck, into his face, and exploded out of his mouth, making a loud violent noise, making her afraid, more red detonating in that cold room than she'd ever known, and when she tried to run, his hand so tight around her wrist she thought it might have broken when she pulled away.

She never saw him again.

He died a week later.

No one offered any reasons why Jonathan was building a bomb in his garage beyond that he was a quiet boy with a bad temper who seemed to like school, liked to experiment with things. No one knew why, but her.

See? I told you, her mother said.

The bell rings now for chapel, jolting Sister Angeline into the present.

She walks back to the bed and puts her habit on over the swimsuit. She forgets to pray as she dresses. Vows slipping away fast. She walks to the chapel, her mind a knotted blur. Inside, the other Sisters smile at her and close their eyes to pray. Sister Angeline tries to pray, tries to be present, struggles to follow the rhythms of the chants, but again and again she fails.

After chapel she reviews the afternoon chore chart, and it's her turn to sweep out the henhouse and collect the eggs. All the time she is sweeping dung and cooing to the startled hens, coaxing them from their perches and stealing their eggs, apologizing each time she lifts the smooth egg and places it into the basket, she is trying not to think about embryos, trying not to think about the day she'd told Jonathan. The day his rage swallowed her love, bruised and twisted it into fear. For eight years she's tried to think what she could have done differently.

She is sweating hard now, and the swimsuit clings to her body, irritating the wounds, and she thinks about whether or not she should meet Gina. Would it be wrong? Of course, she wouldn't swim, isn't ready to explain the rips in her skin, but at least she could see Gina's hidden cove, couldn't she?

Make some friends, Sister Josephine said when she'd dropped her off at the bus station. *Friends are important!*

She's never really had friends. Never felt the need. Preferred to be alone, reading or writing or sitting in her tree. Until Jonathan. Two bullied loners finding each other in science class. She loved his thick black hair and torn denim jacket and the careful way he measured liquids, his precise recordings of data.

They'd quickly become confidantes. He'd told her about his father's disability—how he'd stepped on an IED in Iraq, how hard it was for the two of them to live only on a disability check. His father's anger at the system. His drinking. They commiserated on this—their fathers drinking. His father raged; her father disappeared. And Jonathan understood her fascination with the quantum mechanics of prayer, was as amazed as she was that the earth was flying through space at nearly seventy thousand miles per hour. And he'd loved her eyes, thought the blue and brown of them alluring not bizarre. She never told him about her mysterious energy though; she'd been waiting for the right moment.

After she brings the eggs in, after the Sisters finish lunch, Gina tells them she is off to Angel House. "It's a support house for victims of sexual assault," she says to Sister Angeline. "I visit once a week and lead a Tai Chi practice." And now, "I'll be back by three," she says to no one in particular, but Sister Angeline's heart pulses fast and her face flushes.

Chapter
Twenty-Seven

The light falls from her window to the door in a wide line across the bamboo floor. Sister Angeline paces the illuminated spectrum, back and forth, back and forth. An hour until she does or does not meet Gina. The unnerving clash between devoting the last seven years to prayer, to stillness, to hush, and the rush and thrill of now.

Why haven't I removed the swimsuit?

She slips her hand into her pocket, feels for her rosary touches each bead as she paces, whispering,

guide me, guide me, guide me.

It is when she hears a sound—an appealing sound outside her window, a sound that at once quickens her heart and causes her to stand completely still and press her eyes shut—that she stops thinking and listens.

Coo-OO-oo coo-OO-oo coo-OO-oo

The music of a dove.

Coo-OO-oo coo-OO-oo coo-OO-oo

The golden *O*'s of sound vibrate through the open window,

and she is tempted to look out, to find the dove—it must be perched on the pine near her window, it sounds that close, or maybe it's on one of the yurt frames, maybe her own—but she doesn't want her movements to disturb its call, she doesn't want to lose the celestial melody, the way the second syllable *OO* rises higher and higher until it descends again into a pure hum, and so she holds her stillness, and slowly her body softens and her breath deepens and little by little the tightness in her chest dissolves and the feeling of a lullaby radiates through her.

And it is then, when the dove ends its song, that Sister Angeline receives her answer reverberating on a breeze.

go, go, go

She opens her eyes, squints into the sunlight, and hears the word again.

go, go, go

She is both frightened by and attracted to this reply—there is something about the way her body changes that causes her to ultimately yield, to see what happens. She puts the map in her pocket and a bath towel in the empty brown bag and steps outside.

Immediately, here is Anu rubbing against her skirt. Sister Angeline crouches down, looks into the dog's curious eyes, sinks her fingers into her thick fur. Anu wags her tail wildly, licks Angeline's face, tries to pull the map from her pocket. "Okay, okay, you can come!" Sister Angeline says. She loves this creature and is grateful for her company.

Anu barks and races in circles, and together they head down the narrow footpath to the beach, Anu in the lead as if she knows where she's going. Sister Angeline follows, the fabric of her skirt catching on blackberry thorns tangling through rhododendron branches. The path is steep in places, and at one point, on a descent, she thinks she might not make it, might not have the strength in her legs, but Anu runs back to her, barking as if giving her a pep talk.

Fifteen minutes later they arrive at a small, secluded cove, Sister Angeline winded. The tide is high, the water folding and unfolding into itself like a heart, the air so thick with salt and heat she can taste it. Her breath steadies, and her body relaxes. The elemental holiness of this place opening her and pulling her forward.

And there is Gina, wrapped in a blue towel, standing at the water's edge, waving. "Over here!" Her face a sparkling beam of light. She has the body of a dancer, the top of her spine reaching for sky.

An uneasiness opens in Sister Angeline as she walks toward her.

"You have a suit under all that?" Gina says, smiling.

"No," Sister Angeline lies.

Gina glances at the brown bag.

"My towel. To sit on."

Gina grins. "Hey, no worries about swimming! Maybe next time?" And she drops her towel, lets it fall to the sand. She is wearing a black swimsuit. The fabric stretched tight over feminine curves. The bare unprotected olive skin of her shoulders, arms, and legs exposed.

"Maybe."

"I'm still glad you came," Gina says. "I'm gonna take a quick swim, and then we can talk?" She wades out until the water is up to her waist and then dives under, popping up seconds later for a breath. Sister Angeline watches her swim, the gracefulness of her strokes through the swells, the vague contour of her body surfacing, disappearing, surfacing until she is only a small black dot, and for a moment Sister Angeline panics when she can't see her at all. Even Anu runs back and forth on the shore, barking for her, but now there she is; she has turned and is stroking back toward them, her arms pulling her body forward until finally she has arrived at the shore.

She emerges from the water like a beautiful sea creature, her suit and skin shimmering in the sun, dripping water, her black hair a tangled frizz.

"Whew! Damn, that was cold!" she says, reaching for her towel and drying off, rubbing hard, and Sister Angeline wants to hug her out of relief, tell her she'd become frightened, but of course she doesn't.

Gina walks to a large log, spreads the damp towel in front of it, and lies down, face tilted up to the sun. Sister Angeline follows her, sits on the log, tries not to stare, awed and envious at the ease with which Gina moves her body, feels like she did with the woman in flip-flops—conspicuous and misplaced in her heavy black habit and clumsy black shoes.

Gina rolls over, looks at her closely for a moment, and says, "The least you can do is remove those god-awful oxfords," and she rolls on her back again, uses both arms as a headrest, and closes her eyes.

Sister Angeline, affected by the freedom of her surroundings and Gina's amiability, unlaces and removes her shoes and socks.

How pale and shy her toes look in the gray, roughly textured sand. She curls and uncurls them, pushes them deeper into the cooler depths, the sensation making her feel surprisingly content.

"Do you even know how to swim?" Gina says, her eyes still closed.

"I do," Sister Angeline says, her voice brightening and she is surprised when she tells Gina about the first time she ran through the doors of the YMCA when she was eight, how she'd known something huge was about to happen, the way the pool reflected a perfect aqua, and how her father taught her to swim that day, and how happy she'd been in the water, how happy she'd been to have his attention, to have him look at her the way a parent looks at a child they love. She doesn't say the last thing aloud though.

Gina opens her eyes, turns her face to Sister Angeline. "How could you stand to be shut up for seven years in that cloister—to pray all day and never talk and not be able to swim and take long walks?"

"I— Well, it was a place where I could—" Her body too warm, the swimsuit underneath a sticky, mocking skin. "It—it was a place I could pray, you know, without distraction, with concentration. I could . . ." But now she doesn't want to talk about it. Her toes kick sand over a cigarette butt, and she's beginning to wish she'd never come.

"Was it what you thought it would be?"

She's not able to say where atonement might take her, not able to say how deeply she hopes her reparation will somehow reunite her with the people she loved. If only she'd had more time in her little cell, her private island with no interruptions, where the rhythm of prayer sometimes shifted the floor under her feet and collapsed the air around her and gave her moments of transcending her body, her limitations—where she felt the briefest of releases into a boundless space she can only articulate as floating within the divine. A space so filled with peace and possibility she believed she was drawing closer to touching her baby, her mother, her father, her brother. Though she hasn't yet seen them, the moment so fleeting, she's sensed their existence. Her fear is she may never get closer, never see them again.

"Sister Angeline?"

She realizes she's drifted from the present and turns to Gina, blinking her back into focus.

"Do you want to sit down here with me?" Gina says, smoothing the sand next to her, wiping away a few shells, bits of seaweed. "I mean, you did bring your towel and all. Also, if it's okay, I kind of wanted to ask you something personal, and it would be much easier if I didn't have to keep turning my whole body to look up at you." She tilts her head and grins.

Sister Angeline retrieves her towel from the bag and spreads it next to Gina, sits with her back against the log and her legs straight out. She fixes the fabric of her skirt so only her toes show.

Anu trots over then, done with her beach explorations, and lies down between them. Sister Angeline reaches over to stroke the dog's head. She can feel her shoulders soften, her body warmed by the sun and Gina's companionability. "Okay, ask me something personal."

Gina sits up so her back is against the log too. She brings her knees in and wraps her arms around them. "I'd just really love to know how God called you, how you knew."

Sister Angeline picks up a small gray clamshell and runs her fingers around the concentric rings, the radiating lines of it, her eyes following her fingers.

"When I was a child at school, the nuns spoke about what it was like to be called by God—that you would be visited in some unique way, that you would know it was God, and that sometimes a miracle happened." Sister Angeline turns the shell over and touches the smooth white and violet surface, the colors reassuring.

She tells Gina now about the moth, Ricky, and her father's plane. She tells her how her eyes tingled until she couldn't see anything at all, how an intense heat wrapped around her, how it wasn't a frightening heat—it was like being inside a star or the flame of a candle—and how the most beautiful violet light spiraled around her. She pauses now, catches her breath, inhales the salty air, the feelings of those moments permeating her cells, quickening her pulse. She glances at Gina, who is looking out at the ocean as she listens, and sees that it's safe to keep going.

"I didn't really know what God was then. I just had the images the nuns gave me—you know, the one of an old man in the clouds, pray to Him, raise Him up—but after the experience with the moth, I knew that violet light, that heat, was God. I knew it."

Gina takes Sister Angeline's hands. "Thank you," she says. "Thank you for telling me, for trusting me."

"Thank you for listening, for not thinking I'm—crazy," Sister Angeline whispers. "I've never told anyone before."

Gina breaks off a feathery filament of a bright green bush next to her and brings it to her mouth like a cigarette, breaks off another small piece and hands it to Sister Angeline.

"You're beautiful, and you're the opposite of crazy."

Sister Angeline bites softly on the stem. The sweet taste of licorice, onion, and something bright like spring blend together on her tongue.

"The energy—I felt it when I touched the squirrel and then later with St. Francis. It's— I don't know what to think now or how to feel about it or if I'm doing something wrong or why it comes or doesn't. I mean, it could be a brain disorder, it could be—"

Anu stands and growls at something behind them.

Father Matt.

Sister Angeline rises quickly, glances at her socks and shoes. Gina stands too, commands Anu to stay, grabs her towel, and wraps it around herself.

"Afternoon, Sisters," Father Matt says in a friendly voice, though the edge of disdain remains. He is wearing his black shirt with his white clerical collar and black pants. His forehead and upper lip damp with sweat. "Well, if y'all don't live like you're in a sorority or something," he says. He takes out a handkerchief and wipes his face. "Do you ever pray or is that not hip enough anymore?"

She sees his eyes find her bare toes, linger for a moment. The sand suddenly cold. The air changing around her now, pricking her skin with needles, firing her body with self-consciousness.

Anu shows her teeth and snarls. Gina grabs hold of her collar but doesn't tell her to be quiet.

"Whoa," Father Matt says, putting both his palms out. "I'm just out taking a walk. Though to be honest, I didn't know about this place until I saw you." He nods at Sister Angeline. "You might want to be more careful next time you plan one of your little rendezvous."

Self-consciousness fast becoming guilt fast becoming a blade fast becoming a nauseating feeling.

This is what you get, you stupid girl. You stupid girl with your stupid bare feet and your stupid swimsuit and your stupid longings. He is right, the priest is right, you should have been more cautious, you weak foolish girl, you—

"Seriously," Gina says to him. "What's wrong with you?"

Sister Angeline says nothing. She cannot stop the blade from cutting into her chest.

You could have left your socks and shoes on. You could have

*thrown the swimsuit behind the mirror. You could have devoted
your time to prayer instead of laying out a beach towel, telling
secrets, acting fine, acting like your family isn't dead. You could
have kept your vows.*

Father Matt walks away, looks over his shoulder. "Be careful
of the paths you choose, Sisters. No one said the road to sanc-
tification would be easy."

"Man, he's one arrogant dude," Gina says once he's gone,
not yet releasing Anu's collar. "You okay?"

"We—should get back," Sister Angeline says. "It—it must
be close to—Vespers."

"Don't," Gina says.

"Don't what?

"Don't let him make you believe you've lost your way. Don't
let him make you think you've failed."

Sister Angeline doesn't hold her gaze. The blade still pricking guilt.

"May I offer something?" Gina says.

When Sister Angeline says nothing, only folds her towel,
shoves it in her bag, Gina says, "Have you ever considered that
maybe he's lost his way. Maybe he's failed you. I mean, was that
interaction kind or supportive?"

This thought catches Sister Angeline by surprise. Since the
accident, she has gladly given up the right to exist for a self,
gladly allowed herself to be lulled into obedience, gratefully
become dead to herself.

Gina takes her hand. "Will you—will you wade into the
water with me? Please. I think you'll really love it. I think it
will help."

The two walk across the rocky beach together, holding

hands, stepping around the bundles of kelp, the broken oyster and crab shells, the driftwood, moving slowly, Sister Angeline's bare feet tender. They walk until their toes touch the water, the icy cold of it making Sister Angeline gasp. They step forward inch by inch, the waves washing their feet, soaking the hem of Sister Angeline's skirt. They stop once the water covers their ankles, and then they stand, gazing ahead, the afternoon light falling gold and expansive across the gentle swells, the breeze smelling faintly of a soft green. The hot blade falls from her chest. She watches it dissolve in the water, watches the waves carry the serrated fragments away. She presses her hands to her chest. Tears fall down her cheeks. "Thank you," she whispers.

Chapter
Twenty-Eight

The fifteen-minute bell rings for Vespers. Back in her yurt, Sister Angeline quickly undresses, removes the swimsuit, places it in the bottom drawer of the dresser, puts her habit back on. Thinks about standing in the silver blue, holding hands with Gina. The enormous body of water they'd stood in. Gina's words— *maybe he's lost his way, maybe he's failed you*—running through her mind.

In the chapel now the Sisters, three facing three, fall to their knees, close their eyes, and tilt their heads up. They give thanks for the day, calling and responding in Latin, chanting soft and deep, and Sister Angeline allows the prayers to carry her inward, upward, beyond the confines of time and self. The cat presses softly against her legs and mews soothingly. When the service is over, Sister Angeline steps out of the chapel with a growing sense that she *is* where she needs to be. Even if it means accepting that she might have to leave the Church she's always known. Even if it feels like losing another family.

She walks with the other Sisters to the dining yurt. Alice

links her arm through hers, Gina, Kamika, and Sigrid with linked arms in front of them. Everyone silent. Gina looks over her shoulder and flashes Angeline a smile. Sister Angeline returns the smile, and tears come into her eyes. She is beginning to understand something else. In this place, with these five women who love so easily, there are new reasons to be alive. She thinks of the ones who spoke to her after the accident—her aunt, the doctors, the nurses. When she couldn't conceive of life without her family. When she couldn't understand why she lived and they didn't. *It will get better,* they said. *You'll see, it will get better.*

She thinks, *What if I'd stayed in the cloister? What if I hadn't met these extraordinary women?* She thinks about how Sister Josephine imagined this life she couldn't imagine.

They are almost to the dining room door, when Edith comes from behind, touches her elbow. "May I speak with you?" she says, and Sister Angeline can tell by the tone of her voice that this will not be a good thing.

Edith walks her toward the statue of Mary in the center of the courtyard. Orange calendula blossoms tangle with forget-me-nots around her stone feet. Sister Angeline folds her hands under her scapular, fixes her eyes on Edith's.

"I wanted you to know that the authorities have arrested Amelia's father and placed the two children in a foster home— in Seattle."

"What? I just saw Amelia yesterday. How—"

"Apparently, CPS received more calls yesterday, and they took the children later that evening. We received word an hour ago."

Sister Angeline reaches out to the statue, rests her hand on the stone of Mary's arm. She's so relieved for Amelia, but still, there's something interrupted and crumbling in her heart.

"It's a blessing," Edith says. "They're away from him—they're safe. And just so you know, they said our calls helped, so that matters. Shows that the protocol worked."

Sister Angeline nods. All this information trying to make space for itself under her skin.

"Look, there's nothing more we can do. I mean, if you want, you can probably check in with your friend Carol and ask about Amelia at some point." The dinner bell rings, and Edith turns to go.

"Thank you for letting me know," Sister Angeline says, not moving, sliding her hand down into the open hand of Mary.

Edith turns back to her. "You're not coming?"

"Actually—there's something I need to do. Will you—will you let the others know I won't be there for dinner?"

"I know this is hard for you," Edith says. "But let me tell you something," and she says this with an unusual tenderness. "I was placed in foster care when I was the same age as Amelia— my parents were addicts—stayed until I was twelve, until my parents cleaned up their act."

"Oh, Edith."

Edith waves a dismissive hand. "No pity. My point is that I survived, just as Amelia will. She's got a toughness inside her, a fire. It might not be easy, but she'll make it and be stronger for it. And there's every chance she'll be placed with great foster parents. Now go"—and she waves her hand again—"do what you need to do," and with that she trudges off to dinner.

Sister Angeline slides her hand from Mary's and walks down the beach to the log with the hidden Barbie. Maybe there's a note. She wipes her tears and crawls in. She removes the shells, sticks, and feathers covering the crevasse where they'd wedged the doll.

There she is. She is dirty and her blue eyes more desolate than Sister Angeline remembers. She looks for a note, but there is nothing.

She picks up Barbie and carries her, cradled in her arm, to the kitchen yurt. All the time she is praying, *Please, love, wherever Amelia is, hold her in your arms, keep her safe.*

She calls CPS and Carol reassures her Amelia is in a safe home, though they had to place her brother Jack in a different home because it seemed he had also been physically cruel to Amelia, though it was the father who broke her arm. Sister Angeline says in a trembling voice that she has Amelia's doll and can she mail it to the CPS office, and Carol says she'll be sure Amelia receives it and thank you, that is so thoughtful.

Sister Angeline finds paper, scissors, tape, and a roll of stamps. Takes them back to her yurt. She removes the doll's green evening gown and washes her face and her perfectly shaped body and straightens the three remaining limbs in their sockets. She smooths the knotted blond hair as best she can and puts the dress back on.

Over and over thinking, *How could anyone hurt a little girl, how could a grown man break a little girl's arm, how could a father break a daughter's arm, how could he, how could he.* Her anger a thousand thorns now, and she thinks about the raw of Amelia's suffering, of her own suffering, the way she whips and whips and whips herself, and she thinks again, *Is it suffering if you choose to suffer?* And then, *No it is not*, and she reaches under her bed for the whip.

Furiously, she unbraids the leather ribbons of it. She grabs the scissors and saws and saws the ribbons off, saws until the ribbons are separate pieces falling to the floor. She selects six pieces and cuts them each into six-inch lengths, and she braids three pieces into one bracelet and three pieces into another bracelet. When she's done, she ties one bracelet around her wrist.

She wraps Barbie in protective white tissue and places the doll on the wrapping paper and places the other leather bracelet on top.

Before she tapes the package closed, she writes Amelia a note:

Dear Amelia,

I'm thinking of you and hope you are safe. I will always pray for you. Always. If you ever need anything, please call the convent and ask for me: 360-555-2618. Here is a friendship bracelet I made for you.

Warmly,

Sister Angeline

She folds the note in half and places it under the doll. When she's completed the wrapping, she sticks on twelve stamps just in case. She carries the package to the mailbox, holds it to her breast for a moment, and then carefully places it inside, closes the door, and raises the small red flag like a prayer.

Chapter
Twenty-Nine

It is a Sunday, and there are easily fifty people gathered in the barn to sing and pray. Up front, Kamika, dressed in shades of blue with a violet scarf draped over her loose black hair, plays the harp. Her fingers stroking the golden strings, the music emanating sound waves that weave like secret meanings around the bodies, welcoming them and filling the room with grace and a promise of transcendence.

Sister Angeline dips her fingers into holy water and crosses herself. She takes a moment to absorb it all—the music, the vibrant energy of the people, sunlight pouring through arched windows on every wall, landing on everything. Between each of the eight windows hang Gina's abstract murals. The paintings like stained glass with waves and spirals of blues, greens, yellows, and reds.

She sees Gina now, laying a white cloth across the altar, and even from here she can see the silver rings sparkling on each of her fingers. They've become friends, though they don't meet at the cove—they wouldn't feel safe. Instead they take long walks in the morning and work together in the garden, slowly telling each other about their lives and trying to make sense of things that confuse or worry them, asking each other questions, inching closer to the secrets they hold under their skin.

Sister Angeline's met most of the people here—there's Theo, a young Latino man who used to be Theodora; Henry and Rory with their arms linked, married by Sigrid just a week ago; Holly, a young black woman who grasped Sister Angeline's hand at the market last week, told her she'd been in bed for a month after birthing twins, all the time crying, until her friend Dan got her dressed and brought her here to the barn; and Dan, a thin middle-aged man with a gray ponytail, dressed in a Hawaiian shirt and shorts even though it's October, standing next to Holly, holding her babies, smiling shyly.

There's Conrad and Beth from Madrona Island, who told her they've been married for over forty years and have ferried over to attend the Sunday gathering for the last ten. Conrad telling her that his favorite sermon of Sigrid's was the one about God being madly in love with humanity and how God just wants a great love story! The way Conrad's big hands gently tousled Beth's thinning white hair as he spoke.

Sister Angeline takes a seat on one of the middle pews next to Michael and Lisa. Michael grins at her, says, "Hi!" and scoots over to make room. Lisa whispers across him to her, "Man, it's chilly outside, isn't it? For October, it already feels like January!"

Sister Angeline smiles and nods, draws her shawl tighter across her habit. And now here is Collin. She is surprised to see Liam isn't with him as he usually is. She's gotten to know both of them in the last two months, Collin when he comes to the convent to fix something—they've had easy conversations about the weather, plants, and the wildlife around them, brief exchanges while he's concentrating on his project and she's either doing chores or off to prayer. She likes his relaxed nature and thinks he has one of the kindest faces she's ever seen.

Sometimes she finds Liam at the beach, sitting on the hollow log where she'd met Amelia, and they talk. It's occurred to her Liam is the age her brother Ricky would be now, and that realization caused her heart to ache more for him, to want to help him. She knows what he's going through at school, knows there's a kid who keeps whispering, *Hey, stut stut stutterer* in the hall, knows how the kid incites other kids to torment him too, and that Liam wants to beat him up, wants to beat all of them up, but he hasn't. Yet. He won't tell her the kid's name, and he made her promise not to tell anyone, and she promised, though she's beginning to worry she won't be able to keep the secret.

She kneels now, closes her eyes, breathes in the smells of incense and candles, new hardwood floors, the faint scent of hay. She crosses herself and folds her hands, begins her prayers as she always does, by offering the day to love, to her baby, her mother, father, brother, Jonathan, her past cloister Sisters, her present Sisters, Amelia, the world, the earth, her mind tumbling with prayers until she hears Lisa say, "Father Matt, hi! How nice to see you!"

Sister Angeline's chest constricts. He's never shown up here before. She sees him sometimes at the grocery, the library, and manages to avoid him, but she hasn't interacted with him since that day at the cove, and she was hoping to keep it that way.

"Good morning, Lisa, Michael," he says, his voice convivial, but Sister Angeline can hear it's forced, can hear a jittery nuance of agitation, and the blood rushes from her face. She can hear him sit right behind her, but she keeps kneeling, keeps her eyes closed, doesn't dare move her shoulders or do anything to suggest she has completed her prayers.

Now Sigrid is greeting the whole group, asking that everyone please stand, blessing them with the grace and peace of love. Sister Angeline rises, staring straight at Sigrid, who is opening a spiral notebook to her reading. She does not begin with the Penitential Act, doesn't believe that starting a celebration talking about shame and sin is good for anyone, and Sister Angeline hears Father Matt mutter, "Such a disgrace."

"From Proverbs 4:23," Sigrid says. She always looks so different without her baseball cap. Today she is dressed in a green robe—green, the color of hope and harmony and safety. "Above all else," she says, "guard your heart, for everything you do flows from it." She looks out at them, pausing for a moment. "You have to know what is really going on in your soul," she says into the miniature microphone clipped onto her robe, and the entire group shouts, "Amen!" Sister Angeline does too, quietly, but when she doesn't hear Father Matt say amen, only hears him taking long, loud breaths, his exhales hot through her veil, she begins to panic.

"Swim in love!" Sigrid calls out. "Breathe in love! Breathe out love! Love doesn't care if you don't have your act together! Invite those you love into the truth behind your hurt. We all need someone who knows us inside and out, am I right?"

Heads bob in the congregation.

"Why is it so hard sometimes to love each other? Is it because we don't love ourselves? I mean, if we are to go beyond slapping a *What Would Jesus Do* bumper sticker on our car, if we are to love our neighbor as ourselves—thank you, Matthew!—how can we do this if we don't love ourselves?"

In the far back, a woman shouts, "We can't!"

"That's right. We can't. So it's vital that we love ourselves. It's everything! We must wrap our heart with our own strong hands and bring it to our lips and play it like a silver trumpet." Sigrid clears her throat. "We must look ourselves in the mirror and say, 'I see you and I love you,' until we believe it. We must allow the light to shine into the cracks. Love created you! All of you! We speak often of the need to love others, the need to forgive others, and yet we are so hard on ourselves. If we are to love each other, then we must wrap our own hearts with forgiveness and love. Am I right?"

Sunlight and warm air saturated with late autumn pour in through the barn windows as a groundswell of loud amens reverberate through the room, voices rising and falling like an old beloved song.

Sister Angeline feels emotions bubble up, feels tears on her cheeks, feels Lisa squeeze her hand.

"Shame hates this kind of vulnerability," Sigrid says quietly. "Shame is a burly, intimidating, controlling tool to pull us down and keep us down." She inhales deeply, the microphone amplifying puffs of her breath. "Do not let shame trick you into not loving yourself. Do not let shame trick you into not forgiving yourself. Ever." She swallows, and Sister Angeline can see she is holding back tears. "Do not let shame trick you into thinking you're less than, unworthy, unlovable. You are worthy of being loved. You are worthy of forgiveness. Self-love and self-forgiveness will bring you into a higher expression of yourself. You must align with love—love with a capital *L*!—because that, my dearest friends, is the only thing that will save us."

People saying yes, people nodding and hugging each other, people hoping this story could be the thing that saves.

"Stop! Enough!"

Father Matt.

Everything quiet now.

Sister Angeline hears him leave the pew, watches as he takes a few steps up the aisle. He is dressed in black pants and a black suit jacket. He is wearing his white clerical collar, and in one of his hands, he holds a black leather Bible, which he now raises into the air. "This—"

Sigrid steps away from the altar, her green robe shimmering light, and interrupts him. "Good morning, Father Matt," she says. "This is your first time joining us, and yet I'm sorry to see that you seem quite agitated."

"This," he says again, the Bible looming like a threat, "this is not a Mass, and you"—now he points a finger at Sigrid—"you are not a priest and how dare you pretend to be!"

Disapproval erupts from the pews, the air suddenly dark and muddy. Sister Angeline stares at Father Matt's back, the boiling agitation held in his shoulders, his posture like a military general's.

Michael tugs on Lisa's sleeve. "Mommy, what's happening?" But Lisa only brings a finger to her lips and shushes him, her wide eyes meeting Sister Angeline's in disbelief.

Sigrid says, "Perhaps there's something we can do for you?"

"You—you are not a priest," he says, his voice low. He raises the Bible higher into the air. "Christ chose men as apostles, not women."

"Gender is irrelevant," Sigrid says, her voice steady as the North Star. She walks a few paces toward him. "Mary Magdalene was an apostle," she says. "You know that. You know she was the first witness to the resurrection. You know Jesus sent her to the apostles to tell them he had risen from the dead. That makes her the apostle to the apostles. Am I right?"

"Only men are recognized by the Vatican," he says and turns to the congregation. "Do you understand the pope forbids this woman to offer the sacraments? That she's *excommunicated*? That any sacrament she administers is invalid?" His eyes fervent and bright, though there is also a kind of terror in them, a child's terror. When he looks at her, Sister Angeline instinctively turns her head away, seized by pity for him.

Whispers of discontent move through the church and quickly erupt into shouts of rage.

"She has God's blessing!" a woman shouts.

"Jesus was a feminist!" a man yells.

The hair on Sister Angeline's arms bristling.

Sigrid raises her hand, and the room immediately quiets. She places one hand on the silver cross hanging from her neck and looks directly at Father Matt. "I don't answer to you or the pope."

"You're serving nothing but water and wine and bread," he sputters. "And I—"

"And you are misinterpreting God," Sigrid says. "And interrupting my service. If you can't control yourself, you'll need to leave." She points toward the door. Everyone hushed.

He turns to the congregation again. "Judas did not turn from God overnight, and Peter's denial wasn't the result of momentary lapses of strength. No. Their betrayals had their origins in willful and reckless decisions made for their own power and comfort." He stops to wipe sweat off his face with a white handkerchief from his pocket. "You can't sin willfully and recklessly without consequence," he says, his voice more composed, but agitation still rippling underneath. His finger touches the white square on his collar, while the other hand shakes the Bible. "My Mass, the true Mass, begins in thirty minutes. If you attend, I promise, like Peter, you will be forgiven, no questions asked." When no one moves or makes a sound, he stalks down the aisle, muttering something inaudible.

Chapter Thirty

A slight wind carries the sweet scents of decaying apples and briny ocean across the orchard as Sister Angeline and Gina pick the last of the October apples. There are only a few hanging on to the gnarled branches now, refusing to surrender, but there's enough for Edith to make her signature applesauce for the evening meal.

"Father Matt's interruption at Mass this morning was really disturbing," Sister Angeline says, holding the ladder for Gina, who is plucking the way-up-high apples.

"Dude's seriously messed up," Gina calls down. She's changed into her jeans and Converse sneakers, the blue ones with embroidered yellow flowers, and with her absolute self-assurance, she looks like a teenager. She holds an apple up to the sun and studies it. The red stripe glimmering over the yellow skin of it. The ocean and sky radiating blue behind her. The white-tipped mountains in the distance.

If Sister Angeline had a camera, she would have taken a picture.

The image makes her think about Eve. Her curiosity about

the Tree of Knowledge. How she was tempted by a serpent to eat from it, even though God had forbidden it. How she'd convinced Adam to eat the fruit too, and they'd run off into the woods to have sex. How they'd fallen asleep, and when they'd awakened, paradise was gone.

When she was fourteen, she'd asked her mother about the point of this story. Her mother looked up from reading the latest *New Yorker*.

"Well," she said, "I'd say that just because something looks beautiful doesn't mean you should bite into it, and if you do? Don't blame others. Adam blamed Eve, and Eve blamed the serpent. Blame, blame, blame. No one taking any personal responsibility. It's what's—"

"The snake gets a bad rap," her father had interrupted. "I think we got him all wrong." He was across the room, reading the newspaper and drinking a Corona in his recliner. He'd taken a long swig of beer, shaken his head. "People forget serpents are symbols for rejuvenation." Another gulp. "But you know, honestly? I think Eve knew that. I don't think she was tempted at all. I think she was guided by her own smarts. She wanted to give birth." And when her mother rolled her eyes, he'd said, "I don't mean literally—I'm not a Neanderthal—I mean, birth to, you know, awakening." He drained the bottle. "Kind of a big thing," he said and winked at Meg.

"Seriously," Gina says now, "like friggin' eons ago, Jesus would lay down a law about the gender of future priests for 2015?" She places a few apples gently in the basket around her waist and climbs down the ladder.

Sister Angeline almost smiles. "Aren't you afraid of him?"

Gina steps off the ladder, brushes her curly hair off her face, looks directly at Sister Angeline. Her lipstick the red of the apple's stripes. "I'm not," she says. "He's a classic bully, all bluster."

"But—but bullies can crack." The shiver inside becoming a hammering in her chest.

"Hey. You've said you were bullied. Do you want to talk about it?"

Sister Angeline thinks of Sigrid's words, *Invite those you love into the truth behind your hurt.* But there's been enough turmoil for one day. "No. No, I mean, yes, things happened—maybe another time."

Gina unbuckles the basket from her waist and sets it on the ground. Chooses an apple and takes a huge bite. Holds it out to Sister Angeline. "Bite?"

"No thanks."

"Listen," she says, still chewing. "Don't let him get to you. If he crosses any boundaries, freakin' let him have it." She takes another bite and then says, "Maybe this is part of what St Francis meant when he said, 'Do not fear your rage.' I mean, seriously, if you have to, knee the dude in the balls, literally or metaphorically."

Sister Angeline laughs at this last part. The nerve Gina has; this is what she wants to have too.

Gina moves the ladder to the next tree. "I'd ask you to climb up and get a few yourself, but you know, the whole habit thing you've got going on might trip you up." She tilts her head, looking out from dark lashes, her dark brown eyes warm. "Don't you think maybe it's time you got yourself some jeans?"

But they are interrupted by a man calling Gina's name in the distance. Collin. Even from here, Sister Angeline can see something is wrong. As he walks closer, she realizes he's carrying an animal in his arms, and dread gathers inside her.

Chapter Thirty-One

Collin unlatches the garden gate with his free hand and walks into the orchard toward them, his face desperate.

"It's—it's your cat," he says. "It's Joan."

"No, no, no," Gina cries. "Oh my God, what happened?"

Sister Angeline can see Joan isn't moving, and there's a scarf tied around her stomach.

"I'm sorry, I'm afraid she's—dead," Collin says, his face clouded with pain. "I found her in the ditch close to your prayer box. Looks like a gunshot—size of the hole is pretty small. I've stopped the bleeding, but there isn't a pulse. I'm so sorry."

Gina reaches out, tears flooding her eyes, and lifts the sagging animal from Collin's arms. She kneels on the ground, holding Joan, and gently shakes her, repeating her name over and over as if saying Joan's name might bring her back to life.

Sister Angeline, stunned, kneels next to Gina and places her hand on Gina's slumped shoulders.

Now there is barking, and Sister Angeline turns to see

Anu running through the open gate, running to them, halting when she sees Joan in Gina's arms. She whimpers, tucks her tail between her legs.

"It's okay, girl, it's okay," Sister Angeline whispers, but Anu knows something is wrong, and she circles Gina, sniffs Joan's body. She sniffs the open, unblinking eyes, the nose, the mouth, the chest, the scarf—she pauses here at the scarf as if she knows there's damage under the fabric, her whimper rising in frequency, her cry becoming so forlorn that tears come into Sister Angeline's eyes. Anu's sniffs become more frantic, her nose moving back and forth over the cat's body.

Finally, Sister Angeline reaches down and tugs on the dog's collar. "Enough, Anu, enough," and Anu sits then, looking up at her, still making feeble sounds of pain, her ears completely flattened against her head.

"Oh, girl," Sister Angeline says sadly, stroking her head, meeting her gaze. "You've lost a friend too. Sweet one."

Anu's eyes flutter, and if Sister Angeline didn't know any better, she'd think the dog might actually cry. But now as Sister Angeline looks into Anu's eyes, there is a brightening, the same illumination of the irises as in Amelia's log, months ago. She watches as the blue eye begins to gleam, and now the brown eye, gold flecks flashing like tiny sparklers, and it is then Sister Angeline's own eyes tingle. She holds Anu's eyes with her own, her breath deepening and her sight blurring, her eyelashes blinking slow then fast, and Sister Angeline knows what she must do.

"Gina, could you please lay Joan on the ground?" she says, breathing deep and slow, at the same time her hands trembling. "Collin, will you remove the scarf from her chest?" Her voice sounds faint and unfamiliar to herself.

Breathe. Slow down, breathe.

She closes her eyes, crosses herself, and lays one hand on Anu's head. Inhaling deeply through her mouth, and then with her exhale, an astonishing electrical current flows from the hand touching Anu, a warmth that streams into her arms, her legs, her hips—her whole body yielding.

Come to me. Be with us.

She keeps her hand on Anu's head and slowly places her other hand over Joan. She starts to place her hand directly on the cat but, hesitating, raises it inches above the trauma. She doesn't know what will happen, if anything will happen. She is scared to find out.

Anu barks, and Sister Angeline feels another sudden surge of heat swell from the dog into her hand into her body into the hand she holds above Joan. Inhaling deeply, she makes the sign of the cross over the injury, repeats again and again, *Please be with us,* and then lays her hand fully upon the wound.

"Joan, wake up," Sister Angeline whispers with difficulty, her mouth not feeling her own. "Please wake up, Joan."

The heat surging

surging

surging

through Sister Angeline's hands, and now a twitch, a quiver beneath her fingers.

Keeping her eyes closed, she continues to whisper, her voice strengthening, "C'mon. You are alive. C'mon."

And now in her mind she sees light converge and curl around the bullet. She sees the bullet dissolve into fragments into flakes into glitter into nothing.

Joan makes a sound. It is subtle at first, a faint mew, like a kitten in need of its mother, but then it grows into a longer plaintive meow, and now the cat's belly begins to rise and fall.

Sister Angeline moves her hand to Joan's chest, to the heartbeat.

Thank you, thank you, thank you, thank you.

The heat melts away from her body, and slowly she opens her eyes.

"Joan," Sister Angeline whispers, reaching out in a slight daze and cupping the cat's face in her hands. Anu, wagging her tail madly, licks Joan's entire body.

Collin and Gina staring at Sister Angeline, openmouthed.

Together they watch as Joan tries to stand. She does so unsteadily at first, but soon she is arching her back and stretching her legs. She gazes foggily at all of them, yawns, releases a deep throaty rumble, and rubs against Sister Angeline's knees.

"Holy mother of ocean and sky," Gina says, and the cat, hearing her voice, staggers to her. Gina gathers her up, crying into her fur, "Oh Joan, my sweet Joan."

Sister Angeline wraps her arms around Anu, the dog's entire body relaxed now, her tail a soft, slow wag.

Collin bends down and strokes the cat, separates the fur from around the wound and examines it. "The hole is open but clean," he says, shaking his head. "No blood or anything— excuse my language—but holy shit!"

"I really can't believe it," Gina says, looking at Sister Angeline with awe and affection.

Collin takes off his backpack and brings out a small tube of something, a roll of gauze, and some tape. "Antiseptic," he says, "so nothing gets in and causes an infection." He squeezes some ointment on the puncture opening and wraps a square of the fabric over it. Joan purrs softly.

"Hey, what's going on over there?" Edith yells from a distance.

Sister Angeline, almost too weary to turn her head, sees Edith walking fast through the gate, her black veil blowing behind her.

"For the love of Jesus and Mary, what's going on? Apple pie doesn't bake itself, you know!"

"It's Joan," Gina says. "Someone shot her, but—but she's okay. Sister Angeline—"

"Gina," Sister Angeline whispers, shaking her head in a sort of panic, indicating Gina shouldn't say anything more.

"Shot? What do you mean, shot!" Edith kneels to inspect Joan, and even at arm's length, even in her blur, Sister Angeline can smell alcohol on her breath.

"Collin found her in the ditch and used his epic first aid skills," Gina says, lying with confidence, like a good actress. She points to the bandage. "And she's okay. See?"

Edith looks at Collin, and a flush rises in his cheeks.

"Bullet just grazed her," he says. "Clearly, it didn't touch any vital organs. She's one lucky cat."

"That's it. I'm calling the sheriff," Edith says, rising unsteadily to her feet. "First the squirrel and now Joan. It's one thing to kill a squirrel, it's quite another to try to kill a cat that's clearly a pet, I mean"—and now her voice chokes up as she looks at Joan—"I mean, for God's sake, she's wearing a pink collar."

"Edith, please don't call anyone," Collin says, his broad chest rising and falling. "I—I think it might have been Liam. We had an extremely difficult conversation before Mass. He was upset and didn't want to be with me. So I thought I'd let him cool off, you know, and I went to Mass without him, and when I got home, he wasn't there. I wasn't too worried, but then after a couple of hours, he still hadn't returned, and I went looking for him. I walked everywhere, along the beach, up the road, and that's when I found Joan in the ditch."

"Did you notice if his gun was missing?" Sister Angeline says almost angrily, surprising herself.

Collin takes off his cap and wipes his forehead. "No, I was so worried that I didn't even think of it." He shakes his head. "Please let me find him and talk to him."

"Twenty-four hours," Edith says. "And then I want to know what happened. If it's Liam, we have some serious talking to do—you know that boy needs help. And if it's not Liam, I'm calling the sheriff."

"Thank you, I appreciate it," Collin says, relief and anxiety etched into the weathered lines on his face.

"Edith, I'm going to help look for Liam," Gina says. "Could you take Joan up to the convent?" She kisses Joan's head and gives the cat to Edith.

Something in Edith changes as Gina puts the cat in her arms. Something softens. "My brave little Joan of Arc," she murmurs, rocking the cat. "My brave little warrior." She turns without another word then and makes her way unevenly up the path and through the gate.

"I'll help find Liam too," Sister Angeline says, but she struggles to stand, her hands shaking so violently she thrusts them into her pockets in an effort to contain and quiet them. "I'll take the beach." She has a sense Liam might be at Amelia's log. "Collin, you should probably wait at home in case he comes back."

"You're right, yeah, okay," Collin says. "I just—don't think you should go anywhere. You—"

"Performed a friggin' miracle," Gina says.

The weight of the word *miracle* suddenly too much, Sister Angeline sinks to the ground, burying her face in her hands.

"Oh, honey," Gina says, kneeling in front of her and brushing the veil from her face. "Let me take you home."

"I'll find Liam," Collin says reassuringly. "I know you two have become friends, and for that I'm so grateful, but please, yes, please go home with Gina. I mean, you just saved a life. I can't imagine how you're feeling."

Exhausted. Elated. Terrified.

"Here," Collin says, crouching beside her, "have some water." He holds a glass bottle to her lips. "Open," he says, and he tilts it so that only a small bit trickles in, and something about his gentleness and the cool water calms her, but now the memory of the bullet hole under her palm, the entry wound small as a pearl.

She wipes her cheeks with her sleeves and stands again, stronger this time. "I'm not going home. I want to find Liam," she says firmly. "I've been resting for seven years."

Chapter Thirty-Two

Sister Angeline hikes toward Amelia's log where she and Liam often meet to talk, Anu close by her side. Dark clouds gather above, clutching rain and casting dark shadows across the rippled sand. She takes it slow. She is unutterably weary. She doesn't think about *the miracle*, doesn't have the energy, and if she isn't careful the depth and potential of it might swallow her up.

She thinks instead about Liam—if he could have done something like this. How anger destroys from the inside out. The bullying he endures. She thinks of the girls who bullied her relentlessly about her eyes, the cheerleaders who started and escalated rumors, each rumor a gut punch, a face slap, dirty whispers marking and shaping her days, pushing her to disappear into bathroom stalls, hide in the library like a shelved book nobody ever reads.

How stupidly it had all started—a girl, Delaney, saying loud on the playground, *My mother said your eyes were swapped with a witch's eyes at birth!*

What's wrong with witches, baby? her father asked when she told him tearily, when he'd taken her onto his lap and wiped her cheeks. *And anyway,* he'd said, *that girl doesn't know what she's talking about. Your eyes are a gift. You'll see.*

Later, when she was much older, when the bullying became relentless, she'd researched heterochromia and witches and found various bits of mythology, though nothing was backed by science, so she let it go and kept to herself.

She sees Liam now, standing near Amelia's log, wearing his gray hoodie and black Converse. But as she draws closer, she sees something is very, very wrong. He is only a few feet from Kamika, and he's pointing a knife at her, the silver of it reflecting a cold, sharp light.

Anu growls, and Sister Angeline grabs her collar. "Quiet, girl. Stay by me."

Liam glares at Sister Angeline as she nears him, his eyes red and swollen. "G . . . g . . . go away!" he shouts.

"Sister Angeline," Kamika says, her hands sunk into the pockets of her blue raincoat, her green eyes panicked, her body, still as stone.

"Liam," Sister Angeline says carefully, staying right where she is, "I just saw your father. He's very worried."

"F . . . fuck him," Liam says, continuing to point the blade at Kamika.

"Liam, can you put the knife down? Please?"

Ask open-ended questions.

"Can you tell me what happened?"

He turns, the knife directed now at her. The ache in his eyes. "You w . . . w . . . want to know what happened? M . . . m . . . my father lied to me. M . . . m . . . my whole life. He told m . . . m . . . me my mother died of a heart problem in a hospital. B . . . b . . . but you know how she really died? She was b . . . blown out of a building in 9/11! She died in 9 fucking 11!"

Sister Angeline stunned. Here is the content of the *difficult conversation* Collin mentioned.

"Liam, I'm—I'm so sorry," she says, her chest and throat constricting. "I can't—I can't even begin to imagine what you're going through—"

But Liam is lost inside his pain. "Why didn't he t . . . t . . . tell me?"

"I don't know, I don't know. Maybe he was trying to protect you. He was—"

"Protect me? I'm f . . . fucking f . . . fifteen. Wh . . . why didn't he protect m . . . m . . . my mother? He's an EMT! Where w . . . was he when she was being b . . . b . . . blown out a window by t . . . t . . . terrorists, by f . . . fucking Muslims!" He turns now toward Kamika, the rage on the edge of his skin pushing out hard.

Kamika doesn't move. She is watching, listening.

"Liam, this has nothing to do with Kamika."

"The f . . . fuck it doesn't. Sh . . . she's Muslim, like the f . . . fucking terrorists who k . . . k . . . killed my mother." His words catch, choking on his breath.

"Liam," Kamika says quietly, braced firmly against his words, "I wasn't part of that horror. I was fifteen at the time, your age. I watched the nightmare on television just like everyone else. I—"

But Liam needs to hate someone. His face grim and unyielding. "Are you Muslim? Yes or no?"

Kamika tenses, looks to the clouds, murmurs something in

Arabic, and then looks back at Liam. "Yes. Yes, I am. But Liam, Muslims aren't the enemy; I'm not your enemy. It was Al-Qaida who killed your mother. A very small extremist group. That's who to blame, not Muslims."

"W . . . w . . . why are you even here?" he says angrily. "In the—the convent? It's not M . . . Muslim. How do we know you aren't a spy or a t . . . t . . . terrorist or a—"

She pauses. "For safety. My family separated and went into hiding—"

"Kamika, you don't have to—" Sister Angeline says, feeling a rush of love for her, but Kamika raises her palm.

"It's okay." She fixes her brown eyes on Liam's. "I was a translator for the US Army and was given asylum to stay in America. I needed a safe place to stay, and I found this group of women. I love them, and I love this community, and I feel safer than I ever have in my entire life." Her eyes well and she keeps looking at Liam and he is looking at her, his eyes blinking fast.

"Liam," Sister Angeline says, "she's telling you the truth."

For a long time, he is silent, staring at the knife. He looks at Kamika and then folds the knife into itself, places it back into his pocket. "I'm s . . . s . . . sorry," he says.

In the distance the convent dinner bell rings.

"I'll be going back now," Kamika says softly, her face visibly drained. But first, she steps toward Liam and places both her hands over her heart. "I'm so deeply sorry about your mother, Liam." She nods at Sister Angeline then and heads home, Anu by her side.

After a moment Sister Angeline motions to Amelia's log, and says, "Sit with me, Liam."

They sit. The sound of the waves are loud, the tide is coming in, and a light rain is beginning. And now Liam's shoulders collapse, he cries, and she puts her arm around him.

"It's all right, it's all right," she murmurs, though she knows it's not all right, that life for him will be different now, the before and after of his father's confession, everything weighted with falling mothers and screams and bone dust, his sense of time and space hijacked—

"I was two," Liam whispers, his voice a little boy's. "My f . . . f . . . father said I was two, but I don't remember, he said I was in the d . . . d . . . day care center across the street from the t . . . t . . . towers, he said he couldn't get to me, he c . . . c . . . couldn't find me for t . . . t . . . ten hours, that the teachers took us somewhere in shopping carts. I d . . . d . . . don't remember—why don't I remember?" His breathing ragged gasps.

Sister Angeline whispers, "You were a child, just a child."

"He said I stopped t . . . t . . . talking for a long time after that, and when I did t . . . t . . . talk again, I st . . . stammered."

"Liam! Sister Angeline!" Ahead of them, Collin holds a black umbrella and waves madly.

"Shit," Liam says, sitting up, wiping his face.

"Your father was protecting you," she says. "He loves you."

Liam stands and walks toward Collin. She watches as he walks right by his father and from here it looks like he doesn't say a word. Collin calls to him, but Liam doesn't turn his head.

When Collin reaches Sister Angeline, he holds the umbrella over both their heads, the rain a steady pour now. He's wearing a faded orange rain jacket the same color as his hair. He stops abruptly, draws a deep breath. "I thought it was the right time to tell him, I—"

"Give him time," Sister Angeline says. "What you told him—it's a lot."

"I've really hurt him."

"There's no good time to tell anyone such an awful thing— what matters is that you told him. You told him when you were ready to."

The rain patters hard on the umbrella, and he holds it with both hands. She notices then the scars; there are at least ten, from his wrists to the knuckles of his left hand, and she wonders what happened, if they were part of being an EMT, and her heart opens wider to him.

Silence then as they turn to watch the rain on the water. It is torrential now, coming down in great powerful sheets. The pouring of water from the chalice of sky into the mouth of ocean.

"Collin," she says loudly, trying to speak over the roar, "you should know Liam had a knife. You should know he was threatening Kamika—for being Muslim."

"Oh my God. Oh Christ."

"He'll need help, Collin."

"Yes."

"Go to him. He needs you."

"Yes."

"Before you go though, I want to ask you a favor," she says.

"Anything."

"Could you stop by the convent around ten tomorrow morning? The library yurt? I want to tell the Sisters what really happened with Joan."

He wipes rain from his face. "Of course. I'm fixing the fence there anyway. Just call out to me when you're ready."

"Thank you."

He touches her sleeve. "You're soaked," he says. "Here, please take the umbrella."

She grasps the plastic handle, warm from his hand, looks up at him. His eyes are so blue. "I'm really sorry about your wife," she says.

Chapter Thirty-Three

Sister Angeline hangs the dripping umbrella on a hook outside of the kitchen yurt, her mind whirling in the liminal space of sleep and lucidity. The Sisters are preparing the evening meal, and it smells like seafood and apple pie and contentment. When they see her, everything stops, and the women surround her in a huddle, soft bodies gathering, holding her close.

Sigrid asks if she might remove her wet veil, and Sister Angeline, too tired to say no, murmurs yes, and now the veil, the coif, and wimple are all off, and Alice gently dries her hair with a warm towel. Joan purrs against her legs, and she reaches to stroke her and accepts a glass of water from Gina and drains it, and she is
crumpling
spilling
drifting.

Sigrid says, "Here, sit down, sweetheart, have some soup, you must be starving," and Gina whispers into her ear, "I didn't tell them, don't worry," and now Kamika says, "I told them about Liam—everything is okay."

"It was awful," Sister Angeline says. "You must have been frightened."

"I was. And yet."

"And yet?"

"In some small way, I felt stronger afterward. I've never stood up for who I was like that."

"Sisters, dinner," Sigrid says now.

And once they are all seated around the long wooden table, Kamika opens a book. "I'm going to read from the Qur'an," she says.

Sister Angeline struggles to stay awake, but she thinks she hears Kamika read a prayer to Allah to expand her heart, to untie the knots in her tongue that she may be understood, and the words stream like cool water into Sister Angeline's mouth.

Alice ladles pea soup into her bowl, but it's hard for Sister Angeline to hold her spoon, and now someone offers her a basket of bread, and she shakes her head, the thought of chewing too much, and for a while they are all silent and spooning chowder until out of nowhere Edith says, "If it wasn't Liam, then who was it?"

"There are plenty of people who don't like us," Sigrid says, "and the best we can do right now is pray."

But Edith doesn't like this and says, "Praying won't stop the worst thing!"

And Sister Angeline thinks, *What is the worst thing*, and mothers and babies who die enter her mind, and Edith says, "We're not talking about a kid tearing the legs off a fly here," and she says something about the size of the animals getting larger—*squirrel, cat, what next? Dog?*—and she says she studied this, people killing animals, and what's happening is a real red flag.

It is the word *dog* that makes Sister Angeline jerk alert and stand and say in a panic, "Where is Anu?" but the dog is right there pressing into her side, and she hears herself saying, "I can't stay, I'm not well, I'm going to rest," but she remembers she wants to ask them something and says, "May I speak tomorrow at our ten o'clock gathering? There's—something I want to talk about. I've invited Collin to come too. I want to talk about Joan."

All the women's heads nodding nodding nodding and Sister Angeline's equilibrium

swaying

not solid

suspended

and now Alice is there, holding one of her elbows, and Gina the other, and they are walking outside, and the rain has stopped, and the air is glistening and brilliant with earth smells. Sister Angeline runs her fingers through her hair and how long has it been since she's walked outside without her veil.

Chapter
Thirty-Four

Sister Angeline wakes up still fatigued, and after dressing herself sits on the bed to catch her breath. She doesn't remember this extreme depletion happening the other times the energy arrived, but she knows better than to look for clues and patterns and signs, knows she'll never know the reasoning behind the secret holdings of the universe, the cosmos with its billions of molecules constantly splitting, destroying, creating.

The six women assemble in the library. Sister Angeline watches the scene from behind a tall shelf of books, peeking over the tops of the bindings. She is like an actor backstage, practicing breathing exercises to calm herself, her mind pacing across the small room. It is the audience though, rather than the breathing, that will reassure her most, keep her grounded, make her feel protected.

Gina sits cross-legged on the floor, holding Joan on her lap, and the cat looks so alive and peaceful, it sends a chill through Sister Angeline. Alice reads *A Field Guide to Pacific Northwest Birds* in an overstuffed chair, and Sigrid repairs an electrical outlet near the television, her Seahawks cap on backward and a screwdriver in her mouth.

Edith stands by the window and looks like an oil painting—an anonymous figure in black gazing at rain or maybe at something thousands of miles away or maybe at nothing—her face registering serenity until you look closely at the layers underneath.

Sister Angeline thinks maybe this entire scene might be a dream, might be a painting, and she won't have to confide anything at all, won't have to expose more of herself, but Edith breaks the illusion when she takes her seat, looks at her watch, and says, "Ten o'clock, are we going to start or what?"

Kamika walks into the room then, and she's wearing a pale blue hijab. Her face and body filled with a new composure, light as the gauze covering her long black hair, as if something beloved has been found and returned. Everyone smiles; it's like a homecoming.

"No more tucking into shadows," she says and then sits on the floor. Sister Angeline kneels by her, squeezes her hand, and whispers, "You're so beautiful."

Sigrid screws the switch plate back on now, puts the screwdriver in her red toolbox, and plugs in the television to see if it works. A Geico ad comes on—a St. Bernard climbing on the dinner table and eating spaghetti from everyone's plates. "It works!" Sigrid says, "We're set for the game tomorrow!" and she clicks the television off and grabs a few pieces of paper from the antique desk.

"Before we hear from Sister Angeline"—she gestures to Sister Angeline to sit in the empty chair beside her—"we have two notes from the prayer box and one snail-mail letter to read."

Sister Angeline walks over to the ivory slip-covered chair, the one that's become hers now, sits down, and tucks in a wisp of hair that has slipped out from her wimple. Anu lies at her feet, resting her head on Sister Angeline's shoes.

"You okay?" Sigrid says.

"Yes, I'm fine, thank you."

"Okay, I'll read the letter first," Sigrid says. She puts on her half-moon reading glasses and pulls the note from the envelope.

Dear Sisters,

First, I want to thank all of you for attending the Seattle Pride celebration in July and for your support in working to pass SB 6239 and HB 2516. And while we are all thrilled about the Supreme Court ruling, as you know, there's still a lot of work to do beyond the Love Wins hashtag.

We recently heard all of you share your thoughts on equality at Seattle's Festival of Pride and we were wondering if you all might be willing to speak at our Inter-Island Youth Conference, 7:00 p.m., Friday, March 4, 2016, at the Madrona Island Community Center. I've enclosed ferry vouchers should you say yes, which we hope you will do.

Sincerely,
Tim Zeno,
Deputy Director,
Washington State
Bullying Prevention
Task Force

"So," Sigrid says, "everyone up for speaking again?"

The women all nod, except Sister Angeline, who wasn't there. She'd like to help, though she is unsure what she'd say, and the thought of speaking publicly terrifies her.

Alice is signing something now and pointing to Sister Angeline.

"She would love if you could read her written thoughts at the conference," Kamika says.

"I'd be honored," Sister Angeline says, smiling at Alice, relieved and grateful.

"Okay, great," Sigrid says. "Moving on, notes from the prayer box." The first note is folded into an origami bird. She smiles as she opens up the wings to reveal the words.

Dear Sisters,

Thank you for bringing all the colored paper to the shelter last week so the after-school kids could make origami birds and butterflies. Thank you, too, for making the delicious apple pies! They were very much enjoyed!

I hate to keep asking for things, but I was wondering if you could bring some cough medicine and aspirin next time you visit. We're running low and headed into flu season.

Warmly,
Helen Randolf,
Director of Rose House

"I'll set up an ask at church on Sunday," Kamika says.

"I'll help," Alice signs.

"Great, thanks," Sigrid says. "Okay, last note." She removes the letter from the envelope and unfolds it.

To the Sisters Whom It May Concern,

We support Father Matt, and we won't put up with your pretense. Offering the sacraments has been, without exception, reserved for men, and this fact can't be changed. Take your progressive, liberal ideas elsewhere.

A subtle tremor of anger moves through the room. Sister Angeline watches it land on the faces of each woman, quickening pulses, reverberating into the spaces between them, sparking red under her own skin.

"I mean, what the what?" Gina says, and Sister Angeline thinks then about the gun in her room—will she hold it closer now?

Sigrid's jaw tightens. She folds the letter, leaves it on her lap, removes her reading glasses, and places them in her shirt pocket. "A few bad apples," she says. "Still, be extra vigilant, Sisters. Lock those doors at night. Gina, you keep Joan in your room. Sister Angeline, you keep Anu."

Hearing her name, Anu raises her head inquisitively. "It's okay, girl," Sister Angeline says, stroking the dog's head, though in her heart she feels there's going to be trouble.

"I can't believe you just said *a few bad apples*," Edith says to Sigrid. "As if it's nothing. Lock our doors and we'll be fine. Bad apples or not, it's still a threat, and threats often lead to violence."

Sigrid is quiet for a moment, then says, her voice calm, "I don't think it's *nothing*, but I don't believe whoever is behind this note represents a big group, and they certainly don't deserve a lot of airtime."

"Have you thought about the people who assemble with

us?" Edith says. "Will it even be safe to hold gatherings? Give me the letter; I'm photocopying it and sending it to the sheriff. He needs to know—not that he'll do anything."

Sigrid sighs wearily. "I agree Ferguson probably won't help. He's buddies with Matt and attends his Mass. I highly doubt he'll give it anything but a smirk or say we'd be safer leaving town—he never did agree with our ways. Still, he's bound by law to help." She takes off her baseball cap and rakes her fingers through her short gray hair.

Alice gestures something to all of them now—she'd like the group to pray. Her eyes are quiet but commanding.

Everyone silent for a moment. Sister Angeline expects an objection from Edith, but none comes. Instead Edith stands up and opens a window. A tremendous burst of fresh air blows in, bringing with it the sweet scent of rain layered with ocean salt.

"Yes, prayer is a very good idea," Sigrid says. "Thank you, Alice."

There is a collective deep breath as Alice makes the sign of the cross over the women, folds her hands in prayer, and closes her eyes.

The Sisters do the same. Sister Angeline feels a rush of gratitude for this moment, this small return to the strength and stillness of prayer. She focuses on her breath, consciously inhaling safety and exhaling fear, and slowly, the tightness in her shoulders softens, the current of anxiety dissolves, and a warmth opens.

"Amen," Sigrid says quietly.

"Amen," they all say in unison, and in the moment they all open their eyes, Sister Angeline realizes something remarkable:

she is not alone. Whatever happens, this group of determined women will manage it together, they will find their own way together.

"Okay, Sister Angeline," Sigrid says, "you wanted to talk to us?"

Chapter
Thirty-Five

Sister Angeline's heart thumps no, and *want* is the wrong word, but her head nods a slow yes. She does not want to carry a lie.

"Collin's outside fixing the fence," she says. "I told him we'd let him know when we're ready."

"I'll get him," Gina says, lifting the cat off her lap and hurrying to the front door. She opens it and calls for Collin.

In a moment, he appears, steps in hesitantly, wipes his boots on the mat, and removes his blue raincoat. He's wearing a clean flannel shirt and jeans. "Good morning," he says with a friendly nod.

"Welcome to our library!" Gina says warmly, taking his coat and hanging it outside. "You can sit over there"—she points to a metal folding chair against the wall—"or just stand wherever you're comfortable."

He shoves his hands in his jean pockets and walks toward the bookshelves. Leans against them. He glances at Sister Angeline and gives her a reassuring smile. She smiles back, feels an upwelling of tenderness for him.

"Everyone all set?" Edith says impatiently. "Or do we need to get milk and cookies?"

Sister Angeline touches the gold cross around her neck. Her lips part. She has an impulse to pull her veil across her face. *Why am I so afraid?*

"The story you've heard about Joan's healing isn't all the way true," she says finally. "Something happened—" But the words hide under her tongue, and she looks at Collin and Gina with desperation.

"I didn't save Joan," Collin says. "It was Sister Angeline. Joan was—dead when I found her in the ditch."

"And," Gina says, looking now at Sister Angeline, "can I tell them?"

Sister Angeline nods, smiles faintly, gratefully.

"This is going to sound supernaturally weird and bizarre," Gina says, "but there's no other way to say it. Sister Angeline brought Joan back to life!" She shakes her head of curls, wonder gathering around her big eyes. "She put one hand on Joan and the other on Anu, and well, after several minutes, Joan started to breathe again. I mean—really, it was a miracle." She kisses the top of the cat's head. "An actual-to-God miracle."

Heads tilt and eyes widen. An uneasy silence fills the room, making Sister Angeline feel strange and uncomfortable. She hoped Gina wouldn't use that word again. *Miracle* too weighted, too blunt, too complicated, too exalted with its suggestions of intercessions and divine agency, its insistence on leaps of faith. Too many people waiting for one.

Edith is the first to speak, bringing her brows together in doubt. "A miracle? What in God's name are you talking about?"

All faces turn to Sister Angeline now, and she doesn't know

what to say, how much to tell. She's afraid that in the telling they'll think she's crazy or worse—they'll no longer embrace her. She's afraid she'll frighten the cherished energy away, extinguish it forever, violate the sacredness of it.

Joan unfolds from Gina's lap and ambles over to Sister Angeline. Curls around her legs. It is then, as Sister Angeline reaches to touch her, in the silence of the room, she hears a dove call out. It has the same tone and vibration as the one she heard outside her window months ago.

Coo-OO-oo coo-OO-oo coo-OO-oo

She holds still for several moments, her hand resting on Joan's head, listening, looks to the rafters as if the dove might have found its way into the library, its song that close, but Sister Angeline doesn't see the bird. Still, she hears the coo-OO-ooing, and once again the dove's pulsations ease the beating of uncertainty in her heart. The dove revealed an important friendship to her before. She will trust her again.

"There have been a few times in my life," Sister Angeline says haltingly, "when I've prayed for someone or something to change, and—and there's an energy that comes and fills my body. It begins in my eyes—tiny electrical sparks that multiply"—her voice becoming stronger, more alive—"and vibrate into my chest and spread and spiral everywhere, into my spine and my hips, my legs, arms, hands, and before I know it—" She pauses now, realizes she's talking too fast, thinking how inadequate her words are—she's flying over the ecstatic, mysterious flame of it. "I'm sorry," she says. "It's just really difficult to explain."

It's begun to rain again, and for a moment everything is quiet except the constant sound of drumming on the canvas roof. Alice gets up, takes a knitted afghan from her lap, the fabric woven with the colors of forest and sea, and walks over to Sister Angeline. She kisses her forehead and wraps the blanket around her shoulders.

"In all my years in the Church," Sigrid says in a gentle, reverential voice, "I have never known someone to do something like this, to bring a creature back to life, to perform a miracle." She takes a deep breath and leans forward, the fingers of her hands intertwining. "I think, dear Sister Angeline, you may be a healer."

Sister Angeline's face colors, and her gaze shifts to her hands on her lap, the fingers locked, holding on to each other tight.

"I think we're jumping the gun using the word *miracle*," Edith says. "It's possible Joan was in shock and recovered by the time Sister Angeline touched her."

"No," Gina says angrily. "I know you're a scientist and it's your job to prove things wrong, but Collin's a friggin' EMT and I think he knows what he's talking about." She looks at Collin for confirmation.

"By my estimate," Collin says, his voice matter of fact, "Joan had probably been dead for at least thirty minutes, maybe longer. I took her vitals several times. No pulse. She was cold and becoming stiff. And judging by the location of the bullet hole, so close to her heart, I think she probably died immediately." His face softens now. "I honestly have no explanation for what happened, what I witnessed with Sister Angeline. I've never seen anything—so amazing, so beautiful." His blue eyes move to Sister Angeline, and in his recognition of her, he is suddenly a mirror, and she has a flitting glimpse then of what Sigrid meant when she said, *I see you*, and what her father meant when he said, *My hope for you, sweet Meg, is that someday you will see yourself the way I do—full of power, full of light.*

"Well, not everything that seems impossible to explain is necessarily a miracle," Edith says. She turns to Sister Angeline. "Makes me wonder though, did you ask for God's help, pray to a saint?"

"I prayed to—to the light, and I did feel love's presence deeply." She is flustered, like a guilty person not used to interrogation.

"In Islam," Kamika says quietly, "the ones who perform the miracles are often humans, not gods or saints with divine qualities—humans given a gift from God."

Anu sits up, puts her head on Sister Angeline's knee.

"I am curious, Sister Angeline," Sigrid says, "you said you've felt this energy before?"

Sister Angeline nods slowly, touching her fingers to the rosary in her pocket. "Yes. Once as a child, another when I was ten, another when I was fifteen." She hesitates now, unsure whether to bring up the squirrel and St. Francis. Unsure about how much is too much, unsure if they will accept all this, if they will accept her. But here are Alice's eyes, soft as feathers, telling her to keep going, telling her it's safe. "And I felt it with the squirrel and then again with St. Francis." No one presses her for details, and she's relieved—she's too tired to say more.

Edith gives her an acute, assessing look, then stands and paces the room. "Okay, let's say, for the sake of argument, it was a miracle, that Sister Angeline's a healer, now what? If we say anything to anyone outside of this room, do you know what could happen? Can you see the ferry-loads of people arriving to be healed? The news reporters? The badgering and requests for interviews, publicity shots? The exploitation of the archdiocese?" She laughs. Her laugh is pinched and edged with indignation. "Oh, can you imagine the money they'd send us then!" She turns to Sigrid. "Our life as we know it would be completely changed, our solitude one hundred percent gone."

"Edith," Sigrid says now, "you're the one jumping the gun. Right now the most important question is how can we support Sister Angeline?"

Edith is taken aback. She looks as if she might say more, but she stops herself and returns to her seat.

Sister Angeline stands up. Her legs are weak. She needs to be alone more than anything. She walks slowly to the door then turns. "I know we're a community, that we make decisions together, and I appreciate that, but I'm—I'm not ready for anyone else to know. If I could, I'd like to be alone. I'd like to work, eat, and pray alone for a little while, maybe a week or more. Think this through. Pray about it."

"Yes, of course, of course. Whatever you need," Sigrid says, coming over to her. "We'll be here if you need us."

Alice brings Sister Angeline a folded note. Sister Angeline tucks it in her pocket near her rosary. "Thank you," she says, opening the door. These kindnesses open an ache too deep for her to absorb.

"We love you!" Gina shouts from across the room.

Sister Angeline looks at Collin for a moment; he is still leaning against the wall, hands in his pockets. He smiles at her as if he understands her uncertainty and confusion, and then nods his head and says in a tender voice, "Take care."

She walks back to her yurt, the blanket still wrapped around her shoulders, the rain paused again. Inside, sunlight descends from the windows, but it is cold. She flips the switch on the little propane fireplace and sits on the chair near it, the subdued lapping of ocean outside.

What do I do now?

She pulls the blanket tighter and reaches into her pocket for Alice's note. Unfolds it.

You're at the place between the wound and the healing.
It's a mouth. A womb. An ocean. Follow the questions.

Chapter Thirty-Six

It's the first day of November and the tall beach grasses shiver and the ocean flashes frothy whitecaps. Sister Angeline walks the beach, invigorated by the cold wind and tangy, salty smell. Anu, as usual, runs ahead. Nearby a cormorant stands on a boulder, drying its wings. To her left, the seal—the one with three brown circles on its head, the one that often bobs up during her walks—gazes at her with big childlike eyes, and Sister Angeline wonders for a moment if the seal is lonely, swimming all alone like that, but then she notices there's something about it, a sort of contentment as if it's holding a secret that keeps it warm, keeps it at peace.

She's been alone for nearly two weeks now, praying and fasting—though one of the Sisters kindly leaves her a basket of food and a thermos of tea three times a day, and she sometimes takes a few bites, a few sips. She still collects the eggs and works in the herb garden, pruning, picking, weeding. When she sees another Sister, they exchange only a smile. Her urge to speak to them is strong, but the desire for the insight that often comes to her in silence, stronger.

She worries though, as clarity seems to be avoiding her, the texture of her silence insecure, porous.

She's tried looking deep into Anu's beautiful, mismatched eyes, the dog's face cupped in her hands, tried asking, *How shall we do this, Anu? Where do we go from here?* Anu only watches her quietly, gazing at her with a fierce love. A deeper intimacy grows between them, but not enough to illuminate things for Sister Angeline.

And with each passing day, Sister Angeline's insomnia increases. She thought she'd settle into her solitude, allow the black-and-white of it to help her clarify things, regroup, replenish. She thought she'd been hungering for it—an *it* she has no words for, though the words *oneness* and *touchstone* come close. But she'd forgotten the hazards of isolation.

How a shallow river of doubt can become
a bottomless
pool of grief.

How thoughts can
circle like panicked
yellow-eyed beasts
sneering orange tongues
unable to find a way out.

How voices inside
her mouth can scream
who do you think you are?

But.

When she walks
near the water
catches its rhythm
something
pulls
her away from the
destruction
the dis   integration
urges her
toward light
and shapes her mind
into something like

white clouds
in the shape of fish
swimming.

She comes upon a particularly large tide pool now, crouches low, and stares into it. Red and scarlet anemones the size of her hands unfurl their luminous, fringed tentacles. Miniature crabs rush around, and an orange starfish lies heavy in the swaying green algae. A thin, translucent worm
floats
floats
floats
into the anemone's
pulsing embrace
but now
tentacles jerk
and tighten

and the worm disappears
the wide mouth
closes

moments later
the anemone unfolds like
a delicate flower
as if the worm never existed.

Anu barks at something behind her, and Sister Angeline looks quickly over her shoulder, startled, nervous it might be Father Matt. To her intense relief, it's Collin.

"Sorry. Sorry. I don't mean to interrupt. I didn't mean to startle you," he says, his thick red hair disheveled by the wind.

"Oh," she says, taking a breath to compose herself. "You're not interrupting." Her mouth clumsy and slow after speaking only to Anu for so long.

"How are you?" he says gently.

She digs her hands into her pockets, takes a breath to compose herself. "I'm—I'm not really getting anywhere," she says.

A tiny armadillo-shaped creature the size and color of a piece of rice moves across the arch of her shoe now, then frantically digs itself back under the sand, leaving no evidence of itself.

"Sand crab," Collin says. "You know what's weird about them? They only move backward. They can't move forward or sideways, only backward."

Sister Angeline captivated by this information. The thought of never moving forward. What she wouldn't give to move backward in time, to go back to the way things were before everyone she loved died.

"You know," he says tentatively, "it's almost lunchtime and my houseboat is right over there"—he points to a marina a few hundred yards away—"and I make a mean grilled cheese sandwich and tomato soup combo. Want to join me? We could talk. Maybe I could be of some help—you know, like a sounding board?"

The invitation catches her by surprise, unsettling her. It sounds like he's asking her on a date, and she becomes suddenly very conscious of her vow of chastity. A vow meant to free her from the demands of romantic relationships. A vow allowing her to fiercely devote all her energy to love, to prayer. Like her vows of poverty and obedience, the vow of chastity is a privilege meant to strengthen her soul. She wants to touch her ring now, but she doesn't want her insecurities to become obvious, because what if she's jumping to conclusions?

"You might see Liam," he says as if reading her mind. "He should be home soon."

The truth is she likes Collin. She decides she will continue to trust him. As Gina keeps telling her: relationships are the heart, the core, the mainspring of human experience. *But you have to talk*, Gina would say emphatically. *You have to let people know you.*

"He's over on Madrona Island, working through things with a therapist, a young guy," Collin says. "Liam likes him."

"Oh," she says. "That's wonderful."

"So, lunch?"

"I'm not sure how kosher it is for a nun to be descending into a boat with a man." Her humor takes her by surprise—the way it just comes out of her. She cannot remember the last time she said something light-hearted, something playful.

"Well, Edith comes aboard all the time," he says, laughing.

"She likes to drop a crab pot over the bow, then sit and have a smoke and a beer or two while she waits for things to happen. Sometimes she doesn't even throw the crab pot over. She just drinks and smokes."

The image of Edith sitting on the bow of a boat in her habit, drinking a beer, and smoking makes Sister Angeline laugh too, and this image somehow gives her permission.

"Okay," she says. "Honestly, I'd give anything for a grilled cheese sandwich." She calls for Anu, and the dog bounds over, circling Collin with enthusiasm.

"Hey, girl," he says, ruffling the dog's head. "Hungry?"

Chapter
Thirty-Seven

They walk down the wobbly, narrow dock, Anu trotting in front of them. It's high tide and the incoming waves crash against the pilings and salt-spray flies into their faces. The wind blows harder now, lifting Sister Angeline's veil so that she thinks it might blow completely off and she has to hold it with one hand, making it more difficult for her to keep her balance. Once, she tips a bit, and Collin holds her elbow, his touch startling her. He must sense her unease because he lets go immediately.

"This dock seems like it should be condemned, but it's actually safe," he says loudly, competing with the wind.

Safe? She prays to Mary and tries not to look over the edges.

He stops finally at a huge blue tugboat, the name *Claire* painted in white across the bow. "Converted tug, and she's home sweet home," he says.

Sister Angeline immediately awed by the boat's immensity, the stoutness of it. Everything about its construction announcing determination, safety carved between its curved planks.

It must be at least sixty or seventy feet long and twenty feet high. Three lines thicker than her arm secure it to the dock.

"It's beautiful, spectacular," she says. And then with a smile, "Did you say *she*?"

"Habit learned from my grandfather, a tug captain. He always used the pronoun *she* when referring to ships—I guess most old mariners do, something about women as a mystery of the world, like Mother Earth on the one hand, but needs a man to handle her on the other." He gives Sister Angeline an embarrassed smile. "I know, it's terrible, woman as objects and all that. Sorry. Trying hard to break myself of it." He climbs up and over the railing and reaches his hand out to her.

She lifts her skirt and grabs hold of him—his grip so easy and warm—and steps aboard. Still holding her hand, he leads her to the bow, and they stand there, looking out. The view saturated with vibrating silvers and blues, unceasing motion, shadow, and light blowing wildly unscripted, like gauzy angel wings sailing into and out of an infinite sky, a vast alive body, and Sister Angeline feels exhilarated.

On the beach, two little boys throw rocks into the choppy water, shrieking with pleasure, and abruptly in her mind: Ricky's face, how much he would have loved this boat, this water, this wind, how she would give anything to be standing here, holding his hand—

"Would you like to go inside? Sister Angeline?"

She turns her head slowly, her veil covering her face. She drops her hand from his, and the veil blows from her eyes.

"You're crying," he says, and his arms are around her now, like an offering, like a nourishment, and she doesn't resist, allows herself to surrender, not in a sensual, erotic

ANNA QUINN

quickening-of-pulses way, but as one might with a mother
a father a sister a brother a friend—an embrace where she
wants nothing else but to press into another heartbeat, no
thinking, only release—and she can feel stones falling from
her shoulders. They stay like this for a long time, rocking back
and forth with the boat, until he says, "Want to go inside?
Have some lunch?"

She pulls away gently, returning to herself slowly. The
November sky low and cold, and the air is filled with the
sound of waves crashing on the shore over and over and over.
She looks at his face and considers him, considers whether
anything has changed.

"Yes," she says. "Lunch sounds lovely."

He moves to an arched wooden door behind him. "After
you," and he sweeps his arm into the cabin. She descends three
narrow stairs, Anu behind her, and steps into a large, open room.

She looks around. The ceiling, walls, and floors are covered
in a rich, resonant wood. Daylight pours through three round
windows rimmed in brass. Near her a cushioned bench covered
in green leather surrounds a small pine table with scattered newspaper pages and a box of medical supplies. To her right, a tiny
cast-iron woodstove.

She stands close to it, allowing the heat to soak through her
coat, through her habit, to her skin, and into her bones. Anu
already stretched out in front of it, thumping her tail. Collin
opens a little door in the front of the stove and stokes the fire
until it crackles.

Sister Angeline sniffs the air. "Some kind of fuel?"

"Diesel. She—I mean, this tug—runs on it. Strong stuff."

"I like it," she says. "And I love this space. It's so quiet."

The smell reminds her of the bus that carried her from the southside of Chicago to St. Mary's High School, to her beloved teacher, Sister Blessica. How the young nun would often say, *Ignore the mean girls, tell me about your dreams.*

"Sister Angeline?" Collin says.

"I'm sorry?"

He removes the papers and box from the table. "You should have seen it before we moved in. The decks leaked, gaskets and pumps were burned out, the fuel lines rusted, we filled twenty trash cans with old wiring, the wood in this entire room had to be ripped out, floor planks were rotten." He stops, sets the box and the papers on one of the two neatly made bunks up front, returns, and lights a kerosene lamp on the table. "But you know, it was an eighty-five-year-old working tug, so—" He smiles and fills a metal tea kettle over a large stainless-steel sink.

"You did all this?" She is warm now, removes her coat, and hangs it on a brass hook by his parka.

"I had help. Some good folks around here."

"How long have you lived here?" The boat tilts under her feet, and she puts her hand on a kitchen chair for support.

"You'll get used to it," he says, "the rocking." He sets the tea kettle on the stove and lights the propane. "Fifteen years we've lived here—since Liam was a baby. My grandfather left it to me. I visited him almost every summer as a kid, and let me tell you, coming from New York in July and August, this boat was all kinds of heaven." He pulls a loaf of white bread from a slatted cupboard, some sliced cheese from the small refrigerator. As he closes the door, she notices a magnet on the front of it and reads the words aloud.

But because *truly* being here is so much; because
     everything here
apparently needs us, this fleeting world, which in some
     strange way
keeps calling to us. Us, the most fleeting of all.

"Ever read Rilke?" Collin asks.

"Many times."

"Me too." He turns to her and holds the knife in the air like a sword, like he's giving a performance, his voice deep and dramatic and recites a passage: "'Be patient toward all that is unsolved in your heart and try to love the questions themselves. Live the questions now. Perhaps you will then gradually, without noticing it, live along some distant day into the answer.'"

She claps, and he takes a bow.

"I've always liked those words, at least conceptually," she says. "But—"

There are so many questions that find me and demand things.

"Hey, let's just be here now," he says as if sensing her sudden agitation. "We'll think better after we eat."

"Anything I can do to help?"

"Nah, I got this." And he spreads butter on both sides of each sandwich and then cuts at least a third of a stick and sets it in a cast-iron pan. When the butter bubbles slightly, he places the sandwiches in gently with a metal spatula.

She moves toward the floor-to-ceiling bookshelves on the other side of the room, shelves crammed with volumes of medical guides, novels, and books on hiking, poetry, and nature. She traces the bindings with her fingertips.

"Favorite authors?" he asks.

"Oh—there are so many."

"If you could only take three to an island?" He portions loose tea leaves into a teapot now and pours steaming water over them.

She doesn't answer for a few minutes. Thinks about books she loves. "Okay," she says finally, "I guess I'd take Toni Morrison and Simone Weil and Thomas Merton—and I'd have to squeeze in Virginia Woolf." She watches him get a saucepan from a hook over the sink and empty two cans of Campbell's Tomato Soup into it. "You?" she asks.

He stirs the soup. "Well"—he nods at the bookshelves, his face revealing layers of boyishness—"you can probably see I'm a sci-fi guy, so I'd have to take an Octavia Butler novel and my Asimov trilogy—good ideas there for starting a new colony."

"That's four," she says.

"Makes up for you squeezing in Virginia Woolf." He smiles and sets two fraying green checkered cloth napkins, two plates, two bowls, and two spoons on the table.

She's enjoying this conversation. She hasn't talked about books with anyone for so long—since her name was Meg, since high school English—and for the second time that day, she thinks about Sister Blessica, how she loved books too, was always asking her students questions like, *How would the character be different if this event hadn't happened to her? If you were in the story, what would your relationship be to the protagonist?*

She thinks, too, how her time with Sister Blessica suddenly ended. The principal suspended Meg for frightening Delaney in the lunchroom one day—Delaney, the girl who'd tormented her for a decade—how Meg in a rage had convinced Delaney she really was a witch, told her that if she didn't follow her instructions, something bad would happen. How Delaney had believed her. And how later, alone in her bedroom, Delaney lit a candle and did what Meg had told her to do: pulled three strands of her fine blond hair and held them over a candle's flame.

How the flame caught the sleeve of her nightgown.

How Delaney had remembered to stop, drop, and roll, and survived.

How Meg could barely live with herself after that, how Delaney's arms were so burned with scars she only wore long sleeves. How she could have died.

What St. Francis should have said: *Be very afraid of your rage.*

Sister Angeline sweating now, her legs trembling under her skirt.

"You okay?"

She looks at Collin, bewildered, shaken by the memory.

Collin turns the stove off and motions her to sit at the table. "Our repast is ready!" he says in a charming and chivalrous manner. He pours tea into their mugs, ladles soup into their bowls, places a golden grilled cheese sandwich on each plate. "Oh wait," he says once he sits down. "Grace. Yes?"

She nods, gives a faint smile. Closes her eyes and crosses herself. The soothing smells of ginger and lemon, soup, and toast. The impact of scent suddenly reminding her of a list her aunt gave her a month after the car accident, when Meg wouldn't get out of bed, couldn't think of reasons to live, couldn't stop the horrible images. Her aunt, holding a cigarette in one hand, placed the list on her pillow, taken a deep drag, the smoke rising to the ceiling and curling in a cloud there, and said, "Goddammit, you should be grateful you're alive."

Three Tools to Cope with Flashbacks

#1: Press your feet firmly into the ground.
#2: Breathe in a comforting scent.
#3: Write three affirmations and repeat them each morning.

After her aunt left the room, Meg perched on the edge of the bed. Shivered violently. Watched herself read the list and press her feet firmly into the ground. Watched herself try to breathe in a comforting scent, but there was only the smell of blood and ache and burning screams twisted into cigarette stench. Watched herself rip up the list and throw it out the window, tiny pieces fluttering to the ground like dead white birds.

"—and for this new friendship in a world where many walk alone, amen," Collin is saying, and she realizes she's missed some of the prayer and does her best to blink herself into focus.

"Amen," she whispers.

Chapter Thirty-Eight

"Okay," Collin says, "dive in!" He picks up his sandwich, cheese dripping out the edges, and takes a huge bite, chewing and saying *mmm* at the same time.

Sister Angeline cuts her sandwich into two triangles, dips one of the halves into her tomato soup, and then brings it sopping to her lips. Takes a bite. The luxury and slow melt of it on her tongue.

"So good," she says and immediately dips it again and takes another bite, though she knows after fasting she should practice restraint or her stomach will cramp and reject. Still, she takes a third, fourth, and fifth bite, not even looking up between swallows, and now the buttery triangle is gone. She wipes the crumbs from her mouth and looks at Collin, embarrassed, pushes the plate away, reaches for her tea, and cups her hands around the mug.

"Glad you liked it," he says, chewing and smiling. "You're not eating the rest?"

"That might have been the best sandwich I ever had,"

she says. "And the soup? So good, but I should pace myself."

At the word *good*, Anu comes over and puts her head on Collin's lap, ears pricked.

"Oops," he says, "looking for your treat?" And he rises now and goes to the refrigerator, rubbing the dog's head.

Sister Angeline brings the mug of tea to her mouth, blows on it before sipping. She watches Collin pull out a package of hot dogs, open it, and give one to Anu, who eats it as fast as she can, and she thinks how incredibly thoughtful and generous Collin is—the way he's making sure they are all comfortable, all fed, but also—maybe too much so. Liam told her often how his father was rarely home, how he couldn't say no to anyone who needed his help.

He leaves me alone a lot, Liam said, hurt swimming in his eyes.

She thinks about what it must be like for Collin—to be a single parent, to have lost a wife.

"Collin," she says hesitantly once he's sitting back down. "May I ask about the name on your boat? *Claire?*"

His face dims. The sudden drop of his shoulders. Everything about him sinking. He takes a breath and then says slowly, "My wife. Claire was my wife." Layers of sadness on his face, and Sister Angeline wishes she hadn't asked.

"Collin, you don't have to—"

"I know you're not supposed to change the names of boats," he continues, "but I did, and I'm pretty sure Poseidon would understand. I mean, names matter, don't you think?"

Sister Angeline nods. She doesn't know why this involves the god of the sea, but she agrees names matter.

"And Claire was so beautiful and magical. Nothing with her

name on it could be anything but good." He lifts his mug, then sets it down without drinking. "Claire and I traveled twice from New York to visit my grandfather here before we were married, and"—he laughs a little—"she might have loved this boat more than she loved me. How could I not name it after her?" He runs his hand along the varnished wooden table.

"I'm sorry, Collin." There's so much more she wishes she could say, but the ache of his pain is so intimate.

He takes a gulp of tea, and she can see it's hard for him to swallow.

"It's really good you told Liam about her though."

"I—I didn't tell him all of it." His tone is weary and distant, and he looks away. "I was an EMT in New York as well, and that day, 9/11, I missed the calls from my field supervisor. I'd been out with a buddy the night before, and we—I drank too much. I was going through a bad phase, and I forgot to charge my radio, left my phone in the car." He rakes his hand through his hair, and she can see silver threaded through the red.

"That morning, Claire didn't want to wake me, so she left a note that she'd taken Liam to day care, which was usually my job. She was a travel agent, worked in the North Tower." He hesitates, closes his eyes briefly, then opens them. "By the time I heard the dispatch messages, by the time I arrived at the towers, everything had already gone to hell. Everywhere—" He doesn't break eye contact with her, his eyes watering.

"Collin," she says.

He puts his face in his hands. "God, the screaming and glass and there was so much dust my ventilator wouldn't work—and all I could think was *where is Claire, where is Liam?*"

Sister Angeline is quiet. Blinking tears.

He looks at her again. "Sometimes at night I see her there, Claire, in her office on the phone, helping someone plan their dream trip, but I can't see what happened then—when the jets hit. Did she try to go under her desk? Did she scream? Try to call me? Did she jump or—?" He sits back, his blue eyes wet.

"You're allowed to cry," she says and places her hand over the scars on his.

The weight of being the one who lived.

"And you found Liam."

For a moment, Collin can't speak, his eyes so full of suffering, and when he does, all he can say is, "Yes. Thank God, yes."

There's a continuous beeping sound now near the bookshelves. "Dispatch," he says and rises quickly, wipes his eyes, looks at the message. "Gas leak on Madrona. I'm not needed—just a heads-up."

She's relieved he doesn't have to leave. "Do you get called often?"

"Maybe a few emergencies a day, mostly because we don't have a hospital here and my ambulance is kind of the local clinic on wheels, so they call me for nonemergencies too, like sore throats, stomachaches, allergic reactions, that sort of thing." He turns up the propane under the kettle, clears their dishes, points to her half sandwich. "Want me to wrap it up?"

"Thank you, that would be lovely. Collin—what you do? It seems like a lot for one person."

He shrugs. "Hard to fund things on these little islands, but we've got a pretty great volunteer network. Everybody watches out for each other." He wraps her sandwich carefully in foil.

"And Liam—when you're gone?"

"He's at school mostly and seems okay on his own if I have to go out at night."

Her mouth opens and closes. She wants to tell him Liam isn't okay alone, but she won't break Liam's confidences.

He opens a pink bakery box sitting on the counter. Lifts out a beautiful pie. "Blueberry," he says. "Payment for services rendered—this is from the wife of a man who went into cardiac arrest yesterday. I transported him to Madrona's cardiac unit. Sounds like he's okay, close call though." He pulls a knife from the drawer. "How big?"

She can smell its sweetness, see the blue bursting from the flaky lattice crust. "Just a little."

He cuts two gigantic slices, sets one in front of her and one at his place. "Take home what you don't eat. With that and your sandwich, you're set for dinner." His cell rings now, and he pulls it from his pocket. "Hey, buddy," he says, his whole face lighting up. "Okay . . . yeah . . . no worries, but you'll miss Sister Angeline . . . Yeah, she's sitting right here . . . Okay, I will . . . The session okay? . . . Great! . . . Sure . . . Yes, pizza . . . Okay . . . See you at four . . ." He hangs up, says, "Liam's missed the ferry, so we won't see him, but he says hey."

"Tell him hi back, okay?"

"For sure. He wants me to go to the next session with him— God, I'm so grateful for his therapist. I mean, Liam, man, he's such an awesome kid, you know?" The water is boiling now, and he grabs new teabags, throws them in the pot, pours the hot water over them.

"He's really special," she says.

"And the bullying has almost completely stopped, thank God. I tell you, once that kid Jack left, things seemed to improve big time for Liam. Apparently, Jack was the one egging on the others. Felt bad for him though, and his little sister—heard CPS got involved."

Sister Angeline's pulse quickens. *Jack.* All this time, and Jack was the root of Liam's bullying. It's hard to believe the way threads twist and loop together. She thinks of Amelia then. Hopes with all her heart they are both receiving help, that someone is loving them.

"Liam's therapist," Collin says, "thinks I work too much. Suggested I'm trying to compensate for what happened with Claire."

"And you? What do you feel?" She thinks now of the last seven years, her own deep urge to atone. She is overcome with a sudden, deep sadness.

"Yeah, I'm sure there's something to it," he says, "but hey, we were supposed to talk about you. You said you were stuck, you had questions."

She pokes a blueberry with her fork and watches the juice seep from it.

"I mean, why me?" she says to him, the words tumbling out quickly. "And what if someone comes with their broken-ness and hopes and I fail them? And what if—what if they—"

"Die?"

She nods. The ache and weight of the word making the nod an effort.

He studies her for a moment. "I don't mean to sound cliché here, but why *not* you?"

The sincerity in his face makes some remote part of her want to tell him her whole story, tell him about all the people who died because of her, but she's never said any of it aloud before, doesn't believe there are words.

"I've had people die," he says. "It was the biggest thing I

worried about when I started as an EMT." He hesitates, watching her as if assessing the weight of what he's going to say. "It's as horrible as you think it will be—someone dying while you're helping them. Especially in a small community like this where you know everyone. Did you ever meet Harry Sullivan? He died last week. Complications of his diabetes. I tried to save him, but I couldn't. He was often the one who took care of Liam when I was called for emergencies. He's—he's eaten dinner with us at this table."

"I'm sorry," she says.

"The thing I tell myself is that all I can do is everything humanly possible."

She looks down at her pie, flakes the crust with her fork. "I don't even know if I can do it again—if the energy will come back."

"It's funny for me to say this to a nun," he says, "but you've mentioned you believe that the energy is God and that God is love, so maybe trust a little more? I mean, aren't y'all huge fans of faith?"

She raises her eyes, smiles a little, surprised to feel a flush of relief go through her to have someone so generously encourage her like this.

"You know," he says, "maybe you can tag along on some of my emergency calls? You can help if you feel moved to, in whatever way makes sense." He reaches over, twists the little knobs on one of the round port windows near him, and opens it slightly.

A soft gust of ocean blows in, the salt tingling Sister Angeline's nose. She inhales deeply, and a lightness like a blessing spreads through her chest like a million little breaths waking up cells and reviving the blood in her veins.

"Okay, yes," she says, her shoulders softening. "I think I can do that."

Chapter Thirty-Nine

The day after her conversation with Collin, Sister Angeline walks into the convent library just in time for the morning meeting. She will tell them about Collin's idea. It's been two weeks since she's spoken with them, and she wants to see them. She misses them.

The five women look up when she enters, greet her warmly, each of them stepping forward with open arms, but there's a chill in the room, and she can see on their faces that something is wrong.

"What is it?" she says. "What's happened?"

Gina hugs her and then stands there, wearing her baggy cargo pants and torn purple hoodie, the sleeves pulled over her hands. Her eyes red and swollen. She turns and walks slowly to her chair, folds into it. "I—I found a—dead seal on the beach yesterday," she says, her voice slow and toneless, not sounding like herself, not looking like herself either, but like some lost and confused spirit wandering in from the night forest.

"Shot while resting on a rock," Edith says. "Shot in the heart."

Sister Angeline's body goes cold, her legs crumbling.

No, please no.

"I took pictures—evidence," Edith says, her voice bitter and precise. "Something very wrong is happening."

There's a long silence.

Images form in Sister Angeline's mind: the seal who swam beside her day after day, its great brown eyes, eyes older than time, eyes that know things, things that can't be explained.

"May I see the pictures?"

"Not sure why on earth you'd want to see, but here." Edith scrolls through the photos, holds out the phone.

And there she is. The silvery gray of the beautiful creature tangled lifeless in ropes of kelp and seaweed, a gaping bloody hole in its side. And there on the top of the seal's small head, the three brown circles, the markings of the seal who floated by her on her daily walks. Her companion. The idea that some-one shot her, deliberately killed this innocent living creature, a mammal resting on a rock, makes her sick, makes fire flare in her chest.

"This is—this is—" she says, choking up. She walks to her chair and sits down. "I just saw her, this seal, yesterday."

"What time?" Edith asks.

"Around nine, I think? I'd heard the bells ring for morn-ing prayer."

"I found her a little before ten," Gina says quietly. "I was coming down the path to the beach and heard a strange sound, a loud pop—like a firecracker." Something desperate and disori-ented unravels behind her eyes. "You didn't hear anything like that? See anything?"

Sister Angeline tries to recollect the morning, tries hard to remember if she'd missed something, some sound, some person.

She knows she misses things when she's thinking, preoccupied, praying.

"No," she says finally. "I'm sorry. The wind and the waves were loud, and I don't remember anything unusual. The seal swam along with me for a little while and then disappeared."

Sister Angeline looks at Gina, who pulls the purple hoodie tighter around her face, and she feels she's let her down somehow, feels she should apologize for not having paid closer attention.

"Sister Angeline, there's something else," Kamika says. "Someone put one of the seal's fins in the prayer box"—she pauses, catches her breath—"with a note that said, 'Who's next?'"

Sister Angeline's heart paces frantically.

"We called Sheriff Ferguson," Sigrid says, "and shockingly, he came right away, brought along two Fish and Wildlife folks. He's still saying that without more evidence there's not much he can do."

"He was pretty disturbed," Kamika says. "You could see it on his face. He's also putting an appeal in the paper, asking if anyone can provide information, and going around town today, questioning people—that's something."

Sister Angeline's thoughts fly immediately to Collin, to Liam, worrying that accusations and implications could send Liam into a spin again.

"You're absolutely sure you didn't see anything?" Edith says.

"I walked for at least two hours after I saw the seal, and then I met Collin on the beach. I didn't see anyone else," Sister Angeline says. Should she tell them more? That she boarded Collin's boat? Shared grilled cheese and soup, fears and blueberry pie?

"You met Collin on the beach?" Edith says.

She hates the suspicious tone in Edith's voice. Thinks maybe the reason Edith sits on Collin's boat is to spy on Liam.

"He was taking a walk."

"And Liam," Edith says. "Was he with Collin?"

Anxiety percolates through Sister Angeline. "No. Collin said he was over on Madrona Island, seeing his counselor."

"What ferry did he catch?"

Sister Angeline, infuriated now, surprises herself and raises her voice to Edith. "How would I know what ferry he caught? It was probably close to eleven when I met Collin, and Liam was already gone, so maybe the ten forty, I don't know, and why are you still suspicious of Liam? What do you have against him? He's apologized to Kamika. He's sorry. He's getting help. He's doing really great, he—"

"I just don't believe people can change so fast, especially angry kids, and let's face it, that note sounds pretty damn juvenile."

Alice claps her hands three times and looks at Edith, puts both her palms out and mouths a silent *Stop!*

Edith waves her hand dismissively. "Whatever, whatever," she says. "The sheriff is coming back later, so if Collin hasn't already filled him in, Sister Angeline will need to." She turns to Sister Angeline. "Just the fact that you were down at the beach and saw the seal before it was shot means they'll want to talk to you." She turns to the other women. "In the meantime we can make fliers—get more eyes looking out. Let the killer know we're watching."

"But what is it about Liam?" Sister Angeline says, her voice persistent, edged with broken glass. "Why are you so distrustful of him?"

Everyone silent.

Edith shakes her head, her thick gray brows knitted together in irritation. She sits there, staring at her folded hands, her shoulders slowly collapsing, and she looks suddenly much older than her sixty-five years. But now she straightens up as if she's unfolded the map of whatever she's going to say, as if she's found her bearings. She crosses her arms under her scapular and turns to Sister Angeline.

"It's not just Liam. Kids do things when they're angry. And you can't always tell. It's—" Her face strained now. "When my twin sister, Ellen, was a junior in high school, she was killed by another student, a seventeen-year-old." She pauses, an edge of control slipping away. "Ellen was standing by her locker, talking to a friend, when the boy pulled out a gun." She draws a deep breath and releases it slowly. "He killed her friend too." Her voice sounds far away. "His name was Sean, and he was an honor student, and I didn't know him well, but I knew that he liked the library as much as I did, though I never spoke to him, and that he'd been made fun of because he cried easily." She brings her hands out in the open again, a slight tremble in them as they fold together. "He ended up committing suicide in prison."

There is a long silence now, pangs of sorrow spreading through Sister Angeline, her body understanding the precise shape of Edith's pain, the layers and loss it contains. How people can be harsh, but they aren't really—not deep down. How harsh words can band together, day after day, year after year, can pile up like sharp stones until there is an impenetrable wall around the heart, because there's only so much a heart can take. She thinks of Sean and his rage. Liam and his rage. How with enough mortification and shame, anger can rise to the surface like so many land mines and destroy everything in its path.

"It's just that," Edith continues, "you have to pay attention to the warning signs. If someone had noticed him, had helped before—" She stops and roughly wipes her eyes. "Something is wrong here, someone angry has a gun."

"Edith," Sister Angeline says, "I'm so sorry about your sister. I see why this is upsetting for you. But Liam isn't like that, he—"

"Okay, okay, okay." Edith waves her hand again, her old self returning. She stands up, moves to the worktable. "Let's get to work on the fliers. Find this shooter before the victim is a human."

"Yes," Sigrid says. "Let's get to work, but Sister Angeline, we want to hear about your time away—how we can help. Maybe at lunch?"

Sister Angeline nods but now looks over at Gina, sees she has wrapped her head in her arms and her shoulders are quivering. She kneels in front of her. "Gina," she says. "Look at me."

Gina looks up, her brown eyes filled with bruises and shadow. "I need to go," she says abruptly and rises from her chair and walks to the door. Her legs seem leaden and forced in a way that make Sister Angeline's heart shift. Gina pulls the door open and turns to them. "It's supposed to be safe here," she says tearfully and walks out, leaving a sad hurt in the air behind her.

The women are silent for several moments.

"Something's up with her," Kamika says. "Something more than the seal's death. She's been unusually quiet all week. I tried to talk with her, but she just shook her head."

"She's been missing meals too," Sigrid says.

"I'll talk to her," Sister Angeline says and runs out the door, Anu right behind her.

Chapter Forty

Sister Angeline knocks on the turquoise door of Gina's yurt. "It's me and Anu," she calls. When she hears nothing, she says more desperately, "Please let us in," and finally, she hears Gina moving things away from the door.

Gina opens the door, agitation shivering in her eyes. Anu pushes in and immediately presses her snout into her leg. Gina touches the top of the dog's head vaguely.

Sister Angeline steps inside. The space, usually so light-filled, now dim, the blue curtains closed. The air thick and heavy with the smell of paint. At least five new paintings are on easels, all splashed with jagged shards of only red and black, hieroglyphs of fear and betrayal, the paint still wet, some of it dripping.

Gina bolts the door behind them and reconstructs her barrier of canvas frames and chairs in front of it. When she's done, she picks up Joan and sits on the narrow bed, cradling the cat tightly, rocking slowly.

"Hey, hey, it's all right," Sister Angeline says and sits on the edge of the mattress, their shoulders touching.

"I can't stop hearing that shot, that pop," Gina says, her voice a tight coil. "And when I touched the seal, I could still feel her heartbeat and her chest was heaving so hard and I didn't know what to do." She is rocking harder now.

"You found Edith, you got help, that's all you could do." Sister Angeline wraps an arm around her and surprises herself when she kisses Gina's temple through the fabric of the hoodie.

"Goddammit, who would do such a thing?"

"I don't know," Sister Angeline says. "I don't know."

"Did I tell you I almost shot my father once?" Gina says suddenly, a jolting calm in her voice, and tilts her head toward a revolver lying on top of her nightstand.

Sister Angeline looks at Gina, startled. "By accident?"

"On purpose."

Gina sets Joan on the pillow, and the cat resettles and yawns, curls her tail around her paws. Gina reaches for the gun. Brings it to her lap. Her robin's blue nails an unnerving contrast to the cold steel. She holds the gun in silence and then examines it briefly, turning it this way and that, like a peculiar artifact or a holy relic. Her movements cause Sister Angeline to become rigid as if any slight motion might set the gun off.

"All I wanted," Gina says, "was to protect my mother, you know? Keep him from hurting her." She pauses—her index finger tap tap tapping the metal cylinder of the gun. "I'd waited for a night when my mother had the night shift at the hospital, when he was sleeping," she says, her voice still at a distance. "It was my sixteenth birthday, and I'd gone through how I would do it over and over again in my mind." Her finger curling around the trigger. "Once I was standing there, once I had the gun pointing at him, I couldn't do it."

She stands then, raises the gun, and points it at the painting in front of her.

Sister Angeline thinks she needs to be very careful now, thinks something is breaking inside her friend. "Gina," she says, "I can't imagine how you must have felt toward your father. How much you wanted to keep your mother from harm."

"He broke her arm twice," Gina says, holding the gun with both hands, aiming it straight at a red splatter, but Sister Angeline can see her arms quiver. "He'd beat her up if she ever came home late—beat her up and accuse her of being somewhere else, called her a whore." Her arms shake now. "She was a fucking nurse. Sometimes she had twelve-hour shifts—and to come home to him—"

"My God, Gina. Did he—did he ever hurt you?"

She nods, her entire body trembling.

"Come here. Gina, please can you put the gun down and come sit by me?"

Gina drops her arms, the gun hanging cold by her hip, and turns to Sister Angeline. "It was my mother who persuaded me to become a nun. She said, 'It's safe at a convent and you love God so much. Please. It's safe there.' She gave me a fistful of money and the address of this place. Said she heard about it from a church friend. 'And it's far away from Boston,' she said. And I did want to be a nun when I was a child—what Catholic girl doesn't, right? And yes, I love God, but what I really wanted was to go to art school, have my own gallery, but I didn't have the money for that. I googled this place, and it sounded different. Like there'd be room to do things. Women surviving together. Not bossed around. So I called, spoke with Sigrid, and she told me to come. I said goodbye to my mother and walked out of

the house with my suitcase, my father's gun, and the money."
Her eyes brimming with pain.

"Sit by me."

Gina places the gun back on the nightstand near a blue bowl
of feathers and goes to her. Allows Sister Angeline to hold her.

"I call my mother every week, try to get her to leave too.
But she won't. All she says is 'I can't.' It's like she thinks she owes
my father something or she's not worthy, I don't know. It's—it's
just all so awful."

Sister Angeline gently pulls Gina's hood down and kisses
the top of her head while she weeps.

"I do love this place, these women, this life," Gina says. "I
do. When I took my final vows, it was because I knew I belonged
here. I wanted to devote my life to God and this community."

Sister Angeline can feel Gina returning to herself. "You *are*
wanted here," she says, taking one of Gina's hands in hers. "I
want you here. We all want you here." And then after a moment
she says, "Gina, the Sisters said that you weren't feeling well even
before the seal's death. Did something else happen?"

Gina sits up straight, wipes her tears.

"Matt—" She pauses.

"Father Matt?"

"Yes, but I'll never call him *Father* again."

"What happened?"

"A few days ago in the barn, when I was hanging a new
mural, he came in and latched the door and started acting
creepy, different than his normal, crusading self. He came
up too close to me, touched my shoulder. Out of nowhere
he said he has a cabin, that it's on the church's property, no
one uses it anymore, and he said it's not far, but far enough

that it's really private, and he wants me to meet him there on Saturday—to 'have fun.'"

Gina stands now and goes to the windows and pulls the curtains open. Sunlight rushes in, like a child released to the ocean, immediately changing the tone of the room. But Gina remains benumbed, stares out the window.

"He said if I don't go, or if I tell anyone, he'll ruin our next Sunday gathering in the barn, and every one of them after that." She turns to Sister Angeline. "Like he'll really ruin them. He'll bring people with him—people who hate us." She pauses and catches her breath. "He said he'll leave us alone if I come to him on Saturday, and when I didn't say anything, he touched my hair—he actually fucking curled a piece around his big ugly finger—and said that even if I told anyone, no one would believe me because I'm no one and he's a priest."

Sister Angeline's chest on fire.

"And I just stood there," Gina says. "I just fucking stood there." She shakes her head in self-disgust. "Remember when I told you not to let him bully you, when I told you to stand up to him? Look at what I fucking did. Just like with my father, when push came to shove, I froze—it was like Matt's face suddenly turned into my father's, you know?" Her voice grows high and childlike. "Matt had me in a corner and kept reaching out to touch me with his freaking shiny eyes. I kept praying, *Please, someone knock on the door*, but no one did, and I told him I'd go, I'd meet him there, and then he smiled and unlocked the door, allowed me to leave." Gina breathes deeply. "Now I don't know what to do."

"You know you're not going to that cabin, right?"

"He's serious about wrecking things. I could see it in his eyes. Like he's fucking desperate enough to do it."

"We have to tell someone," Sister Angeline says. "We have to get help."

"No! I would never forgive myself if he ruined what we've built. And he will. I know it."

"But, Gina, if he's doing this to you, he could be doing this to someone else. Let's be smart about it. We have five days until Saturday. Did he say where the cabin was?"

"He said to follow the road, a narrow one, behind the rectory for at least a mile, and then turn at the madrona tree, the one with a carving of a red-tailed hawk on a large stone underneath it, and then I'd see it."

"I'm supposed to talk to the sheriff this afternoon," Sister Angeline says. "Maybe I could talk to him about this, get him to help?"

"Are you kidding me? Ferguson is totally in with Matt. You know that, right? Don't even think about it. Ferguson is another honest-to-God asshole."

The bells ring now for private prayer.

"I should go," Sister Angeline says. "Will you be okay?"

Gina walks to the door and moves the chairs and frames away from it. "Yes. I'll be fine, screw him," she says, a little too calmly, and Sister Angeline can see something has broken inside her, altered her somehow. Gina picks up an Amazon box on a table near the door. "I've been meaning to give this to you," she says with a half smile. "In case you find yourself climbing ladders again."

"My first Amazon box," Sister Angeline says, taking the gift, trying to sound light, making herself smile too. "I'm officially corrupt now, but thank you, I think. See you at lunch?"

Gina nods, and Sister Angeline walks outside, Anu running

ahead. She hears Gina bolt the door behind her, and her heart sinks. She remembers when she first saw this place, how she'd thought that to live here in such beauty would be to live in peace, but she realizes now how naive she was—to believe in such things is to believe violence has boundaries.

Chapter Forty-One

Sister Angeline opens the Amazon box, pulls out a white T-shirt, jeans, and a pale blue bra, tags hanging from the bra that say One Size Fits All and Feels Like a Cloud. She imagines Gina picking these out for her and smiles. She remembers how comfortable clothes like this used to feel. Maybe she will wear them if she climbs a ladder or something. Maybe she'll consider this, someday. Right now she needs to talk to Collin, find out if the sheriff talked to him, to Liam, find out how Liam handled the implications. She won't let herself imagine how he might be responding.

Please, God, be with them, protect them.

She goes now to the kitchen and plucks the phone from its holder. Lunch is still hours away, and the space is empty and quiet, though the faint smell of the morning cinnamon bread is still in the air, soothing her. She looks up Collin's number on the list by the phone.

The phone buzzes twice.

Collin answers.

"Hello? Collin? It's Sister Angeline."

"Are you all right?" he says, his voice tight. "I heard about the seal."

"It's awful."

"Criminal. The sheriff was already here."

"I've been worrying about Liam," she says.

"It's not looking good."

Speaking barely above a whisper, she says, "What isn't looking good?"

"Liam told the sheriff that he left home about ten and walked straight to the ferry, that he hadn't gone anywhere else that morning."

"That's good. right? And his counselor can corroborate he was there so—"

"Yes, but—I couldn't validate that he was on the tug till ten, since I left at seven for an emergency call on Jonas Island and Liam was still sleeping. And when I called him around nine to tell him I couldn't give him a lift to the ferry, he didn't answer, and I left a message, and—"

"And?"

"He never leaves his phone off. Something doesn't feel right."

"Collin, what are you thinking? Liam would never. Also, wouldn't I have seen him?"

"There are plenty of paths to the beach, and a lot of them are hidden," Collin says. "Liam knows all of them. And he could have seen you and hidden behind a boulder or a log. But there's something else—"

"What?"

"He was so incredibly calm when he spoke to the sheriff. Like he didn't get the least bit angry or even annoyed. It was unlike him. He just sat there, completely unemotional, and when he spoke, his voice was—weirdly composed."

"What did he say?"

"That he didn't do it."

"Maybe the therapy sessions are helping?"

A long silence.

"Maybe," he says, and then, "Sorry, gotta go," and he hangs up before she can say goodbye.

Chapter Forty-Two

She slips the phone back into place, feeling sad and distressed—she's never heard Collin's voice this strained before. She stands there for a moment, unsure of what to do next.

Buttoning up her black coat and wrapping a wool shawl around her head, she heads down the trail to the beach with Anu. The November air is cold, her breath pale clouds. She smells the passage between autumn and winter. The point of transition. She thinks of her own period of change in the last few months. What was, what is, what's to come. She's amazed how people adapt. How she's adapted. She realizes she's no longer thinking about how she belongs with her family, her baby, in the stars. She's thinking there might be other ways to belong with them, here. How just a few months ago she couldn't have imagined this thought.

She follows the meandering tide line, the tide rolling out now, leaving seaweed and broken shells in its lacy froth. Sandpipers scatter in front of her, and clams squirt like tiny voices shouting, *I'm here, I'm here!* A great blue heron startles from the tall crimson and gold grasses. It screeches and spreads its tremendous wings and soars into the air.

She reaches the rock where the seal drew its last breath. The sun breaks out from behind a cloud bank, and she witnesses the smooth water change from a leaden gray to a deep cerulean. In the distance the Olympic Mountains rise and widen, the new snow a spreading dome of light.

Along the way she collects shells, glistening stones, and feathers. The bleached skeleton of a tiny crab. A blade of brown kelp. She studies the kelp and notices streaks of green wavering across its surface. When she licks it, the salt tastes a million years old.

She sets the objects on the rock and gazes at them for several moments before arranging them into a circle, the tiny skeleton in the middle. Next to the rock, she clears a place, sweeping away pebbles until there is a small square of sand for her to kneel upon. She blows heat on her cold hands, crosses herself, and closes her eyes. She places her palms on the wet rock and prays for the seal's safe passage to the stars. She prays for Gina's safety. She prays for someone to prove Liam didn't kill the animals. She prays for Collin and the guilt he carries.

She thinks how being the one left behind can gut a person.

And she begins murmuring now, her breath forming small white clouds of voice. She whispers to God about how it happened—the accident; how she'd been sitting with her family in a restaurant and everything was fine, everything was normal, it was her birthday, her sixteenth; how her father was wearing his plaid jacket and drinking whiskey and her mother was wearing silver hoops and blue cashmere and ordering more wine; and how everything was fine, everything was normal, except she could see her father becoming drunk, becoming sloppy, slurring things at the waitress; everything was fine, everything was normal, until she'd asked her mother for a second slice of cake and her brother said, *But you're getting so fat*; and how her mother had looked at her then, and that's when the evening had broken apart fast because her mother knew, in that mysterious, unsettling way she had of knowing things, that her daughter was pregnant; and how her mother said, *You're not keeping it, you know that, right? Right? Right?*; and how she'd stupidly become defensive, said, *I'm keeping her*; and how her mother became louder, her chardonnay rage becoming a tornado, people staring, her father trying to stand and almost tipping over, Ricky biting his lip; and then how her mother had stabbed the car keys into her hand, even though she'd barely just gotten her driver's permit, how her mother had spat, *You think you're old enough to take care of her, then you're old enough to drive*; and how she'd tried to follow the road, telling herself, *It's only three miles, it's only three miles*, but then her mother asked, *How many months*, and she'd said, *Three*, and her mother's words like stones, *It's that boy, that boy I told you to stay away from!* Ricky crying so hard in the back seat, her father slurring, *Calm down, everyone, calm down*; and how suddenly the seat belt was too tight and she thought she couldn't breathe and she worried maybe the baby was suffocating too, the baby inside her, inside her, inside her; and how she couldn't remember if it was her right foot or left foot that eased the gas or pressed the brake—the wheels didn't feel like they were where they should be—and how her mother's mouth was too close, screaming, *I did everything for you* and *How could you*, and how she loved her mother, how she hated her mother, how she'd yelled at her mother then, *I hope you die*; and how her hands had clenched hard on the steering wheel, fury firing everywhere; and how she didn't see the median, didn't know she'd crossed the median, didn't see the semi; and how everything became slow motion became screaming became shattering glass, became silence.

Her mind quiet now. Her eyes closed. She is suspended somewhere between past and present.

And then a voice from within:

You are worthy of forgiveness.

An enveloping force spins and propels through her spine, swims to a place deep inside her, plunges fiercely through dirt and feathers, leaves and stones, until finally, it reaches a place she at once perceives is hers and hers alone—a place filled with a brilliant, magnificent fire.

Slowly, slowly, she opens her eyes, her breath short gasps, her cheeks wet, her hands pressed hard into the rock.

In the distance, a bell rings for the midday meal.

Chapter Forty-Three

The Sisters prepare clam chowder, salad, and sourdough bread to Gregorian Chant playing on Spotify. There is warmth on their faces while they work, but the mood is somber—their sense of safety diminished. They're uneasy about what the sheriff will discover, worried he'll find nothing, and Sister Angeline worries the blame will fall on Liam.

She is relieved to see Gina here, though it is clear she is still not okay—the slow, concentrated way she empties a bucket of butter clams into a red enameled colander, rinses the sandy grit from their mottled gray shells, and drops them one by one into a large pot of boiling water, her body absent of its familiar animation, her eyes dull and expressionless.

Sister Angeline wants to shout, *Father Matt is threatening Gina! We have to help her!* But she knows Gina wouldn't want this, and she understands why. Still, she knows that the Sisters together could protect Gina—if only she can convince Gina of this.

Sister Angeline lifts a large cast-iron pan to the stove now, sparks a high flame underneath, and drizzles in olive oil. "Gina, are you okay?" she says.

Gina shrugs, keeps dropping clams into the pot. "Don't you think it's kind of a cruel thing I'm doing to these little creatures?" she says quietly.

Sister Angeline crushes garlic cloves with the flat of a knife, minces them, throws them in the pan. "From what I've read, they don't have a central nervous system—I think they might be closer to plants?"

"They still have nerves though. And this whole thing about them not being sentient, I don't know, I think it's kind of bullshit." She looks at a clam closely. "See all these concentric lines? Must be fifty of them. They're like tree rings—one for each year of its life. I mean, how sad is that, to survive that long only to be found and thrown into boiling water?"

"Gina, do you want to switch jobs?"

"No, I'm okay, I guess." Her voice subdued. She kisses the clam and drops it in the water, the other shells rattling against the side of the pot, like stones rattled by waves at the shore. "It's all just energy morphing forms anyway, and if it wasn't us, a moon-snail probably would have sucked it out of its shell. I've been thinking a lot about where we draw the line when it comes to sacrificing lives for personal needs, you know?"

Sister Angeline tosses chopped onion and potatoes into the pan, stirs everything around with a wooden spoon. She wants to say the right thing, the helpful thing to her friend. "If we're talking about clams, I honestly don't think there is one answer to where that line is, but I love the way you think." She pours a little white wine into the pan. "Gina," she whispers now, "are you— You're not thinking of sacrificing yourself for the greater good, are you?"

Gina chews on her lower lip. "I'm just thinking through things."

Sister Angeline reaches over and touches the side of her arm. "Can we talk more about this after lunch?"

"I can't today, maybe tomorrow," she says. "There's something I really want to paint, and I need time alone."

Sister Angeline adjusts the flame under the saucepan, pours cream and chicken stock over the onions and potatoes. She sprinkles a little salt and pepper and tells herself to trust what Gina needs to do.

"You still promise not to tell, right?" Gina says, putting the lid on the clam pot and turning to Sister Angeline.

"Of course. Until it's okay with you, I won't say anything. But that's what I want to talk to you about. I really think—"

"I need more time," Gina says with greater agitation, and she reaches for the blue soup bowls and sets the table.

Once they are all seated, Alice sets a carafe of Chianti in the middle of the table and lights an amber votive, and they join hands for grace. To Sister Angeline's right, Gina's hand—a sparrow, a tremble, a flame. To her left, Alice's hand—a raven, a tree, a continent.

Sigrid looks around the table at the five women. "Let's begin with some deep breaths," she says. "The tension in this room is as palpable as an impending squall."

The women close their eyes, and Sister Angeline can feel the expansion and contraction of their breathing, can feel the stored-up nervousness leave their bodies.

"Better," Sigrid says. "I'm also wondering if, after grace, we might eat silently. Use the time to offer a peaceful opening for love to enter, for the Divine to find a place at our table."

The Sisters nod.

"Today for grace I'm going to read from Thomas Merton." She holds *New Seeds of Contemplation*, opens to a bookmarked page, and reads, "'Contemplation is the highest expression of intellectual and spiritual life. It is life itself, fully awake, fully active, fully aware that it is alive. . . . It is a spontaneous awe at the sacredness of life, of being. It is a gratitude for life. For in contemplation we know by 'unknowing.' . . . It is a sudden gift of awareness, an awakening to the Real within all that is real. A vivid awareness of infinite Being at the roots of our own limited being.'"

"Amen," they all say, opening their eyes.

Sigrid pours herself a tiny glass of Chianti and passes the carafe to Edith, who passes it to Kamika, who passes it to Alice, who passes it to Gina, who passes it to Sister Angeline. She pours herself a little bit. It is a ruby red color. She brings it to her nose. It smells like black cherries and something rustic and earthy like oregano.

She thinks now, as the wine ribbons through her body, about the word *awakening*. How her experience at the seal's rock felt like an awakening. She'd felt the deep sense of God as a Being, as a force within her, as a light, a transcendent gift of love. She looks around at the five women, and it is easy to see they have not led her away from atonement, instead they've led her toward a new meaning of it, a new understanding of reconciliation with God and self, God and humanity—of being one with others.

She sees now that Gina is not touching the clam chowder but is poking at her salad. In solidarity Sister Angeline, too, decides only to have salad. She picks up a crisp green apple slice from her small pile of greens, raises it to Gina, and smiles warmly. Gina looks at her strangely and gives her a partial smile, but then returns to staring at her salad, moving the lacy greens around the edges of her plate, and a sense of helplessness spills into Sister Angeline's heart.

Once they are all done, the plates and bowls emptied, Sigrid looks across the table at Sister Angeline and says, "You were going to tell us your thoughts about your ability to heal. Would this be a good time?"

Sister Angeline is caught off guard, the blur of events and anxieties, one thing following another, and Gina under such pressure—should she talk about this?

As if reading her thoughts, her face so earnest and kind, Gina says, "Please tell us. I'd love to know."

Sister Angeline's heart surges with love for her friend. "Yes, of course," she says. She takes another sip of her wine, the silky liquid hesitating on her tongue for a moment before flowing through her, cells opening in its wake.

"I've—I've decided to try to access the energy again—to—to heal others. I want to at least try. And—and Collin had the idea of calling me when he has an emergency. He thinks maybe I could tag along sometimes, and well, I think that's a good idea. I want to try that."

"Brilliant idea," Sigrid says. "I'm proud of you. And don't worry, we'll handle whatever happens with the outside world."

"Wonderful," Gina says softly. "Really wonderful."

"We're here to help in any way you need," Kamika says.

Alice draws her palms together in front of her chest, fingers pointing upward. She bows her head slightly and smiles.

"Like people will keep this in confidence," Edith snorts.

Chapter Forty-Four

As the women leave the dining yurt, a car crunches up the gravel driveway. A patrol car. And now the sheriff steps out, calling to them, "Hello, hello."

Sister Angeline's heart pitches at the sight of him, the red flag that he's a friend of Father Matt's.

"You ready?" Edith says to her.

Sister Angeline nods and whispers a prayer to Mary as she walks by the statue, *Please stay with me.*

"Only answer what you're comfortable with," Sigrid says quietly. "He has a way of getting into people's heads."

"What do you mean?"

"I just think he's here for more than the seal. I think he's checking the climate, trying to find out how close we are to leaving the island—if we're afraid."

"I've got this," Sister Angeline says, her racing pulse contradicting her.

"I know you do," Sigrid says in a way that gives Sister Angeline confidence.

"Well, have you discovered anything of substance?" Edith says to the sheriff as she unlocks the front gate to let him in.

"Just gathering information," he says impatiently, and he steps through the opening. "Tide washed away any footprints that might have helped, and no one seems to have seen nothin'. Need to speak with Sister Angeline." He is a tall man, well over six feet, in his sixties, with a weathered red face and woolly eyebrows. He wears a tan jacket with a shining badge shaped like a star, a gun tucked into a black leather holster on his belt.

Edith motions to Sister Angeline. "You two can use the library."

"Well, you're the other one in the habit," he says in a gruff tone, and Sister Angeline already feels she might lose her nerve. He takes off his rigid hat, exposing a greasy comb-over, and reaches out his hand. "Sheriff Ferguson."

She takes his hand, his knuckles cold as stones.

In the library he removes his jacket, throws it across the table, takes Alice's chair. "Please sit down," he says to her as if the library belongs to him.

She sits and leaves her coat on.

He looks at her, takes a small black notebook and pencil from his shirt pocket. "So what can you tell me that will help us find this seal killer?" he says.

"I—I really have no idea who would do such a thing."

He gives her a long, hard stare. "What time was it when you first saw the seal?"

"I think around nine? It was right after breakfast and chores."

He jots down notes as she speaks. "Why were you walking in that area?"

She reaches into her pocket and fills her hand with rosary

beads. "I walk there almost every day, for exercise, for contemplation." She does not say how much she's grown to love the freedom and peace of this walk, the enormous sky, the beauty and changing colors of the water, the sound of the waves against the shore, the wind against her body, salt like prayers on her lips.

"How much time had transpired between when you left your yurt and actually saw the seal?"

"Maybe ten minutes. It's a short walk to the beach from here, as you know."

"And where was the seal?"

"She was swimming in the water, about twenty feet from me."

"She?"

"It's just a feeling."

"Uh-huh."

"Did you see anyone while you were on the beach?"

"Only Collin."

He cocks an eyebrow. "I assume you mean Collin Whalen?"

"Yes."

"And how much time before you left the seal and went aboard Mr. Whalen's boat?"

She doesn't answer him and doesn't let him see that his question startles her. Did Collin tell him she was on the boat, or did someone else see them together? And why does it seem like he's goading her?

"Sister, I asked you a question."

"I heard you," she says tightly. "Probably two hours or so."

"Have you ever been on Mr. Whalen's boat before?"

Heat rises in her body. "What does my being on his boat have to do with anything?"

"It could have a lot to do with how much you're protecting him and his son. And if you aren't already aware, killing a seal is a crime with a twenty-thousand-dollar fine and possibly a one-year imprisonment, so no small thing. Let me ask again, what were you doing together on the tugboat?"

"We're friends and we were having lunch," she says, even though she means, *Why are you such an asshole?*

"Guess nuns have to have a little fun too."

The quake of anger wants out. She knows this face, this voice. She's seen it in every bully she's ever met. The smug, condescending mocking, the ridicule.

Do not fear your rage.

"And was Liam there, on the boat?"

"No. He was over on Madrona Island at his counselor's."

"Uh-huh."

"You could call the counselor."

"Thank you, but you don't need to tell me how to do my job, Sister, or do you even call yourself that? I notice that's not a thing with y'all."

"You can call me Sister Angeline."

"Okay, *Sister Angeline*, what's your relationship to Liam?"

"He's a friend."

"Kind of young to be your friend, isn't he?"

Everything poisoning fast now.

"Listen," she says. "I'm one hundred percent certain Liam didn't shoot any of the animals. He's a good kid, who lost his mother in 9/11, and he's being bullied at school for his stuttering, but he's getting help."

"Yet he has his own rifle, his father has a rifle, and according to the principal at his school, he's got some pretty significant anger issues. And correct me if I'm wrong, but didn't he threaten one of the Sisters—Kamika, is it?—with a knife? Wasn't he mandated to get counseling?"

"I—I don't know about his counseling being mandated. I'm pretty sure he made the choice with his father. And I know Kamika didn't press charges." She takes a deep breath and breathes out slowly. "I was there, and Liam was really sorry about what happened, and the most important thing is that he's doing well now. Really well."

"How do you know that? You talk to him lately?"

"I— No, I haven't, but I trust Collin, and he feels really positive about Liam's progress."

He writes something in his notebook, then says, "Gina claims she found the seal around 9:30 a.m., but apparently, you'd already walked too far away for her to see you or you to see her, is that right?"

"Yes."

"Did you hear any unusual sounds, you know," he says sarcastically, "like a gunshot?"

"No, it was extraordinarily windy, and the waves were crashing."

"Tell me about your relationship with Gina."

The way he says it makes her cheeks redden. It's becoming increasingly obvious he isn't just here for the seal. "Again," she says, "how is this relevant?"

"I've heard things. Lends to your credibility."

"My credibility?" Her pulse increases furiously.

"Think about it. You show up on this island suddenly, dressed in full habit, yet you don't attend Father Matt's Mass, and according to him—"

"According to him?"

"According to Father Matt, you're having an affair with Gina." He cocks his head, says in a provoking tone, "Does Mr. Whalen know?"

Control yourself.

"Gina and I are friends. I'm not having an affair with her or Collin or anyone," she replies evenly. She holds up her left hand, points to the gold band on her finger. "Already married," she says.

He clears his throat, folds his hands together over his stomach. "I've also heard that you have been practicing witchcraft, is that right?"

What? Who told him that? Did someone see me that day with Joan?

"So why *are* you here?" he asks, leaning forward. "Why *aren't* you in a real convent? You're dressed like a nun, but it seems you've broken every vow, every responsibility to the Church. Why are you with these women who don't call each other Sisters, who attend a sham mass—one a Muslim, one a man. Why—"

Sister Angeline stomach lurches. "What do you mean, *one a man?*"

"You don't know?" he sneers. "Rumor has it the one who calls herself Edith is a man in a nun's suit." He shakes his head. "Makes a mockery of a noble vocation."

"We're done here," Sister Angeline says and stands, hiding her hands in her coat pockets so he won't see the tremor of them.

"Well," he says, "let me just say that if you, all of you, continue to live here and hold your liberal little *masses*, if this keeps up, your lives will be at risk. I'm not saying that as a threat;

I'm saying that as a caution. Right now you're being threatened by someone, and that someone has a gun, and you have
no idea how heartless some of the people on this island can be
when they are defending their values, their religion. They will
do everything in their power to make sure things don't go in
the wrong direction."

She turns to him. "You support them, don't you? You want
us gone too."

His mouth a thin, grim line. "Let's just say I understand
their passion."

"The end justifies the means."

He stands now, and she takes a step back. "I've read the
background check on you, *Meg*."

Her heart skids to a stop. "Background check?"

"The Catholic Church is a powerful entity," he says. "If
they want to find something, they will, and your file is—well,
it's pretty damn interesting. The casting of spells on classmates,
one that led to a girl's arms being burned, your expulsion from
school, your involvement with a bomb maker, driving the
car that killed your entire family. Seems trouble follows you
around. The thing is, *Meg*, we don't want that kind of trouble
around here."

Now something in her gives. Fire arising from within, but
not as a danger, more like a strength, an authority, a power
source.

Do not fear your rage.

She moves closer to him. "Let's be real. We all know these
threats are about a small, hermetically sealed group of misogy-
nists who are obsessed with power and the need to keep everyone
around them second-class citizens."

"You're a disgrace to the Church," he says, practically spitting, his skin flushed.

An unobstructed streak of red races from her chest and out her mouth. "There's a reason people are walking away from Father Matt's church. They're fucking tired of patriarchal megalomaniacs beating the drum of obedience." She walks out now and slams the door.

Chapter Forty-Five

On the way back to her yurt, Sister Angeline meets Edith.

"Well, how was it?" Edith asks.

Sister Angeline takes several hard gulps of air, tears of anger pricking her eyes. "He was awful," she says. "Just awful."

"Come on," Edith says and leads her into her yurt. Sister Angeline has crossed this threshold before—the space as bare and simple as her own. Slightly cold. White walls, white curtains, a narrow bed with a white coverlet and pillow, everything white as a communion wafer. The room unlit except for the quiet flame of the propane stove. On the nightstand, a sprig of rosemary in a white vase.

Edith motions to two wooden chairs in front of the propane stove. "Sit," she says, and then she walks to her dresser and takes out a bottle of whiskey and two chipped mugs. Sets the mugs on the propane stove and pours a little whiskey in each one. "Drink this," she says, holding out the mug.

Angeline grasps the mug's handle, her hands still trembling. She brings the mug to her nose first, cautiously sniffs it. She's smelled whiskey before—of course she has, her father smelled of whiskey always—but in all this time, she'd never tasted it. She tips the mug forward, allows the honey yellow to flow into her mouth, and now a sudden stinging soaks her lit tongue, speeds down her throat, and burns into her chest.

She can see why people might be attracted to this sensation. It is startling, penetrating.

After the heat has hit its vanishing point, she says, "He hates us. That sheriff? He wants us gone."

"Yup. What have I been saying forever? He's part of the good ole boy's network. We're on our own here."

"Aren't you scared?"

"Wrong question. The question we need to ask is, how do we organize without them? I think it's time to tell the congregation. Maybe we all get cell phones. Knock on all the doors ourselves. Enlist help. Lots of things we can do." She takes a gulp of whiskey.

"Do we need guns? Should we learn how to use guns?" Sister Angeline asks, shocking herself.

Is this what fear does?

"There's no world," Edith says, taking another gulp, "no world I want to live in, where women living off the grid on an organic apple farm, praying for world healing, need to use guns. And there's no way in hell Alice would allow it. Her entire life has been devoted to gun control. Nope, guns ain't gonna happen here."

They're already happening here.

"This convent," Edith says, "has been around for forty-two years. The fact that we're only just now experiencing animosity from some in the community tells me this has everything to do with Father Matt. He's the new variable. He's given the haters permission to threaten us, to erase us."

Sister Angeline thinks of her exchange with the sheriff—his tone, his derision and self-importance, how much it matches the tone of Father Matt, and she is angered anew.

"We're not going to let them push us around because we're women," Edith says, draining her mug.

"Edith—"

"What?"

"He— The sheriff implied— He said—"

"What? Spit it out."

"He said you were a man."

The words seem to hit Edith's face like a slap, her fire suddenly gone, and Sister Angeline is immediately sorry she said anything.

Edith stands. She pours herself more whiskey and—Sister Angeline notices—the mug shakes in her hands as she walks to the window, the one facing west, facing the ocean. She opens it with her free hand and stands, staring and drinking, and Sister Angeline doesn't know if she's praying, thinking about what to do, or listening to the swells of breakers crashing loud on the shore. Then Edith moves to her nightstand and picks up the framed photo next to the rosemary sprig. She carries the photo back to Sister Angeline and hands it to her. Sits down.

"That's my twin sister Ellen and me—the sister I told you about. Easter 1962."

In the picture there are two children, maybe twelve or thirteen. The girl has thick blond hair and is wearing a lavender dress and black patent leather shoes. Next to her a red-headed boy in a blue suit and lavender tie.

"My name was Eddie."

Edith's voice, faraway.

"I'd always felt like a girl—since I was the age I am in that picture, maybe sooner." A choked echo flashes across her face. "When Ellen was killed, when I turned sixteen, I knew my parents would have kicked me out or sent me to one of those brainwashing camps or something if I ever said anything. They'd traded their sorrow for a strict Evangelical faction." She pauses for a breath. "When Ellen died, I decided to leave too. Told my parents I wanted to be a priest. That made them happy. Very happy. I told them I was going to a monastery up north—which I did, for a while. Part of me still thought maybe I could pray it out of me, stay a man. But I couldn't. Six years there gave me a lot of time to think, and I only became more and more miserable. It was then a priest I'd confided in offered to help me transition. He helped me get an apartment and stayed with me all the way through the process—the hormones, the surgery, all of it." She pours the last of the whiskey into their mugs. "He saved my life. Without him, I think I might be dead."

"Oh, Edith. What you've been through," Sister Angeline says, her face wet. She is overwhelmed by the pain Edith's endured—the effort, the battle to become herself. The wrongness of anyone blocking her way.

"Somewhere along the line," Edith says, draining her whiskey, "I heard about Light of the Sea, found out it was one of the few places that accepted transwomen, and I realized that's what I wanted—to be a nun, not a priest, a nun, no hierarchies." She is silent now, her breathing slowing into weary sighs. "I owe so much to Sigrid."

Sister Angeline wipes her eyes, clears her vision. "I'm so grateful you are yourself now."

Edith takes the photo and looks at it. "In a way Eddie

died with Ellen. I felt like she took him to heaven with her. She seemed to know all along I was her sister, not her brother. It's like she carried Eddie with her and left all her ribbons and dresses for me so I could live."

They are silent for a long time before Sister Angeline says, "Edith, do you ever want to wear something other than the habit?"

"Come here," Edith says and walks to her wardrobe, Sister Angeline following. She opens it, and inside, hangers of sweaters and pants and skirts—blues, yellows, and greens. On the floor a row of shoes—from athletic shoes to high heels.

Sister Angeline touches the softness of a blue sweater, the rose on one of the skirts. "But I've never seen you wear these."

"I don't. I mean, I try them on sometimes, when I'm alone— I've never worn anything but my habit outside of this room."

"Why not?"

"I'm sure this will surprise you because of my take-no-shit approach to life, but the thought of people looking at me, appraising me as a woman, or worse with pity or speculation or hostility—I haven't been able to do it." She laughs a little. "Not that I'm anything to look at."

"You're beautiful," Sister Angeline says and then shakes her head. "There's a lot of fuck in this world, isn't there?"

Edith reaches over, touches Sister Angeline's hand, and smiles. "It's good that you are saying *fuck* more," she says. "That's a really good sign."

Anu whines at the door now.

"Better get her out," Sister Angeline says. She takes Edith's hand in hers. "I love you."

"I love you too," Edith says.

As Sister Angeline leaves Edith's yurt, she notices a small, framed quote by the door:

When I was thirteen, I heard a voice from God to help me govern myself. —*Joan of Arc*

That night Sister Angeline drapes her habit and veil over the chair and showers under hot water until it runs cold and scrubs and scrubs herself dry and slips under the white sheets of her bed, naked. She falls asleep imagining a world with lives laid bare and whether we would be more at peace with ourselves if we abandoned the masquerades, if it's worth the risk, if it's safe.

Chapter Forty-Six

In the morning Sister Angeline uncovers the mirror in her closet and sets it on a chair. She looks at her strong, lean body and hardly recognizes herself. Her blond hair almost three inches long now and curlier than she remembers. She watches her fingertips touch her shoulders, neck, breasts. Goose bumps rise to the surface of her soft skin, the curve of her waist, the firm of her stomach, the hip bones, the pale bloom between her legs. Her eyes close now, and her fingers dip inside lightly, inside slow, inside deep, until a final shiver and drip of honey.

She opens her eyes and looks at the sight of herself and whispers, *Thank you for saving me.* She looks over her shoulder now, at her back. The scars. The stars. The constellations of reddened connective tissue. Constellations of a time she didn't want to live in her body. Constellations repeating a singular sentence: *I'm sorry. I'm sorry. I'm sorry.*

She thinks, *Who was I in that tiny, silent cell in Chicago? Where did I go when I was there?*

And now, *I don't want to be part of the Church anymore, at least not the Church of the sheriff or Matt or Rome.*

She thinks, *I have a choice now, I know what to do, I know what is right.*

Her fingers touch the gold cross around her neck.

And now she picks up the blue sports bra, pinches off the One Size Fits All tag and the Feels Like a Cloud tag, and pulls the bra over her head. Soft as an Ave Maria.

She pulls on the white T-shirt and jeans, and it's like pulling on a new body or like a body returning.

She sees herself and is surprised she doesn't feel betrayal or guilt. In the cloister she'd become dead to herself. Now she only wants to be herself.

She tucks her rosary in a front jean pocket.

This is the beginning.

Anu whines at the door, and Sister Angeline can see in the dog's eyes, something is wrong. She pulls on her black shoes, grabs her coat and a flashlight because the November sun sinks so rapidly, and she doesn't know how long she'll be gone. She follows Anu out the door, never noticing her new lightness and confidence, how she no longer needs to lift the folds and pleats of her habit, only notices as she follows the dog to Gina's yurt that the turquoise door stands wide open with an upended chair at the threshold.

She rushes into the yurt, her eyes sweeping the room, the space an eruption of chaos. Canvases on the floor, easels tipped over, the sharp smells of paint and thinner and anguish.

She calls Gina's name—no answer.

It's then Sister Angeline notices there is one painting still on an easel—one she hasn't seen before. It is beautiful. Still wet, it is soaked with exuberant reds and loops of yellow and oranges, an indigo-blue burst in the center, the colors radiating desire and flight—a tremendous brilliance as if it isn't a painting at all, but star matter pulsing, splitting open.

This is the first painting she's seen of Gina's that does not have the ragged black line streaking like a knife through the center of it.

She looks around the room, and that's when she notices the gun is not on the nightstand. She opens the nightstand drawer. Only blank white paper and colored pens and a tiny white Bible. She looks all over Gina's art table, moving around brushes, tubes of paint, and rags. She looks under the mattress, under the bed, under and in everything. The gun is nowhere to be found.

Her stomach drops. "Shit."

Sister Angeline hurries to St. Paul's. Maybe Gina is at the church or the rectory. Maybe she thinks she can talk logic and reason with Father Matt. Maybe she'll keep her gun in her pocket.

Sister Angeline walks past farms and fields with cattle, sheep, and round hay bales on one side of her, and on the other: water agitating white froth, like a beast foaming at the mouth.

Now and then a car or truck rolls by, and Sister Angeline waves and half smiles. Locals are used to seeing her walking by the side of the road, sometimes heading to the grocery, sometimes to the library. Tourists often stare at her. She knows how she must look to them—the strangeness of seeing a nun in full habit walking down the road in 2015.

It is then she remembers she isn't wearing her habit. She runs her fingers through her shaggy blond hair and feels at once astonished and strong. Her legs in jeans give her an exhilarating lift, a sense of energy, of determination. She feels strangely, inexplicably, capable.

And now here is the church. Everything dark, except for red votive candles dimly lighting the stained-glass windows. And there is St. Francis. From a distance she can see the golden scar running down his face, luminous in the late morning light.

She thinks about how Gina spoke of fractured things and how they sometimes get restored and in that mending they become sturdier, potent, enduring. How she wants to run to St. Francis, wrap her arms around the statue, tell him she understands his words now, but she must find Gina.

"Be with me," she says to the statue, and the answer to her prayer is a sudden shaft of light from his hand, an offering of strength, of safety inside her rage, and she whispers, "Thank you."

She checks the rectory behind the church now. Father Matt's car isn't in the driveway. *Go to the most dangerous place first.*

Could Gina have gone to the cabin a few days early, to catch Father Matt off guard? She remembers that Gina said the cabin is at least a mile down a narrow dirt road behind the church and to turn at a madrona tree with a carving of a red-tailed hawk on a granite stone.

She walks slowly toward a stand of fir trees behind the church, and here is the road. It is barely wide enough for a car, though it is clear the road isn't a well-worn one—the grass in the center is coarse and tall—and for a moment she hesitates.

Anu runs ahead, nose in the air. Sister Angeline follows, the road becoming more and more overgrown with roots and brambles and shrubs the farther they go. Finally, rounding a corner, here is the madrona tree and the carving of a red-tailed hawk on a granite pillar, the scene prophetic as a fable.

She keeps walking. The crimson and gold leaves crunching under her feet sound too loud. The thick smells of damp earth and sap. A squirrel darts in front of her, and she gasps. The squirrel freezes, looks at her, then races up a pine tree. The sky is overcast, and light barely trickles through the thick canopy of trees.

And now here is the cabin. It is small and ramshackle and surrounded by towering firs and pines. A tilted outhouse nearby. The curtains of the cabin are drawn on the front two windows, blackberry vines tangling on the sills. Sister Angeline scans the shadows within the surrounding woods. The hair on her arms rises. "Stay by me," she says, looking into Anu's blue-brown eyes, eyes that already know what is expected of her. "Right by me."

She moves forward slowly. When she reaches the wooden stairs, she stops and listens. Only crows cawing and branches rubbing and crackling on each other.

The stairs are slippery with moss and decaying leaves. She climbs in a halting tiptoe, each wooden plank creaking her presence. She grasps Anu's collar and says, "Stay quiet."

She knocks on the door, her heart beating violently. When no one answers, she turns the doorknob little by little. It isn't locked. She pushes it open slowly. The hinges groan. She knocks again, calls out, "Hello, anyone home? Father Matt? Gina?" She stands there. Listening. Nothing. Anu presses hard into her leg.

She opens the door a few more inches. Glances around. Deathly quiet. "Hello?" Nothing. She hesitates and steps in.

Chapter Forty-Seven

It smells like any cabin might smell in the woods, musty and damp. It seems it's only one room. A small wooden table and two chairs face a heavy black woodstove, a frying pan and kettle on top of the stove and a stack of logs on the floor next to it. Near the stove a small grimy cabinet holds a white porcelain sink, chinked and streaked with stains. There are no pictures anywhere, only a rain jacket hanging on a hook by the door.

In the far corner, a mattress. It is neatly made with a gray wool blanket and gray flannel pillowcases. Next to the mattress, a floor-to-ceiling pine wardrobe. Near it a window—the curtains slightly open, letting in a slant of light.

It is cold, and she is fighting fear, and she wraps her arms around herself. As her eyes adjust to the dimness, her heart splintering loudly into irregular pulses, she looks around more closely, though she's not sure exactly what she's looking for. Some proof that Father Matt really is a threat, a danger. Anu, too, is poking her nose everywhere, sniffing every nook and cranny.

Sister Angeline opens the cabinet under the sink: an oil lamp, a few white washcloths and towels, a wrapped bar of soap.

She thinks, *What was I thinking to come here?*

Stay. Wait for Gina. She still might show up. She takes a deep breath, moves to the pine wardrobe, and opens its rickety door. She gasps. Shelves and shelves of guns. At least twenty of them, maybe more. Her chest white hot.

It is then, on a bottom shelf, she sees a stack of photos. She picks up the pile and looks at the first one: a naked woman, face up, arms spread wide, legs straight, ankles crossed, on a mattress—a mattress with a gray wool blanket. A blue-beaded rosary trickling across her breasts. The second photo is a different woman in the same crucifix position with the same rosary on the same mattress. The third, a woman with long red hair. It is the young woman from the park—the one with the pink flip-flops. The one who suddenly began crying. Sister Angeline's chest cracks with grief.

And now the fourth woman, Lisa. Beautiful Lisa with her flouncy dresses and big hoop earrings, naked, arranged in the same position as the others. Michael's mother. Her eyes now the color of humiliation. Bruises on her arms from a man relieving himself of his demons.

Shaken, Sister Angeline puts the photos back and closes the cabinet. It is Anu who hears something first, and with her first growl, Sister Angeline grabs her collar.

Heavy footsteps pressing the weak boards of the front stairs.

Chapter
Forty-Eight

Father Matt pushes through the door, bringing a cold draft and hovering shadows with him. When he sees Sister Angeline standing there, he stops dead. His eyes go wide, and his mouth opens, then closes, then opens again. "Whoa," he says, "this is a surprise!" His mouth so quickly a disturbing smirk.

He doesn't look good. Dark circles under his eyes. Unshaven. His hair unwashed. He takes off his black leather coat, hangs it on a hook. His black shirt and pants wrinkled.

He steps closer to her, only a foot between them. He reaches over and touches her hair, despite a low rumble rising from Anu's throat. "No veil today?" he says, his finger meandering down her cheek. "You're not the first girl to tire of playing a nun."

Sister Angeline holds Anu's collar tighter and jerks away. "I'm worried about Gina," she says, her face hot. "I thought she might be here."

His face splits into an obscene grin. "Well, actually, I wasn't expecting her for a few more hours, but hey, if she's that eager, I'm totally open to the three of us—or are you two trading places?"

How is this the same, affable, relaxed man who pulled rainbow scarves from his pocket, now-you-see-it, now-you-don't, delighting a crowd with magic tricks?

"Stop," she says, putting a palm up. "Just stop!" Though she can feel her eyes flicker with indignation, she forces her body to stay composed. She can't leave Gina alone with him—she can handle this.

He lights several votive candles and the woodstove, throws in a log. Motions for her to sit in one of the chairs.

She hesitates but then sits, not wanting to appear frightened, and he sits opposite her, staring at her in the same unnerving way the sheriff had, certain they are the infallible masters. She feels at once exposed and reaches for her veil, but it isn't there. A new delicate reality.

She thinks of the women exposed in the photos—the young woman in flip-flops, Lisa. How he threatened Gina. She thinks, *Do not fear your rage*. And then in a voice as controlled as a mediator's, she says, "Those pictures? In the cabinet, what—"

"You went through my stuff? What the hell— How long have you been here?"

She sees his mouth, his entire face clench, the tight glare of his eyes.

"You wouldn't understand," he says.

"And the guns? Would I understand about the guns?"

He looks at her a moment, blood draining from his face, and then walks over to the gun cabinet and opens it. "Each of these babies serve a critical purpose," he says in a low, cautionary voice. He lifts out a huge gun. Points it at the door. "AR15. Might be the most important firearm in American history." He rubs the shaft of it almost tenderly, his movements slow and precise. "Should the left ever gain absolute power—the distance this can shoot"—he points it at a window—"with its accuracy, the way it reloads itself, the rounds of ammunition it can hold, you can shoot an entire crowd of assholes without blinking an eye." He admires the gun for a few more moments and then places it back in the wardrobe, pulls out another.

Sister Angeline watches him. She doesn't know what this man is capable of, and her body fills with panic. Her hand holds Anu's collar tighter, the dog sitting alert at her side.

"This," Father Matt says, his voice becoming unexpectedly more animated, "this is a Remington 870. Twelve-gauge pump-action shotgun. No one wants to be hit by this bad boy." He sneers now. "Even the lowest level scumbag knows buckshot's gonna hit a vital organ. Got my first one when I was twelve."

"From your father?" she says, thinking she should get him to talk about something other than guns.

"Nope. Asshole left when I was nine. My uncle Frank gave it to me. Taught me to use it. I shot quail and rabbit and squirrels for dinner. Hunting was the one thing I could do that made my mother—" He stops talking now, his eyes going distant, a twist of pain in them for an instant, then he is back and pulling out a smaller gun, one that looks a lot like Gina's, but all Sister Angeline can think about is that he shot squirrels.

"Now *this*," he says, his voice strained as if the pain from his eyes, the aching he'd remembered about his mother, had somehow dripped down his throat, "this little, short-barreled Cobra .38? Well, this is what you want to have in your holster, should your AR15 run out of ammunition."

He's sweating profusely now, and his eyelids are twitching.

"But why—why do you even have guns?" she says as softly

and gently as she can, and when he looks at her, when she sees that he thinks she might understand him, maybe he can trust her, she becomes less afraid, bolder.

He walks back to the chair and sits, the .38 still in his hand. "Slogged my way to working on aircraft electrical systems in the navy." His temples pulse. "Got in a lot of fights, got discharged for unruly conduct. Of course, *they* didn't care *why* I was unruly, *why* I got pissed. *They* didn't care about the assholes in our ranks. I was just trying to help, do my patriotic duty. So many assholes in there, so much bad shit going on." He shakes his head in disgust.

"When I taped a microphone to the ceiling to record the traitors, guess the fuck what?" he says. "They didn't give me an award, just called me fucking crazy and sent me off for another psych test. They didn't care those guys were conspiring against us. Shrink wrote in the report I was having *anger-fueled black-outs*. Total fucking bullshit lies."

He stands, begins to pace, the air throbbing hot with tension, time beating in slow motion. "You know the thing that really fucking pisses me off," he says, waving the gun in the air, "is when investigators spoke with my mother, she fucking told them I was a pissed-off paranoid kid—that I'd always been, that I was racked with conspiracy theories for as long as she could remember. Angry bitch. No one would hire me after that." He sits now, something going slack in his eyes, the shiny glint dimming.

"So you became a priest," she says quietly, trying not to fold in on herself. She's come this far, and *where oh where is Gina?* She prays Gina won't come bursting in, will think to listen at the door, will run for help.

He looks at her. "The uncle who taught me to shoot? Uncle

Frank? He was a priest. Convinced me to go to the seminary. Told me that's where the real power was."

"I assume you're not talking about the power of God."

"Listen," he says, "you can't trust anyone. You gotta take care of yourself. The things you believe in. Your country. Your church. You gotta do whatever it takes."

"Control them before they control you," she says.

A displeased look from him, but then the door of the gun cabinet squeaks open wider. He rises, closes it, but keeps the .38 in his hand.

Once he turns back, she stands, fixes her eyes on his. "You're the one who shot the animals," she says, her voice steady but her hands damp—it's becoming difficult to keep hold of Anu, the dog's body pulsing with adrenaline.

"You know what I think," he says, moving closer, the gun still in his hand. "I think you're here because you want it, don't you? I can always tell when a woman wants it. You're no different than the rest of them."

Anu growls, and Sister Angeline grips her collar tighter. "There's a theory about people who torture animals, cruelly shoot them," she says evenly, a momentum growing within her, out of her control. *Why are you pushing him like this?* Still, she keeps going. It's as if she's speaking to everyone who pushed her into hiding, everyone who taught her she was less than. "I think they're trying to kill goodness," she says. "Mostly their own goodness, whatever is left of it—to destroy what they don't have."

The room too silent, his face so close now, his breathing shallow and fast. "You freakin' preaching bitch. Why don't you just shut the fuck up."

She stands firm. Inside, her entire body pounding.

"Must make you feel pretty powerful, killing vulnerable creatures," she says, "and threatening women to undress and accommodate you." She shakes her head. "What a coward you are—you and your white collar, your camera, your bullets— that you really believe power works like that."

It is then he jams the gun hard into her ribs, making her cry out, making Anu break from her hold. It is then Anu leaps on him, one hundred pounds of muscle and fury taking him down, the dog's mouth becoming a wolf's mouth, vicious and ripping and violent.

It is then Sister Angeline hears the worst sound she's ever heard—a cracking, an explosion—and now a terrible yelp from Anu and now a horrendous thud.

"Anu!" Sister Angeline screams. "Anu!"

Chapter Forty-Nine

"Stay the hell where you are," Father Matt says from the ground, rolling to his side, aiming the gun at her chest, blood spurting from his neck.

"Oh my God! What did you do!" she shouts. "What have you done?" Her eyes wild, horror spilling from her, Anu making choking, strangulated noises, straining for air, the dog's entire body quivering, blood already pooling around her.

"Get a towel," he gasps, holding his hand to his gash, blood leaking from under his palm.

Sister Angeline runs to the cabinet under the sink, grabs the washcloths.

Anu whimpers, tries to raise herself, but collapses. Sister Angeline rushes to her and pushes the corner of a washcloth into the wound, the bullet hole so close to Anu's heart, blood streaming out fast.

"Get the fuck over here," Father Matt says, the gun still aimed straight at her, and the way his voice sounds, the violence and wrongness of it, makes her believe he'd kill her if she doesn't do what he says.

"You'll be okay, girl." She pushes the cloth into the wound a little deeper, the white soaked red, the dog's eyes closing, and her breathing so frantic—Sister Angeline thinks she might lose her.

Father Matt bangs the gun on the floor. "Help me."

She goes to him. She is blurred. Choked. Panic pressing hard. Blood everywhere, his shirt, the floor. She presses the washcloth hard onto the wound with both hands.

"Do—do you have a first aid kit?"

"No," he wheezes.

Anu's tongue hanging out, she's panting fast.

Father Matt's eyes on Sister Angeline, and she can see he is terrified, but the sight of him nauseates her. The full impact of his cruelty hitting her hard—the last soft twitch of the squirrel's tail; the dripping blood on Joan's golden fur; the shimmering seal vanished, the ruined fin; the women's bodies on display, choking false permissions; and now Anu with a bullet lodged near her beautiful heart, destroying her tissues, maybe destroying her forever. How can she help him?

Calm yourself. Remember that bullies hurt deep within them-selves. They are afraid. They need help too.

She lifts her hands from the washcloth, and it stays stuck on his wound. Her hands are cold; she cups them, blows on them, rubs them together. Finally, she folds them in prayer, crosses herself, closes her eyes. Inhales deeply.

"Healing love," she prays aloud. "Come to me."

Slowly, her eyes begin to tingle. "Come to me," she says again, but the tingling doesn't come, it stays faint and faraway, and she thinks maybe she doesn't want to heal him.

She looks at him again. "I—I can't help you with—with that gun in your hand."

"Holy shit," he gasps. "Your eyes. They're blazing gold. Holy Mother of God."

"Drop the gun," she says.

He does as he's told, his fingers slowly opening, and the gun drops to the floor, and she slides it away from him with her foot, and then she gets off her knees, picks it up, walks to the front door, and sets it outside. Another signal to Gina, though it's becoming clear she is not coming, and for that, Sister Angeline is relieved.

Father Matt has closed his eyes, his eyelids bluish and wavering, and she decides he can't hurt her now. She goes to Anu and kneels and gathers her dog's beautiful face in her hands and bends close until their noses touch. "Can you hear me? Anu?"

She holds the back of her hand to Anu's nose to feel for air, but there is nothing. She glances at the dog's chest, but it doesn't rise, it doesn't expand.

"Please, Anu. You are the bravest dog. You are the strongest dog. Please don't leave me."

She wraps her hand over the muzzle and places her mouth over the dog's nose, fills her own lungs with the whole of her being, only skin and breath between them, but still Anu's chest will not swell, will not respond; there is not even the smallest tremble.

Sister Angeline moves quickly to the wound, places both of her hands on it, and there is no heartbeat, only blood and fur sticky against her palms. She crosses herself and prays, "God of oceans, rivers, and sky, please be with me, please be with me," and immediately, tiny golden pins and needles burn her eyes, burn so hot she must close them.

"Anu, we can do this," she murmurs. "Please, girl, please come back."

She presses her hands harder on the opening now, the heat in her fingers intensifying, the yellow-orange energy gathering and rising within her, prickling up and down her spine, heat blazing through her veins, awakening individual molecules and atoms, directing the fingers to remove the bloody towel, coordinating the movements of one hand upon the other over the bloody hole, light spinning white and spiraling yellow and orange and whirling red until

at last at last at last

the wound closes, and Anu's lungs inflate—the lungs filling little by little, the chest expanding, deflating gradually, rising again—and now her tail thumps. The heat diminishes, and the vibrations ease.

Sister Angeline waits until her eyes are cool, and when she can she opens them and blinks and crawls to look Anu in the eyes. And now Anu's eyes open, and her pink tongue reaches out, and she licks the tears streaming down Sister Angeline's face.

A thick gurgling sound emerges from Father Matt. His face, gray. His eyes half lidded, unfocused. The washcloth sopping, the bloodstain near his neck spreading wide and dark on the floor.

Sister Angeline moves on hands and knees to him, exhausted. The sickening copper stench of blood. Clumsily, her hands fatigued, she crosses herself and removes the towel from his wound and, with a dazed heaviness, places both trembling hands over the long gash. Red creeping through the cracks in her fingers.

She draws a deep breath, closes her eyes, and prays.

"Help me. Come to me."

She focuses with as much force and care as she can, and finally, she lets go, and there is a rushing sensation in her mind and a release of tension in her body, unlike anything she's ever felt before.

Her legs and hands suddenly stop shaking.

Her mind lifts from itself.

Her body becomes weightless.

It is then she sees Father Matt as a child. A small boy with curly black hair in front of a red-faced mother—the mother with something in her hand, a stick or a pipe, the mother screaming, *Stand up! Do as I say!* A small boy with big brown eyes looking scared, backing into corners. A small boy wiping his own tears. A mother screaming, *Don't be such a baby.* A small boy standing silent in a doorway, waving goodbye to a father who doesn't turn around, who never returns, who leaves him behind with the mother.

A small boy

who becomes a man

who becomes a weapon.

It is then the force within her transforms to the familiar, the white-hot heat flooding her eyes and body, the thrumming pulse in her ears, the surge of light into her fingers, and again, as with Anu, she can feel the blood slow and the skin around the wound close, and her eyes calm, begin to open, and now her hands lift from the healed wound, the flame inside subsiding until the fire is extinguished.

Father Matt opens his eyes, bewildered and stunned, but understanding something consequential has happened. With effort he brings his hand up and touches the place where Anu punctured the vein. The place that is now covered with a soft, new skin. When he doesn't find the hole, he moves his fingers around in wider and wider circles, his brows wrinkling together, as if maybe he has the location wrong. His fingers go back to the wound, and he touches the skin again.

He looks at her, openmouthed. His eyes well up.

For a long time, he is completely silent, his eyes looking intently into hers.

"Forgive me," he says finally, in a thin rasp, and his head drops, and he begins to weep, repeating over and over, "Forgive me," his tears falling into the pool of blood.

Sister Angeline stays on her knees, one hand holding the other, too exhausted, too numb to feel, not yet completely present in her body, and she watches him weep until he falls asleep.

She crawls back to Anu then and lays her head on the dog's chest and breathes in the rhythm of her pulse until she, too, is asleep.

She dreams.

She dreams her family is still alive. She dreams her father is sitting on a stool in front of her, playing random chords on his guitar, and telling her stories about stars and planets and sea creatures. She dreams her mother is teaching her to catch light in a jar and Ricky is pretending to be a famous ballet dancer. She dreams of reading Rilke with Jonathan on the old sofa in his garage.

She dreams of her baby kicking, the tiny bones of her infant feet making reverberations inside her.

But then the softness of the dream shifts, and it is the day of her family's memorial, and the sun shines too brightly, and her aunt feeds her painkillers in a car. And then she limps with a cane alone across a grassy field to the large gathering. The grass is too green, too velvety, and she keeps slipping, keeps falling. No one sees her fall. No one sees her get up.

Strange men lower the three caskets into three different black holes—seven feet, six feet, five feet. The penetrating smell of fresh earth suffocating her.

Her little brother's child casket in a black hole between her mother's and father's. The priest murmuring, *May the Lord bless and watch over Phillip and Mary and Ricky and give them peace,* as he sprinkles holy water on the caskets, each drop suspended like a sunlit jewel.

Strangers drop colorful flowers like bright songs into the black holes, flowers she can't identify, and someone gives her a yellow flower to throw into her brother's, and the yellow flower has a thorn and draws red, and she flings the flower into the blue and watches it grow wings and fly away.

In the dream she doesn't cry. Maybe it's the fog of Tramadol, but she just stands there, thinking about why the baby doesn't have a casket or a name.

There is a banging now, a relentless banging, and she struggles to open her eyes.

"Hello? Father Matt? It's me, Sheriff Ferguson. I'd like to talk to you."

Sister Angeline blinks into the dark. Only a few candles still burn, barely illuminating the space, casting shadows like so many tongues. Father Matt's eyes are wide and fearful, looking in the direction of the sheriff's voice, but he doesn't make any effort to talk or move.

"Anyone in there?" the sheriff calls. And when there is

no reply, he pushes through the door, another police officer behind him, both with their guns extended in front of them. Both making wide sweeps with their flashlights, the beams of light exposing the spills of blood, Matt slumped against the wall, and Sister Angeline still lying on Anu.

And now behind them, Gina, Collin, and Liam. The three immediately rushing to Sister Angeline, helping her into a sitting position.

"Oh my God, what are you doing here?" Gina says. And then, "Oh my God, you've been shot!" and she is moving her hand around Sister Angeline's body, feeling for an entry wound.

Sister Angeline shaking her head slowly, *No, no, I haven't been shot,* but looking down at herself, her new white T-shirt completely soaked with blood. "It's— The blood isn't mine," she murmurs, her head so murky.

"Sister Angeline." It is Collin. He is kneeling in front of her. He gently takes each of her wrists into his warm hands. She is shivering, and he takes off his jacket and wraps it around her shoulders. He is wearing his EMT shirt, and for a moment she is mesmerized by the badge on his pocket—a blue star with a serpent coiled around a staff in the center of it.

"You all right?" he says, and then, "My God, what happened?"

Before she can respond, Liam says, "D . . . d . . . dad, l . . . l . . . look."

Liam is pointing to the wide-open gun cabinet, the sheriff taping a yellow crime-scene strip across it.

Suddenly, Sister Angeline, too weak to keep her eyes open, slips the room, swimming with

       photos

           guns

      serpents

   bodies

        rosaries

and now someone murmuring, *But why is there so much blood?*

Chapter Fifty

Sister Angeline wakes up to morning prayer bells. She is in her own bed, but she is not alone. Alice, Edith, Sigrid, Gina, and Kamika are gathered in chairs around her, their eyes closed, praying the Rosary in Latin.

Sister Angeline disoriented, confused about why she's in bed, why the Sisters are in her room, praying. Images are coming back to her—the carved hawk, the cabin, the unspeakable photos, the cabinet of guns, Father Matt, the gunshot—Anu! She leaps up, calling Anu's name.

And now here is the sweet creature, paws on the bed, and Edith and Gina help her up, and soon she is licking Sister Angeline's face with enthusiasm.

"You're okay, you're okay!" Sister Angeline repeats, hugging the dog tight, and when she can, when Anu has curled into her side, her fingers search for and find the spot where the bullet entered. The spot warm with a new skin. The skin so warm the heat flows up her arm, into her chest, her neck, her face, forms tears in her eyes.

"She's more than okay," Kamika says, sitting on the edge of the bed—all the women are now. "You saved her life. It's like nothing bad ever happened to her."

"You saved Matt's life too," Sigrid says. "If you had any doubts about your gift for healing, I hope this will clear them up."

For a moment Sister Angeline says nothing, the intensity of what happened in the cabin severe beneath her skin. The heat of touching Father Matt's wound, the way her body wouldn't respond, even though she prayed, her prayers denied, and then her body finally opening. Her heart suddenly pounding, and her mouth asking, "Where is he now—Father Matt?"

"He's in jail," Sigrid says. "They found the guns. Found the photos. Took reports from Lisa, who told them of three other women on the island he'd been assaulting."

"Are you okay?" Gina asks, her huge brown eyes more alive again. "You've been asleep for two days, and I was really beginning to worry and I'm so sorry, this was all my fault."

"What—what was your fault?" Sister Angeline says.

"I lied to you," Gina says, "about meeting Matt on Saturday—he wanted to meet on Thursday, today—and I should have told you the whole truth when we talked. I should have been brave enough to ask for help then and not told you to keep it secret; I was just so worried the truth would put all of you at risk. But then while I was painting on Tuesday, I became so furious about him trying to control me, and I knew the sheriff was interviewing people on the island, and so I called him—the sheriff. Said I wanted to talk to him. I was so upset. I rushed to meet him so I wouldn't change my mind. I met him at Collin's and told him everything, but I didn't think to tell you first, didn't think you would go . . ." Gina weaves her rosary beads between the fingers of both her hands, in and out, in and out, until her hands are completely bound together, the silver cross hidden between her palms.

"It's okay," Sister Angeline interrupts, reaches out, and folds her hands over Gina's. "It's okay," she says again, and in this moment she realizes she is telling herself as well. *It's okay* she felt the rage. Who would she be if she hadn't felt the rage?

Gina closes her eyes for a long moment, then opens them, tears appearing. "I was just so scared. But I'm sorry for lying, and if I had listened to you from the beginning, this would never have happened."

"I'm glad you're safe," Sister Angeline says, her own eyes watering now.

"And we're grateful you are safe," Sigrid says, grabbing a box of Kleenex and passing it to Sister Angeline.

"Collin brought you home in the ambulance," Edith says. "You were completely passed out. You're—lucky to be alive. Not sure going to that cabin was the smartest move you ever made."

It is then Sister Angeline realizes Edith is dressed differently. She's not wearing her veil or her habit. She's wearing a sage green cardigan with a brown corduroy skirt, and her short reddish-white hair is brushed into lovely waves.

Edith sees her noticing and says, "I brought you an outfit too. Couldn't get the blood out of your clothes. Had to toss 'em." She nods her head to a chair, where a pale blue sweater and a jean skirt lie.

The idea of wearing regular clothes is still new for Sister Angeline, and for a moment she's startled, feels a profound pang in her stomach, thinking of her habit hanging in the back of her closet, but then she thinks that even in ordinary clothes, she is still a nun.

"Thank you," she says. "And Edith? You look beautiful."

Edith waves the comment away with a swish of her hand, but Sister Angeline can see by the flush in her cheeks, she's pleased.

"The sheriff said Matt told everyone what happened," Kamika says. "Everything. He admitted to killing the animals and leaving the threatening notes. All of it."

Sister Angeline takes a deep breath and nods. She'd known he would confess the moment he'd begun to weep. She'd watched something change in him, something passing between shadow and light, an awareness of the child within him crying out to be loved.

"And we got a call from the archdiocese," Edith says. "From the archbishop himself, la-di-da. Told us Matt's been relieved from his priestly duties and will be receiving psychiatric help." She rolls her eyes. "As if," she says.

"But now people know about the healing," Sister Angeline says. "What about—"

Alice reaches for her hand and holds it.

In her eyes: infinite tenderness.

In her eyes: love deeply rooted.

"You only have to do what you can," Sigrid says, "what you're able to. We've got this. You've got this, Sister Angeline. We're here for you."

"Thank you," she says, and she looks around at the group. How she loves these women. "And it's Angeline, please just call me Angeline."

Chapter Fifty-One

That night, she stands outside in her nightgown. It is snowing lightly. She stretches out her hands, catching the white flakes. The snow is clean and delicate and touches her hair like tiny doves, and she throws back her head, and the snow melts on her lips, and she feels alive. It is here where she most wants to be. And looking into the sky, the snow melting on her lashes, she realizes the ones she loves will never be gone from her. They will forever be held in sky and ocean together.

And now here is her baby floating above her, and Sister Angeline reaches for her and holds her in her arms, the slight perfect weight of her, and she brings her close to her breast and strokes the silken blond hair.

My baby, my love, she whispers, and she hears the ocean calling, *Hana, Hana, Hana*, and Angeline says, *Yes, that is her name*, and she knows *Hana* means *little flower*, and she knows it's time to let the baby go.

It is then she becomes fully aware of how temporary

bodies are, and in thinking this, a tremendous sadness is lifted, and she releases the infant with joy into a light laced with stars.

Epilogue

Sister Josephine lived in Michigan with her family for a year before writing to Sigrid and requesting to live at Light of the Sea. Working by the quiet of the sea, she wrote essays about her experiences at Tuam, contributing to a growing body of work on the subject. With Lisa's help, she opened a safe house for victims of domestic abuse. She continued to be a close confidant to Angeline and a cherished member of the community until her death at the age of ninety-six.

Sigrid continued organizing protests for five years before she succumbed in 2021, during the global pandemic, to COVID-19. She passed into the stars, surrounded by her Sisters singing to her and praying for a peaceful transition. Sigrid left behind seventy years of striving for equality and guiding others to live kindly with each other and the earth.

Gina became the second prioress of Light of the Sea, leading the Sunday gatherings after Sigrid's passing. She began to sell her paintings in galleries along the West Coast, bringing financial stability to the convent. Her only venture into sculpting, she created a modern representation of the beloved seal. The piece is installed on the rock she died upon as a memorial and reminder that cruel acts happen in this world and must be overwhelmed with acts of love.

Edith's skill as an engineer and her passion for sustainable living served her well as she strived to make Beckett Island 100 percent energy independent. She obtained a grant from the Paul G. Allen Family Foundation to install solar and wind energy that eventually met the needs of the entire island. Edith also managed Sister Angeline's healing practice with skill and an adequate amount of grace under pressure.

Alice lived to be ninety-three years old. She led an initiative in Washington State that provided landmark support to victims of violence and unprecedented protections from gun violence. The legislation was named Talik's Law.

Kamika remained at the convent and organized funding to purchase and renovate the defunct St. Paul's Church. She turned the building into the St. Francis Creative Arts Academy, where she taught music and Middle Eastern culinary arts, Gina taught visual arts and Tai Chi, and Edith lectured on engineering and sustainability. Kamika has yet to find her mother.

Collin continued to live on his tugboat and provide EMT services on the island, eventually setting up an all-island clinic for outpatients needing medical treatment or advice. He often called upon Angeline for her healing, and they remained the closest of friends. He became an artist as well, sculpting intricate metal gates and fences featuring madrona trees. One of his gates was installed in New York City at the First Responder Memorial. He donated it in the name of his wife, Claire.

Liam went on to study political science at Georgetown University. Though he lost his first run for Congress, he succeeded in his second attempt. He plans to return to Washington State and run for governor. Liam and his husband, Mark, purchased a houseboat close to Collin's and stay there whenever they return for visits.

Sherriff Ferguson retired soon after Matt was arrested. He began to regularly attend the Light of the Sea services. Before he died several years later, he asked that Sigrid perform his memorial, which she did, graciously.

Amelia and Jack were adopted by a loving civil rights lawyer and her husband. Jack excelled at athletics and was signed by the Seattle Mariners, where he played first base. Amelia, inspired by her adoptive mother, became an attorney, graduating from University of Washington School of Law and joining her mother's office as a civil rights attorney. She named her first daughter Angeline.

Father Matt was laicized by the Catholic Church. Convicted of twenty-three counts of sexual assault and six counts of rape, he was sentenced to thirteen consecutive terms, totaling 111 years. He was forever altered by the night at the cabin, witnessing two miracles, one of which saved his life. While in prison, he wrote a screenplay called *Father*, which was made into a highly publicized film. He donated all his earnings to Light of the Sea convent. He died in prison with sixty-six years remaining on his sentence.

The cabin Father Matt used was left to decay, becoming the home of any wild creature who wandered in. When the roof fell and the walls buckled, the Sisters gathered to remember the pain and to celebrate the love and courage that intervened, then burned the remnants of the structure to the ground, sending prayers of thanks and celebration into the smoke.

Angeline became a full-time healer, curing and saving hundreds of lives each year. Anu remained at her side until her natural death in 2026. Two additional yurts were added to the convent to house people who came seeking Angeline's help. Angeline discovered she was able to heal wounds, broken bones, and burns, but not cancer or other diseases. The Vatican frequently requested permission to send emissaries to verify her miracles, but Angeline always turned them away. She was known to touch the statue of St. Francis often.

Acknowledgments

To the feminist writers who came before me and cultivated my thinking and voice, particularly Dorothy Allison, Maya Angelou, Hannah Arendt, Octavia E. Butler, Simone de Beauvoir, Kate Chopin, Audre Lorde, Edna O'Brien, Elizabeth George, Christine de Pizan, Toni Morrison, Ursula K. Le Guin, bell hooks, Zora Neale Hurston, Doris Lessing, Susan Sontag, Gloria Steinem, Clarissa Pinkola Estés, Mary Ward, Adrienne Rich, Alice Walker, Simone Weil, Jeanette Winterson, and Virginia Woolf, but so many more.

To all of the nuns I've ever met, who in small and large ways influenced my identity and writing, particularly those whom I've known personally—Sr. Rosa, Sr. Mary Catherine, Sr. Regina, Sr. Anne, Sr. Therese, Sr. Philopena, Sr. Mary Helen—and those whom I've known through reading articles, essays, and books: the Sisters of Selma, Nuns on the Bus, Sr. Mary Corita Kent, Sr. Megan Rice, Sr. Jeannine Gramick, Sr. Teresa of Ávila, Sr. Donna Quinn, Sr. Joan Dawber, Hildegard von Bingen, Sr. Mary Antona Ebo, Sr. Simone Campbell, and many more, who have dedicated their lives to creating inclusive communities and pathways toward equity and social justice.

To Erica Bauermeister, Louise Marley, Susan Brittain, Karen Sullivan, and Peter Quinn for their gracious and constructive feedback about this book in its early and later stages.

To the phenomenal team at Blackstone Publishing, particularly Corinna Barsan, Jesse Bickford, Sarah Bonamino, Bryan Barney, Deirdre Curley, Alenka Linaschke, Ananda Finwall, Bryan Green, Jason Green, Jennie Stevens, Addie Wright, Josie Woodbridge, and Jeffrey Yamaguchi.

To my superb agent, Gordon Warnock, whose enthusiasm for my work is unwavering and who forever reminds me to dream big.

And lastly, thank you to my sons, who keep me afloat, and my husband Peter, who forever and ever affirms my deeper yes.

To the sisters at Our Lady of the Rock Monastery on Shaw Island, where I spent a heavenly period working on this novel, sitting every afternoon in their beautiful chapel listening to women sing the Divine Office in traditional Gregorian chant.